GALLAGHER'S CHOICE

A MONTANA GALLAGHER NOVEL

MK MCCLINTOCK

Trappers Peak Publishing

Montana

Copyright © 2013 MK McClintock
All rights reserved.

Published in the United States of America
Trappers Peak Publishing
Bigfork, Montana

McClintock, MK
Gallagher's Choice; novel/MK McClintock
ISBN-10: 0615601685
ISBN-13: 978-0615601687

Cover design and formatting by Potterton House Author Services
Mountain Barn © designwest | iStock
Woman and Horse | Dreamstime

Edited by: Magnifico Manuscripts, LLC

PRINTED IN THE UNITED STATES OF AMERICA

For my grandmother, Elizabeth.
Your heart is as big as the Montana sky.

AUTHOR'S NOTE

Dearest Readers,

Is it possible for me to love the Gallaghers even more? I believe it is. Even though this story concludes what I'm calling a trilogy in the Gallagher series, you have not seen the last of this remarkable family. Ramsey is a nice balance of tough and sweet. He missed out on a lot, but he's been lucky when all is said and done.

Eliza is a contradiction of stubborn pride and levelheadedness. She loves her family, her life, and does what has to be done. I love the steadiness of both Ramsey and Eliza, which is why I believe they are a wonderful match. The present dangers may now be resolved, but the adventure doesn't end here.

-MK

Montana Territory
October 1883

I won't be far behind you. Ramsey's words echoed through Eliza's thoughts. When she had asked for time to prepare her family for his return, she didn't expect this much time. *There's something I have to do,* he had told her. They now had more to lose than ever before—a new generation of Gallaghers lived at Hawk's Peak.

I won't be far behind you.

Eliza had been able to hold off the inevitable tongue-lashing she knew her brothers wanted to deliver, but she'd be unable to forestall them much longer. For now, she could be grateful their ire was directed elsewhere.

"You remember what we talked about, Eliza?" Ethan glanced briefly at his brother and then looked directly at her.

Eliza nodded. "I remember, but just this time."

"We'll take what we can get, sis," Gabriel said.

"That's settled then." Ethan stood to move from behind the desk. "Gabriel will take two men and head north, and I'll take two more and head south, just in case Jeb misinformed us. If we leave tomorrow, we may be able to catch up with Hunter, or at the very least, discover exactly where he's going. The rest of the men will stay here—we still have cattle to look after and we're not leaving any of you alone. Now, I'll go out and let the men know the—"

"Rider coming in!" someone shouted from outside. Ethan rushed to the window and Gabriel quickly joined him. The snow had stopped, and now the cold air misted around the mountains. Eliza stood beside them and saw the lines of the horse and man as they raced over frozen earth toward them. Something familiar stood out about the rider, and Eliza moved to the railing in an attempt to see more of him. Broad shoulders filled a dark coat, open to show the heavy woolen shirt beneath. His brown felt hat remained in place despite the speed of his ride. Long limbs fell on either side of the magnificent stallion—a horse familiar to Eliza.

The rider came to an abrupt stop in front of the hitching post and lifted deep green eyes to the three on the porch. Gabriel heard his sister gasp and turned to her, but her eyes remained on the man sitting atop a thoroughbred similar to his Zeus.

"What's going on?" Gabriel faced his sister. "Do you know this man?"

Ethan hit the side of Gabriel's arm and walked to the edge of the porch. "Take a closer look, brother."

Gabriel did and when the man stared back, seven years slipped away. "Ramsey?"

"Sorry I'm late, Gallagher." Ramsey remained on his horse. "I had a devil of a time with the weather through the pass."

"What are you talking about?" Ethan's gaze shifted back and forth between Ramsey and his sister. Both continued to stare at each other. "We heard you'd be coming out this way, but as I live and breathe Ramsey, I didn't believe it."

"I could have used an extra week, but Gabriel's friend, Jeb, said you needed a marshal fast. He found me on the trail outside of Bozeman."

Eliza finally spoke up. "What does that have to do with—oh my."

Ramsey moved the edge of his heavy coat aside to reveal the small, round silver badge pinned to his wool vest.

"How is that possible? You didn't say—"

"There's a lot I didn't tell you, Eliza." Ramsey dismounted and tied his horse to the post. He took a moment to glance around at the men approaching from two sides. "I'm glad to see you have numbers," he said and moved up to the porch.

Gabriel leaned against the railing. "You're the marshal?"

"When?" Eliza took a few steps toward Ramsey.

"Just after you left." Ramsey smiled at her. "I figured it would come in handy."

Once, years ago, they had called Ramsey a friend. Whenever they happened to be on the same trail or in town at the same time, they enjoyed Ramsey's company. Why Ramsey worked for Hunter was a question asked more than once among the Gallaghers. It wasn't until later that they discovered the possibility that Ramsey was Nathan Hunter's grandson.

Eliza had never imagined that their family would be joined with Nathan Hunter, but when Brenna Cameron had showed up in Briarwood a year ago, looking for her grandfather, no one could have stopped the events which followed. Brenna may have been the granddaughter of their fiercest enemy, but love was determined to win, despite everything. Marrying Brenna was the smartest thing Ethan had ever done, and Eliza happily called her "family."

Ethan stepped forward and slapped a hand on Ramsey's shoulder. "You have some explaining to do."

"I know that, but there's something else I have to do first."

The front door slowly eased open, and Brenna poked her head out and looked at her husband. "Will our guest be joining us for breakfast?"

Ethan lifted her hand from the edge of the door and pulled her outside.

"It's as cold as the Highland hills out here, Ethan."

Ethan removed his coat and draped it over his wife's shoulders and leaned down. "There's someone you need to meet," he whispered against her ear.

"Who might that be?" Brenna stepped back into her husband and gasped. "Faith, but it can't be!" Brenna stepped forward toward the image of her father as she remembered him from her days as a child. "Are you really here? Is it truly you?"

Ramsey stepped forward and turned all of his attention to the woman before him. He lifted his hands to her face, one on each side, and raised her tear-filled eyes.

"It's really me, Brenna."

Brenna looked at Eliza. "This is your doing? You found him."

Eliza smiled at her sister-in-law. "He was easier to find than I thought."

"I'm just sorry she had to come all the way to Kentucky to find me, but I'm grateful she did." Ramsey shared a momentary glance with Eliza before turning back to his sister. "I would have come back, but I'll admit that Eliza was the motivation I needed to see you."

Brenna stepped back from him. "You would have come here without telling me?"

Ramsey didn't hesitate before answering. "I wish I had the answer you'd want to hear." He looked over at Ethan and Gabriel, who waited patiently while he spoke to Brenna. "I heard about your troubles and planned to do what I could—without telling you," he admitted.

Ethan looked fondly at his sister. "Eliza has a way of changing a person's way of thinking."

Ramsey nodded. "Yes, she does."

Brenna drew his attention with her quiet words. "Tell me

you're staying."

Ramsey saw the unmistakable pleading in Brenna's eyes, and yet he refused to make a guarantee on the unknown. "I don't know yet."

"If it's time you need, I'll understand. I won't ask for what you can't give. We're nearly strangers, but I hope we can change that."

"So do I." Ramsey returned her smile. Brenna's warm and genuine smile was a foreign sensation. In Kentucky, he had called the Tremaine family his friends, but they knew only what little he had shared over the three years he'd known them. When he had left his grandfather's ranch seven years ago, he built a strong barrier around the part of him capable of feeling real emotion. Whether that barrier would crumble remained to be seen. He couldn't predict what would happen while he was in Montana, and he refused to cause his sister pain by making promises he wasn't sure he could keep.

Brenna interrupted his thoughts. "Grandmother is here."

Ramsey shifted his focus to the house and then to Ethan. "What happened?"

"Hunter went looking for her, and we thought this was the safest place for her. She was here when Mabel passed and chose to stay."

"It'd be best if she is told before I see her."

Eliza waited for the small group to move into the house, and yet Ramsey and Brenna remained transfixed outside. The morning sun offered little light and no warmth. Eliza looked up to the sky and watched the heavy gray clouds settle comfortably around the mountain peaks. In those few moments, it wasn't the promise of a heavy winter that loomed in the air or the struggles that lay ahead with Hunter and his men. A brother and sister had been reunited, never having known the beauty of that special bond.

Eliza looked at Ethan and then to Gabriel. She understood that bond. Her chest constricted, and the need to walk away overwhelmed her. Stepping toward Ramsey's horse, she took the reins from Jake, who had been the closest ranch hand when Ramsey rode up.

"I can look after him, Eliza," said Jake.

Eliza shook her head. "I'd like to see to him."

Jake tilted his head at the edginess in her voice but released the reins and stepped back as she turned the horse toward the stable.

"Where's she going?" Gabriel stared after his sister's retreating back.

Ramsey turned momentarily away from Brenna to watch Eliza walk away with his horse. He looked back to his sister and smiled. "There's something I need to do, but I'll be back soon, I promise."

Brenna nodded. "I'll let Grandmother know you're here."

"Thank you." Ramsey squeezed Brenna's hand as he imagined a brother would do. He nodded to Ethan and Gabriel, then walked quickly over the snow-covered ground to follow Eliza's boot prints.

Though a good size, the stable was now crowded with more than just the horses for which it had been built. When Ramsey had stopped off in Briarwood, Loren, the storekeeper, told him about the barn burning and the housekeeper's death. He had met Mabel only once but remembered talk of her kindness in town. She had been part of the Gallaghers' family, and they had lost her because of his family.

Eliza turned at the sound of boots on wooden planks but continued with the task of removing the saddle and blanket from Ramsey's horse. She heard him come up behind her and watched his hand smooth over the stallion's back.

"Thank you for looking after him."

Eliza nodded and picked up a horse brush out of a nearby bucket and slowly moved the soft bristles over the animal's shoulder. Ramsey covered her hand with his, halting her progress. She lifted bright blue eyes to his green. He didn't release his hold on her hand or the brush.

"I'm sorry I couldn't tell you everything. I had to be certain it would work out," he said quietly. "After everything I failed to do for my sister, for your family, I wanted to be certain there was no way out this time for my grandfather."

"It's easier to call him Hunter."

"You're forgetting that's also my name."

"It doesn't have to be." She slid the brush down the horse's side, forcing Ramsey to release his hold on her. "You were born a Cameron."

"I haven't earned the right to use their name."

"I imagine Brenna would see things differently." Eliza set the brush in the bucket and pushed Ramsey out of the way. She moved his horse into the last empty stall and checked the water and feed before closing the gate.

Ramsey stepped forward to run a hand over the horse's muzzle. He gave Eliza his full attention, as though nothing else mattered but what she might say.

"Have you once stopped to think that perhaps you've suffered as much as your sister?"

"That's ridiculous."

"Why? Because she's a woman? Because she suffered at the hands of the man who is kin to you both?"

"She could have—"

"Died? Yes, she could have been killed. We've all come close, and we've all lost people important to us." Eliza concentrated to prevent the tears from filling her eyes. "This isn't about what the Gallaghers have suffered. We'll get our justice, but don't compare your losses with Brenna's because from where I'm standing, you've lost as much, if not more."

"Eliza, how in the hell can you say that? She lost everything!"

"If I thought it were possible, I'd beat some sense into you!" Eliza took a deep breath. "You both lost parents, you both lost the chance to know each other, and you both have a grandfather who destroyed your lives." Eliza calmed down enough to close the distance between them. "You had to live with a horrible man, and then when you discovered the truth, you had to live with the knowledge that you had parents and a sister you might never know."

Ramsey nearly turned away from her, but Eliza gently brushed her fingers over the light growth of hair on his jaw. "You've suffered enough, but if we help each other, we can end the suffering of both our families."

He lifted his eyes to study Eliza. "Have your brothers ever told you you're bossy?"

She laughed. She didn't know what else to do, and it felt wonderful. "All of the time."

"Thank you," he whispered, leaning into her and resting his forehead against hers.

"Brenna is waiting, and I imagine your grandmother now knows you're here," Eliza said quietly after taking another deep breath.

Ramsey nodded and pulled back. He held out his arm to her. "Walk with me?"

"I generally get to know a fella before I go strolling on his arm."

He smiled. "Perhaps we could skip a step or two."

Eliza considered him carefully, uncertain if he was responding to her light humor or if he was serious. She slid her arm through his and walked beside him through the snow to the house. Her eyes shifted briefly to the remains of the burned barn.

"I am sorry for your loss," he said softly. "I know she meant a great deal to your family."

She didn't respond, and they continued to walk in silence. Eliza struggled daily with the knowledge that their continued fighting with Hunter had led to Mabel's death. Their housekeeper, Mabel, had been a surrogate mother when theirs passed away, but more importantly, she had been their friend, and Eliza still ached from the loss. When they reached the porch steps, she stopped and faced Ramsey. "Do you really believe that badge you're wearing will make a difference?"

Ramsey lowered his arm. "It can't hurt. Better to do this on the right side of the law."

"My brothers want to see this end as much as I do, but they've tried to work within the law and that hasn't done us any good."

"I didn't ask for the badge with the thought it would scare my grandfather into turning himself in," Ramsey said.

"Badge or not, there are going to be more deaths before this is over."

Ramsey placed one leg up on the first step and leaned into Eliza. "Let's make sure it's not one of us."

The front door opened, and Ethan stepped partially over the threshold that held the outer door. "If the two of you are done catching up, we'll have that talk now, Eliza."

Eliza briefly looked at Ramsey. "I'll see you at supper."

"No, he's coming too," Ethan said.

"I will, but there's something I have to do first," Ramsey said.

Ethan studied him a moment and then nodded. He left the door ajar but walked back into the house, and Eliza knew he expected them both to follow.

Ramsey stepped up next to Eliza on the porch and held open the door. "I've always thought it best to get the hurting over quickly."

"Clearly you don't remember my brothers," Eliza mumbled and walked past Ramsey into the house.

In the years he'd known the Gallaghers, Ramsey failed to receive an invite to Hawk's Peak. He'd been friendly with Ethan and Gabriel and had always noticed Eliza, but as a member of the Double Bar outfit, he had never expected an invitation. Nor did he blame the Gallaghers for not extending one. His grandfather had practiced the art of underhanded deception, but Ramsey remained on the Double Bar for all of those years out of loyalty to his grandmother. When he left, it was with the hope of protecting everyone else. A mistake he couldn't change, but one he hoped to make right.

Ramsey now walked through the Gallaghers' home and realized the wood and stone construction was merely protection from the elements. The people within those walls gave the structure life and meaning. He envied the warmth and kindness he saw in the small framed photographs on surfaces smelling faintly of beeswax. The worn rugs muffled the sound of his boots and attested to years of good use by a large family. The welcome scents of home cooking wafted from another part of the house and reminded him of the days before his grandmother ceased her efforts to make a home for his grandfather.

He watched Eliza walk toward a room off the left side of the hallway. She turned to face him. "Are you coming?"

He nodded. "In a minute. Where's Elizabeth?"

Eliza smiled and pointed to a large open door farther down the hallway on the right.

"I just need a minute."

"My brothers will wait," she said and disappeared into the library.

Ramsey stopped under the doorframe that led into the kitchen and took a moment to watch the woman who had loved him all the years of his life. Every time he suffered emptiness at the loss of his parents, or of never having known his sister, he remembered everything Elizabeth had sacrificed for him. The pain he experienced of life without his family filled him, but Elizabeth's love he carried with him during the ten long years he'd been away.

A younger woman walked in behind him. "I'm sorry, sir; I didn't know anyone else was here." Her words caught Elizabeth's attention.

"Brenna told me you'd come," his grandmother said, and though she didn't move, she looked at the young woman. "It's all right, Isabelle. This is my . . . grandson."

Isabelle glanced quickly between him and Elizabeth, excused herself, and quietly left the room.

Ramsey stepped toward Elizabeth and lifted the towel from her grip. "I gave you a lot of cause not to believe I'd come back."

"I didn't give up hope."

"No, but perhaps I did." Ramsey's eyes skimmed over the face that had brought him years of smiles. "I need to take care of something with Eliza and her brothers, but I want to talk— soon."

"I'd like that, Ramsey." She hesitated a moment and then pulled his larger frame into her arms. Elizabeth pulled back and said, "I don't imagine her brothers are waiting patiently. Go, we'll have our time."

Ramsey studied her for a moment longer, squeezed her hands, and exited the kitchen.

When he returned to the library, he paused to study the occupants. Ethan stood behind the oak desk and waited with hands splayed on the desk's surface. Gabriel stood next to him, his arms crossed—neither man said anything. Ethan indicated the empty leather chair next to the one Eliza currently occupied. Her eyes met his briefly—they both knew what this was about— and they didn't have long to wait

Ethan leaned forward, his large hands bracing his weight, his eyes intent on Eliza. "We know better than to question your reasons for doing what you do. You've had some foolish ideas in the past, but never did I believe you would sneak away like you did."

Eliza objected. "I didn't sneak—exactly. I left a note explaining where I'd gone."

"Much appreciated," Gabriel said sarcastically. "Listen, Eliza, I wanted to thrash you when I first realized what you'd done, but I was willing to wait until you returned and explained why."

"You know why. I believed finding Ramsey was necessary."

"And it couldn't wait?" Ethan's dark blue eyes conveyed his disappointment. "You couldn't have told Gabriel?"

"Gabriel wouldn't have allowed me to go alone any more than you would have. He couldn't go with me and leave the ranch unattended. It was the logical choice."

Ethan paused in his questions for a moment, and Eliza imagined him reenacting the scenario, except this time with both him and Gabriel cognizant of her plans. Though in Ethan's scheme, she would have been locked in her bedroom until they thought she'd regained her good sense.

"Do you really believe going the way you did was logical?" Ethan's voice calmed. "If something had happened to you, it could have been weeks or months before we knew about it."

"Whether or not I believe it was the best choice doesn't matter now. I believed it at the time," Eliza said. "I made a decision and once I do—"

"You don't let the idea go," Ethan said. "No matter how foolish." Ethan exhaled and lowered his head, his voice quiet. "When Gabriel showed me your telegram, I tamped down the worry because I thought you'd turn around halfway there and come home. When you didn't . . ."

"Worrying you is the only regret I have, but I can't change what I did." Eliza stood, and Ramsey followed suit. She was immensely grateful he remained quiet, but it was easier knowing he was there. "I know how much you both wanted answers when I first returned, but then Mabel . . . then too much happened. I'll answer all of your questions, but please just know that I was always safe."

"We're all we have," Gabriel said calmly. "Just don't do anything like that again without telling us first."

"I promise," Eliza replied.

"Can't say that we're done with you, Ramsey," Gabriel said, shifting his focus.

"I expected not."

"I'm going to trust Eliza when she said nothing happened, but she was gone long enough to require sleeping under someone's roof." Ethan turned to Eliza. "Unless of course you stayed in a hotel."

"Ethan—"

Ramsey looked briefly at Eliza, his expression telling her that his turn for explanations had come.

"Yes, we slept under the same roof, but only a few nights, and I assure you we were not alone. My friend, Nathaniel, his sister, Mallory, their father, and a house filled with servants can attest to that."

"The Tremaines," Ethan said quietly.

Ramsey nodded. "Eliza told me about the letters you received from them. They had only meant to help you in finding me, but you weren't the first to come looking. They kept me out of their plan for fear that Brenna wasn't who she claimed to be, that she wasn't the sister I'd told them about."

"Wait a minute." Confused, Gabriel asked, "Who else was looking for you?"

"For a long time, it was my grandfather—Hunter. Once he realized I'd left without telling him, he sent telegrams to sheriffs in towns close by and then as far as Wyoming and the Dakotas.

I only learned of it because I knew two of the sheriffs."

"He never found you?"

"He came close, once."

Ethan nodded, and then turned to look at his sister. "Would you mind giving us a few minutes alone with Ramsey?"

Eliza looked from Ramsey to her brothers. "I thought you had questions."

Ethan turned his attention back to Ramsey. "We have plenty of them."

Eliza's eyes met Ramsey's and he nodded. Understanding that he was now the one requesting for her to leave, Eliza looked once more at her brothers with a look that undeniably warned them not to blame Ramsey for anything she had done.

Once Eliza closed the door of the library, Ethan invited Ramsey to sit down while he settled himself in the chair behind the desk. Gabriel stepped across the room to occupy the place Eliza had vacated.

"We were surprised when Eliza showed up here alone."

Ramsey turned to look at Gabriel. "I couldn't take her where I was going, and she was anxious to return home. Knowing what's happened since, I can understand why she didn't wait. It didn't sit well with her—being away so long. I'm the one who convinced her to stay on a few days when she likely would have left the day after arriving."

"I'll admit I still don't understand what prompted her to go so suddenly," Ethan said. "But, we've learned to trust Eliza's judgment. Scolding her as we did—"

"I wouldn't have done differently if she were my sister."

Ethan focused on Ramsey with eyes more worldly, yet otherwise identical to Eliza's.

"But she's not your sister."

"I won't deny there were times we found ourselves alone," Ramsey said, choosing his next words carefully, "but even if time had allowed for something to occur, nothing would have happened."

"I believe you," Ethan said after a moment. "In fact, I'm grateful you were there when she arrived."

"I imagine she's capable enough to have dealt with whatever circumstances arose, had I not been."

Gabriel's light laughter seemed out of place, considering the conversation, but Ramsey envied his ability to lighten the mood. He remembered Gabriel as the Gallagher who could charm his way into any woman's heart, laugh at his own shortcomings, and still have the strength to get the work done or die trying. "She likes knowing she's unreadable."

"She usually is." Ramsey's tone turned quiet and serious. "There were moments I thought I knew exactly what she was thinking, but whenever I believed I'd caught up to her, she'd already thought five more steps ahead of me."

"That's our Eliza—damn frustrating." Ethan leaned back and crossed strong arms over his chest. "You went to some trouble for that shiny metal you pinned to your chest. Care to tell us how or why? We all know we'd do what has to be done with or without a badge."

"The how isn't important. But as to the why—the badge has its advantages."

"Care to elaborate?" Gabriel asked.

"No." Ramsey leaned back into the chair, looking carefully between Ethan and Gabriel. "I'm going to ask you both for something I haven't yet earned, but I need you to trust me."

Silence met Ramsey's request as both Gallaghers contemplated his request. Moments of speechlessness filled the library, the only sounds coming from the thick walls, reminding them the ranch house lived.

"I don't mean to state the obvious, but you've been gone a long time, Ramsey," Ethan said. "I'll admit I'd be hesitant to trust you without explanation, but Eliza trusts you, and for now, that's enough for me."

Ramsey slowly nodded. "I appreciate that, and I hope you'll feel that way later."

2

Eliza hesitated only a moment after closing the library door behind her, weighing the guilt she'd feel about eavesdropping over her desire to know what they would say without her in the room. Guilt soon overpowered her desire to stay. She walked down the carpeted hallway, following the fragrant path to the kitchen. The domestic scene she happened upon pushed away one of the dark shadows that had hovered around her heart since her brothers and the men laid Mabel in the ground. Elizabeth and Isabelle stood over the long wooden table—one kneading bread, the other stirring a thick creamy batter.

Elizabeth still surprised Eliza at times. Decades of marriage to Nathan Hunter had made her strong, and despite her past hardships, Elizabeth was a beacon of hope and faith in the future. Isabelle had been a joyous addition to the family when she agreed to an unexpected marriage proposal from Gabriel, but since her brother and his new wife decided to make their union permanent, Isabelle had moved easily into the life of a Gallagher, as did Isabelle's younger brother, Andrew.

"This is one of the moments I almost wished I'd learned how to cook." Eliza stepped into the aroma-filled room. "I can't do much, but feel free to put me to work."

"Your company is enough, my dear," Elizabeth said, her

warm smile inviting Eliza to join them at the table.

Eliza welcomed the chance to not feel so alone—a foreign feeling. Alone is a state she'd always embraced, but since finding Ramsey, alone began to feel more like lonely.

"Where's Brenna?"

"Andrew wanted to help her put Jacob down for his nap." Isabelle wiped a stray blond hair from her forehead with her arm. "Ever since Brenna and Ethan brought their baby home, Andrew has been enthralled with the boy. Andrew didn't have a chance to be a big brother before our mother passed, so I think he enjoys having a baby cousin."

"Doesn't Andrew have a birthday soon?"

Surprised, Isabelle looked up. "He does."

Eliza answered the unspoken question. "Gabriel mentioned it. We could use something to celebrate around here."

"Odd to hear you say that," Elizabeth said. "You've given up on your quest for justice so easily?"

"Not a chance," Eliza replied quickly, "but that doesn't mean we can't give Andrew a normal childhood, and if I remember correctly, that means celebrating birthdays."

"Don't you worry, child, we'll make his day a grand one."

"Gabriel and I have already planned for Andrew's gift," Isabelle said and set down the bowl of whatever she'd been stirring.

Eliza watched with interest. "Is there really not anything I can do to help?"

Elizabeth's skeptical glance told Eliza what she already knew—she didn't know how to cook. Elizabeth handed her a small bowl filled with eggs.

"You're strong. Whip those up good until they're fluffy."

Easy enough, Eliza thought and began doing as instructed.

Isabelle pulled out a chair across from Eliza. "Will you tell me about Kentucky?"

Eliza's whipping of the eggs slowed until the yolks barely moved in the bowl. "It was certainly different. Perhaps like your home in New Orleans."

"I've never been anywhere except Texas and here," Elizabeth said, her eyes encouraging Eliza to share.

Sighing heavily, Eliza set the whipped eggs aside. "I'd never been anywhere either. My mother wanted to send me to finishing school, but with the help of my father, we convinced her it wasn't necessary. Up until leaving for Kentucky, I'd never been on a train, or even had the desire to be on one. Hawk's Peak was always home—I didn't need anything else." Eliza cleared her throat and smiled at the other women. "It was an adventure."

"Gabriel mentioned you sneaked away," Isabelle said. "How?"

"Ben drove me in the wagon to Briarwood." Eliza blushed. Ben Stuart had worked as a loyal ranch hand at Hawk's Peak long enough to have asked her a few questions, but Eliza left that part and her little lie to Ben out of her confession.

"How did you get to the train?" Elizabeth was as curious now as Isabelle.

"I hired a wagon and driver."

Isabelle raised a brow and sat straight in her chair. "I hate to say this, Eliza, but I can understand your brothers' being upset."

Eliza picked the bowl of eggs back up and stirred them. "I know I deserved the talking to they gave me in there, although they weren't as unyielding as I thought they'd be."

"Was the journey worth the trouble you went through?" Isabelle cut a slice of bread from the loaf sitting in the center of the table and spread honey over it.

Eliza stared at the stream of steam cascading up from a heavy black pot on the stove. "It was worth all of the trouble and then some." She leaned forward, directing her question to Isabelle. "It's incredibly hot there, and my skin always had a sticky layer to it. Was it like that in New Orleans?"

"Oh yes." Isabelle laughed and set down the rest of her bread before she choked on it. "I can only imagine how tired the housemaids were at the end of each day. My mother insisted on bathing twice a day and that cool water be kept in her room at all times."

Eliza smiled at Isabelle's description of her entire experience in Kentucky. "There are far too many people in that part of the country for my taste. It certainly wasn't the size of St. Louis, but I hadn't expected quite so many people in Lexington. The horse farms were magnificent—so different from our ranches."

"A few miles outside of New Orleans, landowners built beautiful plantations with wide columns and driveways so long you couldn't see the house from the road," Isabelle said nostalgically.

"That sounds like the Tremaines' horse farm," Eliza said. "I always thought Hawk's Peak to be grand, and by Montana standards it certainly is, but nothing compared to what I saw out there. They had more servants in one home than anyone could possibly need."

"The practice of too many servants extended through most of the South." Isabelle scooped a gooey batter into the tins Elizabeth set in front of her. "The slaves outnumbered the landowners, and regrettably, they used those numbers to their advantage."

"Did your family ever—"

"Keep slaves?" Isabelle finished Eliza's question. "No. Gratefully, my parents didn't believe in the practice."

"Did your journey to Kentucky produce anything worthwhile?" Elizabeth glanced at Eliza. "Was there not anything to entice your return?"

"I wouldn't mind seeing the horses again, but no—everything I want is here."

"Everything?"

Eliza heard more than that simple one word in Elizabeth's

question.

"I'll admit, I hope Ramsey stays," Eliza told the older woman. "You didn't appear surprised when he showed up. My brothers dragged us into the library before he had a chance to say much to Brenna or to see you. Yet you're in here cooking, exhibiting greater patience than I could if my grandson was in the same house and I hadn't seen him."

"I always believed Ramsey would return someday." Elizabeth walked to the stove and lifted the lid from the black pot. Picking up a long wooden spoon, she stirred what smelled to Eliza like vegetable soup. "I suppose I have secrets of my own to tell, but I owe it to Ramsey and Brenna to tell them first."

Eliza slowly nodded. "I understand."

"But what I'd rather hear about are these horses you seem to admire so much." Elizabeth smoothly changed the subject. "Isn't Gabriel's horse from one of those farms?"

"Oh yes, I remember he mentioned that when he was telling Andrew about Zeus!" Isabelle said. "He promised Andrew he'd take him there someday."

Eliza looked at both women, aware that they had deftly turned the conversation back to a less invasive subject. She realized answers about what Elizabeth might or might not have kept secret all these years would have to wait, if she ever heard them at all. But somehow, Eliza wanted to know everything she possibly could about Ramsey's life and his past if she was somehow going to help him—and her family. She may overstep her place as family friend, but the matter of Ramsey's life choices and of those around him were important to her.

"Speaking of Andrew," Eliza said, acceding for the time being to drop the subject of Ramsey. "Do you have any objections if I give him a little something extra?"

Isabelle's warm smile attested to her joy in speaking of her brother. "Of course not," Isabelle replied. "I'm touched you would think of him."

Eliza stared at Isabelle. "He's family," she said simply. The hint of moisture in Isabelle's eyes surprised her.

"Andrew would be delighted," Isabelle said, quietly clearing her throat. "What did you have in mind?"

"Actually, I need to ask you and Gabriel if—"

The clatter of a heavy pot hitting the kitchen's wood floor brought Eliza to attention. She turned and knocked over her chair to reach Elizabeth. Eliza carefully rushed around the contents of the heavy iron pot, which had only moments ago sat bubbling on the stove.

"Goodness, Elizabeth!" Isabelle knelt to help. "Are you all right?"

Eliza watched Elizabeth nod, but when she reached out and pulled the woman away from the spilled soup, Elizabeth's small, sturdy body trembled. Eliza tried to coax the older woman into a chair at the table, grateful that the noise wasn't loud enough to bring the others into the kitchen.

"I'm just clumsy, dear," Elizabeth answered Isabelle and lightly brushed away Eliza's efforts for help. "Heavens! That was half of dinner."

Eliza heard her quietly exclaim and exchanged a worried glance with Isabelle.

"We'll have this cleaned up quickly enough," Eliza said. "There's plenty of meat and vegetables."

Isabelle rushed to the pump at the sink. Eliza moved over to help her.

"This pump can be stubborn in cold weather. There's a supply of white cloths in the cupboard above where you found the bucket." Eliza watched Elizabeth slowly kneel on the ground next to the spill, using the single cloth she had with her to mop up the mess. Isabelle walked away to find the towels while Eliza pumped water from the stiff pump. With the bucket filled, Eliza carried it across the kitchen and knelt across from Elizabeth. Isabelle set a small pile of old cloths next to them, and they quietly worked together to clean up the floor.

When the last of the soup had been cleaned up, Eliza moved closer to Elizabeth. "Are you certain you're all right?"

Elizabeth looked up briefly before accepting Eliza's help to stand. "I don't know what happened. My vision went blurry for a moment, but then I was fine."

"You're most likely tired," Eliza said calmly. "You should go upstairs and rest."

"But dinner."

"Isabelle and I will take care of dinner."

"You can't cook."

Eliza pursed her lips at Elizabeth's obvious statement. "I'll manage. Now go and rest and we'll finish up."

Elizabeth walked slowly from the room, and Eliza turned to Isabelle. "Can you cook?"

"I'm not much of a cook, but I believe Elizabeth had enough fixings set aside to make more. We can manage that much."

"Manage what?"

Eliza and Isabelle turned at the sound of Brenna's voice.

"I just passed my grandmother on the stairs. She told me she was lying down for a spell."

"She's overdoing things," Eliza said. "We're taking over kitchen duty for the evening, but today I've become glaringly aware of my inadequacies in the kitchen."

"Jacob's down for a bit, so I'm all yours."

"Do you cook?"

Brenna glanced around the kitchen and then looked at the other woman. "Not well. Should I find Ethan?"

Eliza felt an unexpected urge to laugh. "I don't think he'd be of much help right now. He and Gabriel have sequestered themselves in the library with Ramsey. We can get by."

"What are they doing with Ramsey?"

Isabelle set a bushel of potatoes on the table and handed Eliza a small knife. She took that to mean she would be peeling.

"Tell you what, Brenna. Would you mind peeling and I'll fix biscuits?"

Isabelle smiled. "You know how to prepare biscuits?"

"It's a trail food staple," Eliza replied simply. "As to what my brothers are doing with Ramsey, I don't know. They gave me a brush down and then asked to speak with him alone."

Eliza watched Brenna's expression turn from curiosity to worry. "I can't imagine it's anything to worry over, Brenna."

"I can't seem to help but worry these days," Brenna told her. "With my family at the root of your family's troubles, it's certainly worrisome."

"Hold it." Eliza dropped the scoop back into the flour crock and sifted in the remaining ingredients. "You're beginning to sound like Ramsey, and you're both wrong."

"It's not always that simple."

"It is actually." Eliza continued to stir together the biscuit fixings, then floured a section of the table. "True, Hunter is your family, but we're your family first—don't forget that." Eliza finished rolling out the biscuit dough and shook her head at the haphazard shape of her biscuits. She softly laughed. "This is easier to do on the trail. I never appreciated the work it took for Mabel to feed all of us. Preparing for breakfast after supper and preparing supper after breakfast—no wonder she spent most of her day in this kitchen."

Isabelle handed Eliza a biscuit cutter board. "Your mother never wanted you to learn?"

"She did, but I wasn't a great student." Eliza held up the board. "I preferred to cook only what I would need on the trail, which isn't much. What is this, Isabelle?"

Isabelle held back a smile. "Our cook had one. You're

supposed to use it to cut the dough."

"Do you know how?"

"It can't be that difficult."

Eliza shook her head and set the board aside. "That's what a knife is for."

"Speaking of being out on the trail," Brenna began, "did you really sneak away just to find my brother?"

Eliza slowly nodded.

"Thank you," Brenna said softly. "I didn't have my grandmother's faith that Ramsey would appear someday."

3

"Do you know what you're asking of us, Ramsey?"
Eliza held a hand up when Ethan moved closer to Ramsey. She didn't believe for a moment that her brother would do anything he'd regret, but she'd just as soon be certain of it.

"I'm certain Ramsey has a reason for what he's asking," Eliza calmly told her brother, though she looked at Ramsey. "Let's give him a chance to explain."

A clatter at the door turned everyone's attention to the entrance of the library. The men stood, but Ramsey rushed to take the tray from Elizabeth.

"You ought not to be doing this, Grandmother." Brenna leaned forward. "We don't need—"

"Of course I should and I will and you do need it." Elizabeth followed Ramsey and hovered near him until he set the service on a small serving table in the corner of the room. She looked around at the occupants of the room. "Please, don't let me stop the conversation."

"You should be here for this," Ramsey told her.

"Nonsense. I'll be in the kitchen should you need anything else." Elizabeth quietly departed, leaving six pairs of eyes watching her leave.

"She must slow down, Ethan."

Ethan looked down at his wife. "You try and tell her that."

The worried expression his wife wore had him adding, "I'll take care of it."

"Now that everyone has been nicely distracted, we can get back to Ramsey's explanation."

Ramsey's eyes briefly met Eliza's before he spoke to everyone. "I know waiting is not something anyone wants to do, but if this is done the wrong way, outside of the law, someone could end up in jail. Hunter has managed to escape imprisonment for years. There has to be a reason for it."

Ethan eyed Ramsey carefully. "You think someone on the 'right side' is helping him?"

Ramsey nodded. "I do."

Gabriel released Isabelle and stood. "I'm willing to believe it, but what makes you so certain?"

"Acquiring this badge wasn't the only goal. With it comes access to resources we wouldn't have otherwise." Eliza's eyes met his and he prayed she could help him with her brothers. They weren't going to be pleased. "With those connections, I found out that my grand—that Hunter is also wanted in Texas. He managed to escape imprisonment there, too."

"I'd like to know how you came by that badge." Gabriel poured himself half a measure of whiskey from a bottle on the sideboard. "They don't just give those out."

"A man owed me a favor."

"I don't care about any of that right now." Brenna stood and walked over to her brother. "What happened in Texas?"

Ethan walked up and put a hand on Brenna's shoulder and whispered, "Don't do this to yourself."

Brenna ignored her husband. "I want to know. Our mother was in Texas before she met our father, Ramsey. Hunter left soon after. What happened? Did it concern our parents?"

Ramsey lifted Brenna's hand into his, and her muscles tensed. "Our mother was engaged to another man when she met our father."

"I know that."

"This man was killed not long after our parents left Texas."

Brenna shook her head. "No, they wouldn't have—"

"I know that. The young man's father accused Hunter, and the sheriff backed him. Apparently there had been an immense fortune at stake. One Hunter had borrowed against before the marriage took place."

"Then how did he get away with it?"

"That sheriff retired ten years back, but he remembered all of the details from the murder. He was going to arrest Hunter, but word came down from the governor's office to leave Nathan Hunter alone."

"The governor—"

"Died fifteen years ago."

Eliza's eyes darted from one occupant in the room to another before finally settling on Ramsey.

"Perhaps waiting is a wise choice."

All eyes turned to Brenna. She sat forward, her hands moving to armrests on the chair. "I realize that I'm new to this family, but what Ramsey is saying makes sense."

"You can't be serious?" Eliza was almost afraid to think of the consequences of backing down. "After everything Hunter has put us all through, what he did to you, how can you want to back off?"

Ethan looked at his sister with the hope of calming her down. "Listen, Eliza, don't—"

"I don't want to back off, Eliza, but I'd like the rest of us to go on living!" Brenna inhaled a deep breath and stood. She had commanded the attention of the room. Stepping toward Eliza, she lifted her sister-in-law's hands into her own. "I love you. I love all of you. We've all failed to stop my grandfather, and no one understands more than I do the harm he has done. If Ramsey has a new course of action, I would like us to consider it."

Eliza stared for a moment into Brenna's glistening eyes and embraced her. "I love you, too." She stepped away and then turned to Ramsey. "What did you have in mind?"

"I owe you an explanation."

Elizabeth continued to knead the bread dough on the surface of the table. "You don't owe me anything, Ramsey."

"I left you there. With him."

Elizabeth removed her hands from the dough and wiped the flour from her fingers on a white cloth hanging from her apron. She motioned Ramsey to sit at the table, and she walked to the stove and filled a tin mug with hot coffee from the pot. She set the mug on the table in front of him and sat down. "You didn't leave me anywhere. If you'll remember, I told you to leave."

She lifted his strong hand onto her lap and covered it with her own. "I knew his character long before you were born, child. I did everything I could to stop him from taking you from your parents. I failed my grandchild because I couldn't protect you. I knew the only way for you to have a good life was to escape him."

"You could have come with me."

Ramsey watched quiet tears fall from his grandmother's eyes. "You had to go far and fast. That journey was not for me. I've been happy these past years, child. Never believe differently."

"I love you." Ramsey lifted her hands, still strong from years of hard work. He studied her a moment. "Something is bothering you."

Elizabeth sat back in the chair and folded her hands on the table. "When did you know about Brenna? Was it something I did or said?"

Ramsey shook his head. "Nothing you did. I learned about her after I left."

"But if you knew about her, why not go to her?"

He hesitated and then answered. "That's the explanation I owe you, but Brenna deserves to hear it first."

"She's patient, waiting for you to go to her."

"I know, and I will." Ramsey squeezed her hands. "It's early, though, and I'm not staying here for nothing. I told Ethan I'd join the first shift of men with the cattle."

"Don't wait too long."

"I won't." Ramsey stood, pulled his hat and coat from the iron hook by the back door of the kitchen, and walked outside into the cold morning.

Two days had passed since the night Ramsey revealed his plan, a plan not everyone was convinced would work, but one they agreed to try. A fortuitous blizzard had halted any immediate action of revenge as every able-bodied soul on the ranch worked to ensure the livestock survived. Bitter, howling winds and glacial temperatures forced everyone to work in shifts, returning to the main house for warmth, hot beverages, and a quick meal. For two days, each man barely slept more than a few hours before heading back into the cold. Elizabeth kept the coffee brewed and hot water on the stove for those who preferred tea. Gabriel and Ethan insisted their wives remain inside, so they set to work helping Elizabeth in the kitchen, kept the fires going, and looked after the children.

A heavy rope had been connected from an iron loop attached to the house, just off the kitchen door. The other end of the rope sloped across the snow-covered ground to another iron loop attached to a post next to the water pump. Each time one of the men came back to the house, he filled a bucket from the outside pump and brought it inside for whoever ventured in next.

A blast of cold air whipped into the foyer when Gabriel slammed the front door. Ethan experienced the same frustration and turned to his sister. "We'd worry a lot less if you remained inside, Eliza."

"You know I'm capable."

"We all know you're more than capable." Ethan studied his sister a moment. "Promise me you'll be careful out there. We haven't seen one this bad in years."

"I promise."

Ramsey came up behind them, shrugging into his coat. "Ready, Ethan?"

"We both are."

Ramsey looked at Ethan. "Is it worth the fight?"

Ethan smiled and shook his head. "Not today." He set his hat securely on his dark hair, pulled his collar together, and stepped out into the biting cold.

Ramsey watched as Eliza pulled on a thick shearling over a cotton shirt, leather vest, and wool pants. The pants weren't a surprise considering how involved she was with the ranch, but they looked tailored-made for her frame. "Ready?"

"Let's go." Ramsey held open the door and followed Eliza outside.

Ramsey watched Eliza closely, admiring her ability to work alongside the men, no matter the conditions. The ranch hands respected and trusted her—a great accomplishment for a woman on the western frontier. The world was rapidly changing, and Montana was not immune to that change, but life still proved challenging for women. A person wouldn't know it, though, to look at Eliza.

Halfway through the first day, they'd lost only two cows, but they had a tough struggle ahead if they wanted to make it through with the majority of their stock intact. Ethan and Gabriel decided that at least one of them should be out with the hands, so they made sure to go back in, only as the other was coming out. They'd left Eliza out of their discussion but kept a close watch, and each of them tried to drag her in when they returned to the main house for the break. Ethan managed to locate her, keeping watch over the herd with Ben and Colton. She didn't put up much of a fight when he insisted she go inside. Ethan attempted to shield the exposed part of his face from the blowing snow, and the expression his sister wore worried him. Careful to stay behind her back to the stable, they dismounted and moved the horses into stalls. Tom stepped into the stalls and covered the horses with blankets.

"It's a bad one, Ethan," Tom said. "Ain't seen it this bad since that big one in '77."

"I know, but we'll get through it just as we did back then." Ethan looked around the stable. Filled to capacity since the large barn burned down, the burgeoning building had barely enough room for the horses. Any extra space had been filled with smaller livestock to protect them from the snow. They had enough dry timber under the lean-to by the stable for most of the structure. The rest they'd have to order from Loren. The animals couldn't remain suffocated as they were, huddled together without room to move comfortably. "How long do you have left in here? You might want to sleep if you can."

"I'll be swapping with Jake soon. Just as soon keep the animals company. I ain't too tired yet." Tom looked at Eliza. "You all right?"

Eliza managed a tight smile. "I've been better, but this beast of a storm has to let up soon."

Tom cast a worried look to Ethan and handed him a lantern. "Just checked the rope—good and tight."

"Appreciate it." Ethan guided his sister to the stable doors, nodding to Tom when he opened the doors to the outside. The lantern blew out halfway to the house, but they made it from the stable with all of their extremities and hats covered in snow.

Elizabeth looked up from the stove, and Brenna stood up from the table. "Goodness, child, get that coat off and come sit by the hearth." Elizabeth rushed Eliza over to the fire and looked at Ethan disapprovingly before turning back to Eliza. "Why must you be so stubborn?"

Eliza allowed herself to be led to the fire and have her coat pulled off. "I'm all right. Believe me, I've been through worse."

"That doesn't mean you should be out there in this mess," Ethan said, shaking off his own coat and hat near the door.

"No one should be out in this mess," Eliza said. She accepted the hot cup of coffee from Brenna and turned back to look at her brother. "I'll warm up same as you, then head back out."

Isabelle walked in the room with Andrew. "Elizabeth, Andrew would like to ask—oh my, Eliza!"

Eliza faced Isabelle and then looked down at herself. "What's wrong?"

"You look a tad peaked."

"I'm well enough." Eliza turned and told everyone in the room the same thing. "I'm all right. Has anyone seen Ramsey come in? It's been a while since he's lived through a Montana winter."

"He came and went about two hours ago. I'd best check on Jacob." Brenna kissed her husband, whispered something in his ear, and left the room, shuffling the hair on Andrew's head when she passed him.

Isabelle cast a worried glance toward Eliza but led Andrew to the table. "Andrew has a question to ask you, Elizabeth."

"And what may I do for you, young man?" Elizabeth smiled at the young boy, who looked shyly back at her.

"Do you have some bread with honey?"

"Do I have bread and honey?" Elizabeth grinned and motioned to the chair next to Isabelle. "I have bread fresh from the oven. Sit down there with your sister and I'll fix you a slice—with honey."

Ethan watched Eliza's back as she faced the fire, seeming to ignore everyone in the room. He knew better. Eliza rarely missed anything that went on around her. He walked across the room and stood next to her, the fire warming his cold limbs.

"Don't bother asking me to stay here when you go back out, Ethan."

"Wouldn't think of it, but it wouldn't hurt for you to sleep a few hours."

"The day isn't over, and we need all the bodies we can get to fill the shifts." Eliza listened to Andrew's laughter from behind and stepped closer to her brother. "Tom is right. This is a bad one. We're bound to lose more than a few before it's over."

Ethan turned away from his sister and set his coffee mug on the table.

Elizabeth wiped her hands on the edge of her apron and began to heat milk for Andrew's chocolate drink. "You're going back out so soon?"

Ethan moved to the back door, where his coat and hat hung next to his sister's. "As Eliza said, it's a bad one."

The kitchen door opened, and Colton stepped inside. Breathing heavily as the snow and wind whipped behind him, he said, "There's trouble."

"Eliza, stay here," Ethan said.

"Not a chance." Eliza pushed Ethan out the door, pulled on her coat and hat, and followed the men.

4

Ramsey held firmly onto one end of the struggling steer; Kevin held onto the other. Caught in a loose stretch of wire, the steer stumbled over itself, unable to see through the thick curtain of snow. Now free from the wire, the steer lunged forward, and the edges of Ramsey's heavy shearling fell open. Beneath the dark wool shirt, his skin chilled, and his thoughts unexpectedly shifted to Eliza. He had caught sight of her hours ago, watching over the cattle. He knew she toiled alongside the men all year long, but he'd never seen her work until now.

"Kevin!" Ramsey's voice carried through the wind. They'd saved this steer, but they'd already lost four to the storm. He didn't want to add a body to that count. "Kevin!"

"Here!" Kevin approached from behind, leading Ramsey's horse behind him.

Ramsey lifted himself into the saddle, fighting to keep the wide-brimmed hat on his head. He leaned as close as he could to Kevin, his words fighting the storm. "Let's do one more sweep then—"

Howling wind and vibrating moos from the herd couldn't drown out the gunshot. The barrel blast resonated through the storm, the echo ricocheting off the mountains. He motioned his mount forward, propelling it through the nervous herd. *Don't move!* Ramsey silently willed the cattle. A path swept through the snow, parting before him. A horse minus rider pranced in Ramsey's path. The cattle, sensing or catching the scent of something they didn't like, moved into each other, temporarily blocking Ramsey's movement. The gun at his hip slid out of the leather. Three gunshots urged the confused cattle to move away from the sound. Ramsey jumped down from his horse, aware of faint shouting coming from multiple directions. His knees hit the ground, and he lifted the still body into his arms.

It wasn't supposed to happen this way.

"Eliza."

Go away.

"Eliza, sweetheart."

They want something. Why can't they just let me go?

"She can't hear you, Gabe."

"The hell she can't."

They want to argue now? Was that my scream?

"You better know what you're doing, Ethan."

Yes, he'd better. Wait, why did the pain stop?

"Is she out?"

It's not supposed to happen this way! I want the pain back!

"Wait, she's back."

"Stay with us, Eliza."

Brenna? Finally someone sensible.

"She's opening her eyes."

"Ramsey?" *Good grief I sound awful. Can they even hear me?*

"Ramsey."

"I'm here."

Ethan and Gabe moved slowly aside, watching Ramsey as he knelt next to the bed. Elizabeth's shaky hands smoothed the white sheet and handmade quilt up and over Eliza's body, covering her partial nakedness and bandaged wound.

"I saw you. In the snow," Eliza whispered hoarsely.

"Oh dear, that's Jacob. Excuse me," Brenna said quickly and left.

Brenna's soft voice floated to Eliza's ears from the end of the bed, but Eliza focused what little strength she had on Ramsey. "Thank you," Eliza whispered.

Ramsey reached just under the edge of the sheet and interlaced his fingers with hers. Leaning close he softly said, "I thought we'd lost you, before we had a chance—"

"Thank you." Eliza's soft voice faded and her eyes slowly closed. Her steady breathing filled the silence.

"She'll be all right," Ramsey said quietly. He hesitated for a moment, knowing her brothers stood behind him, but leaned forward and brushed a soft kiss on her forehead. He stood and faced Ethan and Gabriel. "She's going to make it."

Ethan rubbed his sister's blood on a white cloth and focused steady eyes on Ramsey. "Because of you." His eyes lowered to his hands. Faint color remained. "I'm going to clean up and then go and hold my son." When he looked up again, his eyes shone. "Thank you, Ramsey."

Gabriel watched his brother leave and his wife enter. "Is Andrew asleep?"

Isabelle nodded. "He wouldn't let go until I promised him his Aunt Eliza would be all right." She walked to Gabriel and slipped her hand into his. "Please tell me I didn't lie to him."

"It looks like she'll pull through." Gabriel leaned down and kissed his wife. "How are you?"

Isabelle shook her head. "I've tried to erase the image of her limp body in Ramsey's arms." She turned to Ramsey. "When I saw you on the other side of the door, I thought it was a dream. Her face, paler than the snow falling behind you—"

"You behaved like a seasoned nurse on the battlefield," Ramsey said.

"I'd just as soon not relive it." Isabelle then spoke softly to

Gabriel.

After a few moments hesitation on Elizabeth's part, Isabelle was able to coax the other woman from the room. Brenna's grandmother had been a general, commanding everyone's movements during the crisis. The moment Eliza had opened her weary eyes, Elizabeth couldn't keep the tears from her own.

Alone now with Gabriel, Ramsey indicated the chair next to the bed—the chair Ethan had sat in when he dug the bullet from Eliza's body. "Do you mind?"

"Of course not." Gabriel stepped closer to the bed and sat carefully on the edge. He allowed his eyes to roam her face, searching for signs of pain. "We give her a hard time. She puts up with everything we throw at her."

Ramsey remained silent and watched Gabriel watch his sister.

"The truth is she holds us all together." Gabriel looked away from Eliza and focused on Ramsey. "When our parents passed, Ethan and I swore that if we never had another reason to keep this place going, we would do it for Eliza. She had to go and prove she could do everything we could—some things better."

Ramsey leaned forward in the chair and said, "I'm sorry I left all those years ago, Gabe. I'm sorry I wasn't there to stop Hunter."

Gabriel lifted his moistened eyes to Ramsey. "Strange to hear you call him that."

Ramsey looked over at Eliza. "Someone recently told me I was born a Cameron, not a Hunter."

"You couldn't have done anything. We were all young and not experienced enough to handle Nathan Hunter. We almost lost Eliza once before. You were there this time to make sure that didn't happen."

"Does anyone know what happened?"

Gabriel shook his head. "When Kevin finally found Ethan and me to let us know she'd been shot, half the men were out trying to keep the cattle from scattering. You and Kevin seem to have been closest, but he said only you heard the gunshot."

Ramsey nodded, silently agreeing but distracted. "You said you almost lost Eliza once before. What did you mean?"

"She hasn't told you?" Gabriel shook his head. "No, she wouldn't have shared that story."

Ramsey edged closer, his eyes on Eliza's pale skin. He waited, not having the right to ask, hoping he wouldn't have to.

Gabriel knew his wife waited for him, but he focused on Ramsey. "What happened in Kentucky?"

"Nothing you'd disapprove of."

"Anything we should know?"

Ramsey sat back in the chair, his eyes settled on Eliza. "I don't know yet."

Gabriel nodded. "The story isn't mine to tell, and she's likely to lay into us both when she finds out."

"And she'll know?"

"Lesson one. Eliza always knows everything eventually." Gabriel looked down at his sister. "You'll want to stay with her a while, I imagine."

"You don't mind? I'm not family."

"If we minded, you would have been run out the moment you rode up." Gabriel leaned across his sister, careful not to brush against her, and kissed the top of her head. "You get better, Eliza," he whispered. Turning back to Ramsey, he said, "Ethan will be in soon to sit with her. We'll talk. And Ramsey, you are family."

A dim light filled the room, one Eliza instinctively recognized as a late sunrise on a winter morning. Her eyes fluttered a few times while her mind evaluated the options. Wake and accept the searing pain in her side, or close her eyes against the light and hope the pain dwindles. The pain made the decision for her, and a soft groan escaped her lips. She smoothed her tongue across the surface to moisten them, but her parched mouth offered no relief. Blue eyes finally opened fully, and she turned her head away from the window to search for relief. A small pitcher sat next to a short glass. Eliza closed her eyes again. Movement from close by disturbed her attempt to return to slumber. She wanted to smile when the sound of water flowed into the glass, but the pain extended to every part of her body.

"This is going to hurt, but I need you to sit up just a little."

The edge of the glass met her lips. She drank slowly, temporarily satisfying her dry mouth.

"A little more, Eliza. You need to drink all of it."

Her eyes opened and she hoarsely said, "You're bossy."

Ramsey smiled. "We've already established you hold that title." He pulled the glass away and set it on the small pine table. Smoothing the hair away from her forehead, he sat on the edge of the bed. "One of your brothers will be back in soon."

"How . . ." Eliza paused a moment to clear her throat. "How long have I been out?"

"Three days, in and out. The women have been taking shifts looking after you."

Eliza's hand crept under the blanket and searched for the bandage wrapped around her middle. She pushed the quilts away, but her long blue nightgown covered the wound.

"You lost a lot of blood." Ramsey reached over and spread the quilt back over her. "Ethan managed to remove the bullet."

"That explains the pain."

"We couldn't get Doc Brody out here with the storm. Ethan sent one of the men into town to fetch him today."

"I don't need the doctor." Eliza attempted to raise herself. "My body aches everywhere. I need to get out of this bed."

Ramsey gently pushed her shoulders back against the pillows.

"You're not going anywhere," Ethan said from the doorway.

He stepped inside and crossed the room. Ramsey moved away, allowing Ethan to take his place on the bed. Leaning forward, Ethan kissed her forehead. "You scared us good this time."

"Just keeping you sharp, big brother."

"It's not funny."

Eliza sobered. "I know, but it feels better to make light of it than try to remember what happened."

Ethan slowly exhaled. "You don't remember what happened? Nothing?"

Eliza shook her head. "It's blurry. The thick snow made seeing anything difficult." She shifted. "May I have some more water?"

Ramsey poured water into the glass and handed it to Ethan.

"I can do this, Ethan." Eliza slowly raised herself and accepted the glass. She lifted it to her lips and took a tentative sip, then full swallows before Ethan reached over and took the glass from her outstretched hand. "Thank you."

"You should rest."

"I've rested enough." Eliza's weak arm wouldn't have stopped Ethan if he chose to leave, but he remained at her side. "I didn't see who it was, but I saw someone or something through the whiteness. I heard the gunshot and a moment later fell off my horse. I thought, for certain, the cattle would trample me." Eliza turned her head and looked up at Ramsey. "Then I saw you."

"You can thank him for being in this bed rather than buried beside . . ." Ethan paused.

"Mabel? Mother and Father?" Eliza's clear blue eyes met her brother's and held them. "That won't happen."

"Damn right it won't." All eyes turned to Gabriel who walked into the room followed by Elizabeth.

"Gabriel."

"Don't 'Gabriel' me. Ethan may be taking it easy on you but that's only because he's the one who had to pull the bullet out of your side." Gabriel stood at the end of the bed and looked across at his pale-faced sister. "If I have to lock you up myself and toss the key into a manure pile, I'll do it, Eliza."

"I imagine she could do with a proper bath," Elizabeth said and looked at the three men. "Don't you have cattle to look after?"

Ramsey grinned at his grandmother.

"Ramsey?"

"Yes?"

"Thank you."

Ignoring her brothers, Ramsey stepped to the bed and leaned down, placing a light kiss on Eliza's cheek. "Any time." The sound of his boots on wood flooring followed him from the room.

"You, too," Elizabeth said, looking at both men.

"This discussion isn't over, Eliza," Gabriel said. "But I'll wait until you can walk before thrashing your hide."

Eliza found the strength to form a small smile. "I love you too, Gabe."

5

Ramsey understood the expressions on the other men's faces when he walked passed them. *They'll want an explanation—one I can't yet give them. One I can't yet give myself.* He wouldn't deny the effect Eliza had on him, but he refused to promise anything to her, or to himself, until this whole mess ended. The memories of her from their younger days remained, but when he saw her in Kentucky, he couldn't disregard the years in between—the years after he had abandoned everyone. The Gallaghers welcomed him back into their lives, and his sister was a gift. He knew returning to Montana was inevitable, but he meant to do so quietly. He'd concocted a plan over the years, one which would allow him to return, remove the threat, and leave—no one realizing he had been there. Eliza changed those plans when she chose to search for him. He now knew what he'd been missing during those years—a family. People to love and who return that love. Nathaniel Tremaine had been a good and loyal friend to Ramsey, even after Ramsey told him about his grandfather and about leaving his family and friends behind in Montana. However, he had lacked a family—until now. Ramsey knew leaving would never again be an option, but to ignore that there were circumstances beyond his control would be foolish.

Someone, somewhere, had breached Hawk's Peak, taking

advantage of the savage storm in order to carry out devious deeds. With no military service or appointment from government, Ramsey had called in a favor when he petitioned to become the new territorial marshal. Governor Robinson had hesitated when Ramsey first entered his office and asked to assume the role of U.S. Marshal in Montana Territory, but how could a man refuse a request from the one who saved his life?

Ramsey had been willing to use his history with the governor to accomplish his goal. When the team of horses pulling the governor's carriage had careened out of control, the driver jumped from his seat in an effort to save his own life. Ramsey had been riding nearby when he witnessed the young man's leap. The horses turned abruptly, causing the tongue to break. Ramsey was unable to reach the carriage before it went over the river's edge and plunged into the water. He pulled his horse to a stop near the river and dismounted. Water had nearly covered the top of the carriage, and he had to shoot the door handle to release it. By the time he surfaced with the unconscious man, two workers from a nearby field had arrived and helped pull them both from the river. Ramsey visited the governor the following day in the hospital, only to learn whom he had saved. Governor Robinson told him that if he ever needed anything, not to hesitate asking. Ramsey took full advantage of Robinson's offer.

Fortunately, the governor had influential friends in the right offices of government, including the current governor of Montana. Ramsey's appointment was a temporary one, a month if they were lucky, until the new marshal came to retrieve the badge. That fragment of information he had kept to himself. The Gallaghers would know soon enough of the time constraint, but presently that concern was his alone.

Alone now in his room, Ramsey pulled a thin stack of documents from one of his saddlebags. His position gave him access to information he may not otherwise have found.

Regrettably, little was known about Tyre Burton, except that he seemed to have as much interest in the Gallaghers' downfall as did Nathan Hunter and willingly carried out Hunter's orders. Ramsey's search came up empty after three full days of reading through archives and sending telegrams to marshals in territories Burton may have visited. Then fortune came from a sheriff in Wyoming. A reformed gunslinger himself, the sheriff remembered Burton and offered up what he knew. The sheriff had managed to avoid death for nearly fifty-seven years, three of those memorable years in the company of Tyre Burton. He wrote stating that if Ramsey caught the blue-eyed Comanche, "Make it hurt."

The blizzard subsided, and now only light snowflakes fell together in a heavy mass, carpeting the ground and covering the cattle in the low pasture. The cold continued to welcome anyone who stepped outside, but the winds had diminished and the tired workers of Hawk's Peak, at last, rested their weary bodies.

A warm fire flickered in the kitchen hearth. Silence surrounded Ramsey. The last of the family had retired more than two hours ago, and though his body cried out for sleep, he had been the last one to gain some reprieve from the arduous work. Unable to shut down the thoughts shifting around in his mind, he chose instead to feed the fires as the Gallaghers slept.

"Thought you would have turned in." Ethan walked into the kitchen and passed Ramsey on his way to the stove. He poured himself a cup of coffee from the half-empty pot and lifted it in the air. "Thanks for keeping this hot."

Ramsey nodded, but his eyes shifted and moved to the window.

"And thank you again for saving Eliza."

Ramsey had yet to erase the image of Eliza lying on the ground from his mind. Whoever had shot at her was either a superb shot or a clumsy one, but he'd bet there was nothing clumsy about what happened. The shooter couldn't have known who he was aiming at unless they were right next to the rider. Assuming the shooter had seen Eliza, he chose exactly the right person to draw a reaction from the rest of them. If Ramsey had seen the shooter, or had proof of anything, he would have made an arrest or pulled off the badge to mete out frontier justice—whatever was necessary. The shooter could be Tyre Burton, or it could be a random cattle rustler. Ramsey wasn't ready to believe that, but he couldn't rule it out.

As unruly as the territory still was, the law didn't condone vigilante justice. Ramsey was willing to kill to end the fighting, but it also fell on him to see that none of them went to prison in the search for justice.

Ramsey finally turned to Ethan, watching his old friend sit across from him at the long wooden table. "Any man here would have done the same."

"But not any man was there." Ethan took a long drink of coffee and set the mug on the table. "Gabriel told me about your conversation."

Ramsey said, "I've been such a fool. I knew what Hunter was capable of, but I never imagined he'd allow—"

"You've been gone a long time, Ramsey, and we've had our share of altercations over the years. Hunter has crossed some lines, but there's a part of him I know fears what we would do to him if anything happened to our family. When Hunter's men raped Mary, they were careful not to do the same to Eliza. He escalated the attacks when he took Brenna and then Andrew, and I imagine he's sweating over those failures. But something has been bothering me about these latest incidences." Ethan leaned back in his chair. He appeared relaxed, but his body remained tense.

"As though someone is working on his own?"

Ethan nodded. "Did you suspect this before or after you arrived?"

"Some of what I learned before arriving explains how he's managed to stay a step ahead."

Ethan's hard stare met Ramsey's. "Do you know where he is?"

"I have an idea," Ramsey answered carefully. "I know what he's put your family through, but this should be my fight. I should have stayed and stopped him a long time ago."

"Like hell!" Gabriel stood in the kitchen doorway, his tall frame only inches from the top beam.

"What he said." Ethan indicated Gabriel. "What are you doing up?"

"The inability to sleep seems to be contagious." He eyed the coffee pot on the stove. "Any left?" He didn't wait for an answer but walked over, poured a cup of the thick brew, and took a swallow. "This is horrible."

Ethan raised an eyebrow when Gabriel took another drink and sat down next to him.

"Now, where were we? Yes, like hell, this is just your fight."

Ramsey's thoughts drifted to the woman sleeping upstairs—bandaged, bruised, and nearly killed. "Who's with Eliza?"

"Isabelle couldn't sleep either," Gabriel said and assured them. "I checked on her before coming down. She's holding her own."

Ramsey nodded.

"There's something between you," Ethan said quietly. "We've all seen it."

Ramsey didn't deny it. "If I make it through this, I'll let you know."

Gabriel sat forward. "Are you planning on getting in the way of a bullet?"

"If that's what it takes to end this." Ramsey looked at both brothers, his eyes unwavering, his conviction firm.

Strong fingers glided back and forth over the worn surface of the gold pocket watch. For nearly five years, it had served as a reminder for what he had lost, and what he never had the chance to know. Shadows of a dark past consumed him, and mistakes haunted him. He had only three regrets in his life, and he was now presented with the opportunity to rectify two of those. His life wouldn't have to be defined by what he failed to do in the past. When he rode away from the Double Bar Ranch and his grandfather, he promised himself never to return. His home had been whatever place on the map his horse and feet took him. He finally had a second chance to be part of a family—a real family. Ramsey questioned whether or not he deserved them—or their forgiveness. Eliza assured him there was nothing to forgive, but he disagreed. There was at least one person who deserved the truth and one person whose forgiveness did matter.

Ramsey walked through the quiet halls of the house, absorbing the details around him. The stalwart beams above and sturdy floor below were determined to withstand time. Hawk's Peak was a testament of the rewards available to those willing to persevere on a wild and remarkable land.

He believed his actions altruistic, a concern for his sister and her happiness. He attempted to justify remaining hidden from his sister, but the glaring truth emerged with each passing year— his own fear. Fear that he would disappoint her, or worse, that he would be angry for the life she received, and the one he did not. The day came when he could finally move past his fear. Years of hard work endowed him with an appreciation for the land. The Gallaghers had remained, fighting for what their family had built.

The silent study welcomed him, a room fit for men and women who earned their station and knew it. A room where ideas blossomed and responsibility weighed on the shoulders of people willing to pursue their dreams. Brenna sat on one of the upholstered chairs near the window, a book open in her lap, her eyes fixated on the dwindling sunlight outside the window. He had often imagined what it would be like to truly know her. Seeing her for the first time when he rode up to Hawk's Peak, his heart knew he had found home.

"I hoped to find you alone."

Brenna turned from the window, and a slow smile appeared on her face. "Pleased I am you did. Join me." Brenna stood and moved to the settee, motioning her brother to sit beside her.

Ramsey walked across the woven cotton rug and sat next to Brenna, the space between them filled with past secrets and present questions.

"We've been otherwise occupied these past days, and I'll admit I've almost felt as though you've been here, always. Then I realize I know so little about you or your life during the years we've been apart."

"It's not a story I can tell in one sitting, but I promise I will tell you all of it."

"You plan to stay? You won't leave again?"

Ramsey wondered at his good fortune.

"I'm not leaving." He closed some of the space between them and covered her hands with his. "You deserve more answers than I can give right now, but will you do something for me?"

"Anything."

"Will you tell me about our parents?"

Tears of sadness filled Brenna's eyes even as a slow smile lit up her face. "What you ask is simple, and it would bring me great pleasure to tell you of our parents. Where do I even begin?"

Ramsey enjoyed her smile and was grateful for the easy way she accepted him and welcomed him into his life and heart. "Just a memory for now. Your favorite memory."

"There are so many . . . oh goodness, Ramsey, I'm sorry."

Brenna sobered. "Sitting here with you, knowing we're together . . . for a moment I forgot we'd ever been apart."

"My life may not have been like yours, but it wasn't a bad life, Grandmother saw to that. I hold no ill will toward you or our parents for events beyond their control."

Brenna reached up to wipe the tears from her eyes, and then her lips curved into a warm smile. "I can't seem to help it. These last few days have been horrible for everyone, and yet I'm truly happy in this moment." Brenna leaned over and hugged her brother, surprising him. "Now, my favorite memory. When Papa gave me my first horse."

Ramsey listened intently to Brenna's retelling of her childhood story. Her words told him how much she loved their parents, and how good they had been to her. He no longer envied her the life she had been given. Rather he was grateful to their parents for loving Brenna so much.

"Did you ever leave Scotland before you came here?"

Brenna shook her head. "I always wanted to, but Father lost his interest for travel after Mother's passing, and I never felt right to leave him alone." Brenna hesitated a moment. "Did you go to a university?"

"I left here at a young age, spent a lot of years wandering, but I read a lot. Picked up enough here and there to amount to what I would have learned in school."

"When did you know about me? About your family?"

This time Ramsey hesitated, and not because he didn't want to tell her, but because he would have to explain why he didn't seek her out sooner.

"I knew for certain nearly two years ago, but about five years back I found this." Ramsey reached into his pocket and pulled out the gold pocket watch."

"That's Father's!" Brenna reached for the watch. "How did you get this?"

"It arrived here in Briarwood one day, general delivery. I was in Kentucky at the time, and Loren was kind enough to send it out."

"I don't understand. Mother gave him that watch on their last anniversary before she died. He wore it every day." Brenna smoothed her fingers over the surface of the watch, much like Ramsey had done. "He sent it to you. What did he tell you?"

"Nothing," Ramsey replied. "No letter, no explanation, but the watch is engraved."

Brenna opened the watch and rubbed the inside of the lid. She read the inscription out loud. "Always our hearts entwined." The tears began again, softly, but were accompanied by a small smile. "They meant it. Never a moment of their lives did they not truly love one another." Brenna lifted bright green eyes to her brother. "How did you know who sent it if no letter was enclosed?"

Ramsey leaned forward. "I wondered who would send me something which held such personal value, so I tried to trace the package. The original postmark led me to a lawyer in Boston, but he would tell me only that he acted on behalf of a client. Nathan Tremaine was traveling to Boston to meet with a group of politicians. I asked to go with him, hoping the lawyer would speak with me directly if I showed up."

"Father's lawyer, the man I met when I first arrived from Scotland. He is from Boston." Brenna leaned forward. "Did you speak with him then?"

Ramsey tilted his head slightly and studied her. "Not exactly." His face took on a slight pink hue. "I may have convinced his secretary to speak with me."

"Ramsey—"

"That's all I'm saying. She didn't tell me much either, except that the package arrived from Scotland. I may have heard Grandmother mention my father was from Scotland, but I had already left the Double Bar and attempting to contact her would have been too great of a risk."

"What changed two years ago?" Brenna wished now more than ever to know how her brother knew of her before she knew of him.

"That Boston lawyer sent me a letter to tell me of Father's illness. Before I had a chance to reply, I received another letter informing me of his death . . . and of a sister."

"I regret you had to learn of us that way."

Her guilt weighed heavy on him, but the guilt was not her burden to bear. "There was more to the letter—something the lawyer told me you didn't know about."

Brenna sat forward, intent on what he would say next.

"It's about our inheritance."

"But I already know about that. I have Cameron Manor, and they left me money in Scotland and here in America."

"Not that." Ramsey shifted slightly. "I don't know how, or even why, but they left a substantial fortune for us both, here in America."

"Goodness," Brenna whispered. "How substantial?"

"Your children and their children will never want or worry."

"I didn't know," Brenna said. "I wouldn't even know what to do with such a large amount."

"Neither do I. I've lived simply and have done well enough for myself, working on ranches and horse farms, but I was instructed to give you your portion. I haven't touched any of it, hoping I'd gain more answers."

"I'll give you all the answers I can, but it will take time to share the years we missed."

"And I want to know all of it, I do," Ramsey said, "but I'm more interested in making sure you and your children have a wonderful future."

"You will have a wonderful future, too. I hope you believe

that."

Ramsey smiled. "I'm working on it. Listen, about the money—"

"I don't have a personal need for it," Brenna said, "but if you're intent on not using your portion, then I'm certain we can put the money to good use for our families." Brenna looked up when Isabelle appeared at the door with Jacob in her arms.

"He's wanting his mama." Isabelle hesitated, but then walked into the room. "I'm sorry if I interrupted."

Brenna lifted her son into her own arms and smiled down at the fussy child. "Apologies aren't necessary."

Ramsey watched his sister doting on her son. An image formed in his mind, and his thoughts returned to the injured woman upstairs.

"If you'll excuse me, Jacob needs a change." Brenna turned back to her brother when she reached the doorway. "We'll speak later?"

"We will." Ramsey watched his sister leave, then gave his attention to Isabelle. She appeared to be waiting for him. He'd barely had the chance to speak with her since his arrival."

"Is everything all right?"

"I do have a favor to ask you."

Ramsey turned to Isabelle. "Anything."

"I've occupied Andrew upstairs most of these last few days; I thought it best with everything going on. He'd much rather be outside, even in the cold."

"I haven't spent any time with him, I know."

"He's been asking about his new uncle." Isabelle smiled. "I'm afraid having all of these men around has him behaving in ways which befuddle me at times."

"Say no more." Ramsey briefly looked out the window. The rare blue winter skies beckoned. The cattle would require a reserve of endurance from them all over the next few days. Ethan had told him they'd lost nearly a dozen head, but Andrew wouldn't understand that. "I can spare some time this afternoon. The sky has cleared up enough. Why don't he and I go riding? Wait, does he ride?"

Isabelle laughed softly. Her refined accent, a mix of southern genteel and cultured French soothed him. "At every opportunity."

"Then you let him know to be ready after lunch," Ramsey said. "If you'll excuse me, I'd like to speak with Eliza."

"Elizabeth was sitting with her when I passed by her room earlier. Eliza looked to be giving her a difficult time."

Ramsey's full lips curved into a half smile. "Grandmother can hold her own against Eliza; don't you worry about that."

6

"I'm not staying in bed."

"Do you need another blanket, dear?"

"I mean it. Just a little privacy so I can dress would be appreciated."

"You're not cold then? Perhaps just a sweater."

"A sweater would be nice for when I go downstairs."

"No sweater then."

"For heaven and—"

Ramsey listened intently from the hallway, suppressing his laughter. *She's one hell of a woman*, he thought, although he couldn't decide to which woman he referred.

"Elizabeth, I appreciate your help, truly I do," Eliza said calmly. "And don't take this the wrong way, but please get—"

"Good to see you awake, Eliza," Ramsey said, quickly stepping into the room.

Eliza's eyes looked him over curiously and he wondered if she was attempting to figure out how long he had stood there listening.

"Awake yes, but apparently not well enough to leave this bed." Eliza stared at Elizabeth's retreating back.

"I'll be back to check on you later, dear" Elizabeth said upon exiting the room.

"Your grandmother is impossible."

"Interesting," Ramsey murmured. "I was going to say the same of you."

"I heard that."

"You were meant to hear it." Ramsey walked across the room and moved a wooden chair from its place against the wall and set it next to the bed. He occupied the chair and looked over his shoulder at the door. "How long do I have before one of your brothers walks through?"

Eliza glared at him. "Plenty of time, I imagine. They both came in earlier to annoy me with talk of the ranch. Your grandmother told them I would be fine, so they went out to work—where I should be right now."

"Weren't we just talking about you being impossible?"

Eliza shook her head. "You were doing all the talking. I'm just going crazy."

Ramsey sobered. "I don't know you well enough yet to know if you're using that pluck of yours to avoid talking about what happened or if you're just this ornery."

Eliza fiddled with the edge of the quilt but remained silent.

"I'll take that to mean you're avoiding the subject."

Eliza's barely audible sigh was followed by a slight frown. "That's probably a fair assessment."

"We don't have to talk about what happened, not yet at least."

"I want to," Eliza said, "if only to clear the foggy images hindering my thinking." Eliza shifted in the bed to rest most of her weight on her uninjured side. "As a consequence of my unwanted convalescence, I've replayed that night many times. I do remember seeing something. At first I thought it was a bear or mountain lion after the cattle, but the closer it came, the taller it became. By then I knew it wasn't an animal, but the next moment I was on the ground, then in your arms."

Ramsey kept his worry to himself. Battling Nathan Hunter

and his men didn't mean they had to put their lives on hold. When Ramsey first made the choice to return to Montana, it was with the belief that he might not survive the encounter with his grandfather. He prepared himself for that—he had nothing to lose. Now he had everything to lose, and dying was no longer an option—nor was allowing Hunter to torment them further.

"I promise you'll be out of this bed soon. We'll find whoever did this to you, and you'll be back tormenting your brothers on the range before long."

Eliza smiled. "I do believe you're saying that with the hope I'll cooperate with Elizabeth and remain in bed for the rest of the day."

"You read me too well," Ramsey said, almost pleased.

"You and my brothers could all smooth talk your way through a grizzly fight if necessary. You're just sometimes obvious about it."

"I'd bet on the grizzly in that encounter." Ramsey laughed. "You, on the other hand, might stand a chance in such a confrontation."

"You've made your point."

"I didn't realize I had a point."

Eliza tilted her head and smiled at him. "If I'm strong enough to withstand a grizzly attack, I'm strong enough to hold my tongue with your grandmother and remain in bed, but that doesn't mean I have to be happy about it."

Ramsey no longer smiled, but he was curious. "How do you know what people mean, when they don't say what they mean?"

Eliza shrugged. "I don't think about it," she said and ended the line of questioning before it went further. "Will you be joining Ethan and Gabriel today?"

Ramsey nodded. "For a few hours. I promised Isabelle I'd take Andrew riding this afternoon." Ramsey checked the hour from the clock on the bureau. "Speaking of time, I'd better head out and take my shift with the cattle. I can't be late for Andrew." He stood and moved the chair back against the wall. Ramsey hesitated only a moment, then walked back to the bed and lifted Eliza's hand into his own. He gently kissed the smooth skin, lingering for a moment and allowing his warm breath to caress her skin. Her hand jerk slightly, but it remained in his. An easy smile spread across his lips. The confusion he saw in her eyes pleased him.

He wasn't done teasing her. "If you're a good girl, perhaps I'll convince Elizabeth you're well enough for me to carry you downstairs to dine with the family this evening."

Eliza considered him for a moment and pulled him closer. "If I'm a good girl?"

The soft down pillow ripped open when it met the top of his head. Eliza's broad smile shone through the floating feathers.

"You have remarkably good aim for someone with your injuries, and you've ruined a perfectly good pillow." He looked at the half-filled feather pillow sitting by her side. "I supposed I deserved that." Ramsey laughed, then leaned over and kissed her soft skin again. "Until our next delightful encounter." His smooth laughter followed him from the room.

Eliza settled down under the feather-covered quilt. The laughter came without any encouragement.

"Appreciate the help, Ramsey," Ethan said, riding up alongside Ramsey's sable stallion.

"I'm not here to sit and do nothing," Ramsey replied. He looked across the pasture to the burned rubble left from the old barn. "Do you plan to rebuild it?"

Ethan nodded. "It won't be easy, considering what happened there, but we have stock to consider and they can't share the smaller stable all winter. You ever raise a barn?"

"A few. My hands and back are here for whatever you need."

Ramsey made certain no one else was nearby before continuing. "There's something I've wanted to discuss with you, though I can't say this is the best time."

Ethan's gaze followed the landscape of the land his family never managed to conquer, but somehow found a way to make peace with it long enough to build a life. Every stone was set and board cut, not because of timing, but because life waited for no one. "I've come to realize there's never a better time for everything. What's on your mind?"

Ramsey studied his brother-in-law a moment, grateful his sister had found someone worthy of her or at least as worthy as any man could be of a good woman. "I finally sat down with Brenna this morning."

"About time," Ethan mumbled, and then looked over at Ramsey. "But it just so happens she told me about it when I stopped off at the house earlier."

"About the money?"

Ethan nodded. "She doesn't need it or want it."

"I know she doesn't and neither do I," Ramsey said. "But it's there, and if you're willing, I'd like to invest that money in Hawk's Peak."

He'd caught Ethan's full attention.

"You can't be serious." Ethan stared at him. "Brenna didn't know how much exactly, but from what she understood, it was quite a large sum."

Ramsey shrugged. "It is substantial."

"Can't let you do that," Ethan said, shaking his head. "Look around you. Sure, we have our struggles like any other rancher in the West, but thanks to my father's astute investments and the strong foundation he gave this ranch, we don't want for anything."

Ramsey watched as a few of the men slowly made their way back to the bunkhouse, while others rode their horses over the snowy ground to the pastures for the next shift. "I haven't suggested this because I believe the ranch needs the money."

"Why then?"

For a moment the startlingly deep blue eyes staring back at him belonged to Eliza. Ramsey pressed forward. "My offer comes with two reasons. Mallory Tremaine, my friend's younger sister from Kentucky, happened to mention that Eliza was interested in buying up some of the stock from their farm. I've seen Eliza with horses, and she's magnificent. I know this is primarily a cattle operation, and horses are a tremendous expense. If she decides to start a horse operation, assuming you and Gabriel support her, I'd like the funds to be there for her."

Ethan remained stoic. "Your second reason?"

"My grandfather is going to try and get a hold of that money any way he can."

Ramsey watched Ethan's body tense and admired his ability to appear unmoved. "You're certain?"

"Nothing else makes sense," Ramsey replied, but a doubt of uncertainty remained. "If the money is invested entirely into Hawk's Peak, it remains in part with Brenna as your wife, but it would be protected, as would she and our grandmother."

Ethan sat on his stallion, considering. "And you believe if there isn't any money for him to ransom for, that he'll simply move on?"

"I didn't say it would be that easy." Ramsey turned slightly in the saddle and watched Gabriel ride toward them. He added, "Hunter will hate us even more than he does now, but it might just be the beginning of the end."

"End of what?" Gabriel brought his gelding to a halt.

Ethan looked at his brother. "End of Hunter."

"I'm listening."

"We'll talk more this evening after supper. I suppose we'll need to carry Eliza down. I doubt Elizabeth will allow her to walk down the stairs yet."

Ramsey smiled to himself, remembering his earlier conversation with Eliza. He would gladly carry her anywhere.

Gabriel addressed Ramsey directly now. "Isabelle tells me you're taking Andrew riding this afternoon?"

"Isabelle has a way of getting a man to agree to something he didn't realize he wanted to do."

Gabriel grinned. "Only with people she likes and trusts. You've made an impression on her, and not on only her."

Ramsey glanced up at the sky, cloud cover blocking the sun. He pulled out his pocket watch. "I promised Andrew I'd take him at two o'clock."

Sobering, Gabriel said, "Do me a favor and ride west, away from the Double Bar."

Ramsey nodded. "I'll keep him safe."

"Do I get to hold the reins, Ibby?" Andrew danced and kicked up snow onto her dress. They walked together toward the stable and corral, where Ramsey and Gabriel waited.

"We'll see, Andrew, now stay close." Isabelle was more cautious around the smaller stable. The constant coming and going of ranch hands, coupled with Andrew's exuberance, could lead to disaster if he wasn't watched.

"There's the young cowboy." Gabriel lifted Andrew into his arms, then tossed him in the air.

A shrieking giggle escaped Andrew's lips. "Again!"

"What, and keep you from your ride?"

Andrew squirmed in Gabriel's arms now, eager to get down. "I get to ride the horse!" When Gabriel set him back on the ground, he turned to look up at Ramsey. "Uncle Ramsey, do I get to hold the reins?"

"If it's all right with your sister, I think we can manage that," Ramsey replied with a smile and looked at Isabelle. "We can fashion a rope to the bridle for me to hold, and he can keep the reins."

Gabriel's agreement soothed Isabelle's worried expression— somewhat. "They aren't going far, and Ramsey is about as good with horses as they come."

"Is he better than Aunt Eliza?" Andrew asked, having heard the interchange.

"Ah, well, he just might be," Gabriel replied, "but don't go telling your aunt that."

Ramsey detached the rope from the mare's saddle, one of Eliza's old saddles, and attached one end to the mare's bridle. He held the other end while Gabriel lifted Andrew onto the mare's back. Gabriel tied the ends of the reins and handed them to Andrew.

"You hold onto those real tight now." Gabriel folded Andrew's fingers around the reins. "Don't pull or move them too much unless Ramsey says."

"Okay, Gabriel." Andrew whipped his head around, looking at the animal. "I haven't named this one yet!" Andrew exclaimed.

Ramsey laughed. "Do you name all of the horses?"

"Gabriel said I could." Andrew looked thoughtful a moment. "Do I get to name your horse?"

"It just so happens he doesn't have a name, but do me a favor and make it a good one." Ramsey led the mare by the rope to where his stallion was tethered. With the rope in hand, he mounted, careful to keep enough length so his horse didn't rub against Andrew's leg.

"I get to ride out there, Ibby!" Andrew pointed toward the snow-covered pasture.

"You just be careful and mind Uncle Ramsey," Isabelle said, once again worried. She leaned into Gabriel and quietly said, "He's so young, Gabriel, and he hasn't left this immediate area before. Are you certain—"

"Ramsey will watch him."

"I'm not worried about that, but you know how excited Andrew can become."

Gabriel slipped an arm around his wife. "First, it's really too cold for you to be out here any longer, and second, Ramsey is likely one of the best people I've ever seen with a horse." They watched Ramsey and Andrew ride past the cattle, heading east away from Double Bar land and the herd.

"I saw plenty when we were all younger. I wasn't speaking for Ramsey's benefit earlier—he just may be better with a horse than Eliza." Gabriel grinned down at his wife. "But I'll deny it if you ever tell her."

Isabelle smiled slowly when her husband guided her in the direction of the house. "If only I had a good reason to keep quiet about this little confession of yours."

Gabriel looked down at his wife, their feet leaving indents in the snow. "You've been spending too much time with Eliza. Not a woman alive I've ever known who can manipulate something the way she can." They reached the front steps of the long deck, and he pulled her closer. "You're just lucky I like to be manipulated."

Isabelle's soft laughter followed them inside.

Andrew held the leather reins while he gripped the saddle horn. Not an easy task for the young boy, but his wide grin said he didn't mind. Ramsey rode alongside him, keeping a close watch on the boy while scanning the area around them. He could hear some of the men out with the cattle and smell the welcoming smoke from the chimneys. They moved at a slow walk farther from the buildings but always within sight. Ramsey led them toward the trees and smiled when Andrew pointed to the deer, prancing across the meadow. A whisper of snow began to fall but only enough to touch their skin softly from time to time. The bright sun shone overhead, but the brutal cold of winter still surrounded them. Andrew didn't seem to notice the stream of fog from his mouth every time he spoke. Ramsey reached over and lifted the borrowed bandana so it covered the lower part of Andrew's face.

"We won't be able to stay out here much longer, kid."

Andrew started to speak through the cloth but lowered it enough so his lips were free. "A little longer, please?"

Ramsey compromised. "One more loop around and then we'll head back in. Perhaps your sister will fix us both some hot chocolate." Ramsey turned them away from the tree line and back toward the ranch, though it was now far in the distance. "Have you thought of a name for that mare yet?" he asked Andrew.

"Snowflake!" Andrew held onto the saddle horn tightly with both hands. "She's white and pretty like snow."

"I'd say that fits her nicely." Ramsey smiled. "How about this big guy here?"

"I still have to think." Andrew peered over at Ramsey. "Does he like to run fast?"

Ramsey remained silent.

"Uncle Ramsey?"

"Yes?" Ramsey said absently, his eyes focused on the open area to the west.

"Does he run fast?"

Ramsey ignored the question and moved his horse next to the mare. Reaching over, he lifted Andrew from the saddle and set him down on his lap. He secured the mare's reins and slapped her on the rump.

"Snowflake is running!" Andrew clapped, but his delight was short-lived.

"Hold onto me tight," Ramsey said firmly, then with one arm wrapped securely around Andrew and the other holding the leather straps, he urged the animal into a run. Snow flew up behind and around them with every stride. The first of the gunshots missed, but another one hit Ramsey's hat, knocking it from his head. Ramsey sensed Andrew's fear and heard the boy's frightened sobs, but he continued to run the horse as quickly as he could over the snow. He lowered his head and covered Andrew with his large body, hoping for the best.

7

The first gunshot echoed through the valley, alerting the cattle and men to trouble. Kevin, Henry, and Colton, being the closest, first noticed the horse without a rider, then a short distance behind it, Ramsey's stallion. The stallion soon caught up with the mare, and both animals raced toward the stable.

"Coming in!" Colton and Henry rode toward Ramsey, firing off shots in the direction of the ones coming toward them.

Gabriel ran from the stable and caught sight of the horses. Another gunshot resounded through the air. *Andrew!* Gabriel ran back to the stable to get his horse, but Ramsey reached the corral. The mare continued past them a short distance before Ramsey managed to gain the lead and pull around in front and stop her. Gabriel ran to Ramsey and Andrew and quickly lifted the boy from the saddle. Ramsey turned his horse to go back out.

"What the hell are you doing?"

Ethan rode up then, having heard the gunshots from the south grazing lands.

"The bastard could have killed the boy," Ramsey said.

"Son of a—" Gabriel held Andrew's shivering body in his arms. "Go."

Ramsey urged his horse away from them, heading for the men still firing shots off into nowhere. Ethan hesitated and ran his eyes over his nephew.

"He'll be all right."

Ethan nodded and followed Ramsey. Seconds later, his stallion caught up to Ramsey, cutting him off. Neither horse appreciated the interruption in their run, nor their close proximity. "You're not doing this alone."

"They're not getting away this time!" Ramsey's horse pranced beneath him. "I won't be the reason my sister becomes a widow."

"Follow me." Ethan turned his horse, and Ramsey followed him toward the trees. The shooting continued, but they soon rode out of range and into the woods. The men pulled their horses to a stop, both animals anxious for more, yet willing to allow their riders a temporary respite.

"Let's get something out of the way. Normally I wouldn't bother explaining myself, but considering we're kin, I'll reassure you only this once. I have no intention of ever allowing Brenna to live her life as widow."

"Fair enough," Ramsey said. "You want to tell me why we took for the trees? Granted it's been a number of years, but Hunter usually kept a close watch on the forested edge of his land."

Ethan watched the tree line. "He used to, but perhaps we'll get lucky."

"Risking this on luck?"

Ethan stared at him a moment. "Does that bother you?"

"Not at all," Ramsey replied. "Heaven help my sister."

"Why's that?"

"She married a man as crazy as I am." Ramsey guided his stallion forward through the trees. They moved effortlessly, the horses' steps muffled by the layer of snow covering the forest floor.

"I estimate at least five minutes since the shooting stopped." Ramsey's muted words carried no farther than Ethan. "He's likely gone, though I imagine not far." Ramsey lifted the flap of his saddlebag and pulled out a brass and leather telescope.

Surprised, Ethan watched Ramsey focus on the snowy fields, then commented, "Fancy."

"Gift from an old friend." Ramsey studied the landscape through the glass. "Got him, and he's moving fast."

Ramsey left the confines of the trees first, Ethan close behind. Their powerful horses moved swiftly through the snow, quickly gaining ground and closing the distance between them and the riders. Once close enough to be heard, Ramsey shouted out for the rider to halt. Turning slightly, the rider responded with three haphazard pistol shots.

"One more chance!"

The rider carelessly fired again, this time losing his grip on the reins and his balance in the saddle. He slid from the running horse and landed on his side in the snow. The impact slowed him down for a second, but then he lifted his pistol with an unsteady arm and fired another shot at the men. Ethan and Ramsey both fired back, one or both of them hitting the man's palm. The quiet of the land was disturbed by the man's screams echoing over the fields.

"Will your men come?"

Ethan shook his head. "I told them to stay back."

Ramsey stepped toward the screaming man, and once upon him, Ramsey paused. "Dirk?"

Dirk stopped shouting for a moment, but his face remained twisted in pain. "Ramsey? We thought you was dead."

"I find that difficult to believe. You shot at me."

Dirk frantically shook his head. "I didn't know it was you, I swear I didn't."

"I'm not sure I believe that," Ramsey replied. "You've managed to make me madder than hell, so tell us the truth!"

"No, I swear!" Dirk rocked back and forth and pulled his bleeding limb to his chest while blood dripped onto the stark white snow around him. "I didn't know it was you!"

"It's been a long time, Dirk, and I didn't trust you back then either."

"Damn it to hell, I didn't know! I thought you was one of them bloody Gallaghers!" The effort to appeal for his life failed.

"Wrong answer." Ethan's stony response barely reached Dirk's ears, but he heard it and realized his mistake.

"I was just doing as I was told."

"By whom?" Ramsey asked.

"You know who. He thought you was dead too!"

Using the bottom of his boot, Ramsey pushed Dirk back into the snow. "And the boy you almost killed?"

"He ain't dead, is he?" Dirk spat at them.

Ramsey grabbed him. "Where is he?"

"You go to hell, Ramsey, and you, too, Gallagher!"

Dirk's confidence faltered, and Ramsey regarded the pallor in the other man's face. "You don't have a lot of time left, Dirk. You're losing blood." Ramsey's soft voice contradicted the hard glare in his emerald-colored eyes.

"You gonna leave me like this?"

"Where is he?"

Ramsey watched the fear in Dirk's eyes increase, but he realized the man might tell them only lies.

"You'll get me to the doc?"

Ethan stepped forward and stood on the other side of Dirk. "That was my nephew you nearly killed out there today."

"He's the brat Hunter told us to take."

Ethan paused and then said, "You weren't one of the men at the cabin."

"'Course not. I just as soon kill the little bastard."

Ramsey stood and said, "Last chance, Dirk. Where is he?"

"He'll kill you when he knows you're alive."

"That's my problem."

"I'm in a bad way here." Dirk tried to cover his wound but failed to stop the bleeding. "I need the doc."

Ethan leaned down, aiming his pistol at Dirk's chest. "I'll do you one better. I'll make it quick."

"Ethan." Ramsey's firm voice was meant for his brother-in-law, but Dirk saw a possible ally.

"You ain't gonna let him kill me?"

Ramsey pulled the edge of his long coat back, catching Dirk's attention.

"You're a marshal?" Dirk attempted a smile, but he lacked much strength to form the expression. "No matter what I say, you gotta help me 'cause you're the law."

"And what is it you want to tell me?"

"Hunter'll kill you." Dirk then turned to Ethan. "And you filthy Gallaghers. He'll get all of you, even that new brat of yours." Dirk managed the beginnings of a laugh. "You'll all be—" One punch by Ethan's strong fist was all it took to silence Dirk.

Dirk lay unconscious and quiet. Ethan raised his eyes to meet Ramsey's. "It's a wonder we haven't had more company from the Double Bar."

Ramsey shifted his eyes to focus on the area behind Ethan. "Could be they aren't there, or it could be they were told not to come. Either way, we have to get him to the doctor."

Ethan nodded and holstered his gun. "I'll ride back. The snow isn't too deep; we can get a wagon out of here."

Ramsey followed Ethan's movements as he mounted. "Ethan."

Ethan stopped, then looked down at Ramsey and the wounded man.

"As much as I'd like otherwise, we have to get him help. I'll patch him up the best I can, but hurry."

Ethan's stallion found his footing and sprinted across the snowy field. Ramsey slowly turned back to look at Dirk, sprawled out on the snow. "You're just lucky I'm not my grandfather." He trudged through the snow to his horse, and pulling the knife from his belt, cut a section from his rope. Ramsey shrugged out of his coat, the cold knifing through to his skin. He carefully cut a slit in the fabric near his shoulder and ripped the sleeve from his shirt. The rope didn't tie easily around Dirk's arm, but it worked well enough to stem the flow to the wound. Ramsey managed to stop the bleeding and wrapped the remaining shirt sleeve around Dirk's hand.

"You're a heap of bother, Dirk," Ramsey said aloud. "By the time I see you're shipped off to prison, you'll have wished you'd stayed far away from Nathan Hunter." He finished bandaging Dirk, covering the wound with snow and continued speaking to the supine man. "You may end up with a bit of frostbite, but you just might keep the hand." Ramsey looked over the prostrate body and swore. He returned to his horse for his coat and folded it over. As carefully as he could manage, Ramsey lifted Dirk's head and placed his folded coat under him, creating a barrier between the man's head and the snow. "You'd better have something good to tell me when the doc finishes with you."

"He still alive?"

"Thanks to the snow." Ramsey moved out of the way to allow Henry and Tom access to Dirk. "The cold kept him from bleeding out."

"We aren't going to have much daylight." Ethan jumped down from the wagon. "I sent Colton into town to fetch Doc Brody."

"Think the animals will mind sharing the stable with him?"

"Ben offered his room off the bunkhouse. I almost hesitated, but I wasn't about to let him into the main house. The doc can treat him, and then we'll transport him to the jail."

"He's a mite one," Tom said, once all four men pushed Dirk

into the back of the wagon.

"Not too puny to shoot at us." Ramsey tied his stallion to the back of the wagon and climbed in, then covered Dirk with a wool blanket and heavy canvas. "He's as set as he's going to get."

Ethan nodded and climbed onto the wooden seat of the wagon. Henry joined Ethan on the bench, and Tom took a place in the back with Ramsey.

Tom looked at their prisoner and then lifted skeptical eyes to Ramsey. "Don't seem worth the trouble."

Ramsey grabbed the wagon's edge as Ethan guided the team carefully through snow. He glanced back at the patch of bloody snow and automatically reached out to brace Dirk when the wagon jostled. "Men like him rarely are, Tom, but a life is a life." Ramsey turned his head, his eyes meeting Tom's.

"He almost killed you, Ramsey, and the boy. I don't understand. He's barely alive."

Ramsey watched the sun slowly caress the mountain peaks. Ramsey was aware that Ethan and Henry listened. "Have you ever killed a man or looked down the barrel of a gun?"

Tom shook his head. "No, sir. It don't look like much fun either."

"No, it's not." Ramsey chuckled unexpectedly. "This land isn't for the fainthearted. But there are too many men already who can answer 'yes' to both questions. Better if you stay wondering."

"You don't wonder?"

"No, I don't." The evening light cascaded from the sky, touching the ranch as it slowly appeared in the distance. Ramsey turned away from Tom, his eyes focusing on the open land, surrounding them on three sides. The mountains rose up above the trees and formed a barrier between them and whatever world existed on the other side. He shifted and looked forward when the wagon rambled toward the bunkhouse.

"I came as quickly as I could." The doctor preceded Colton into Ben's one-room cabin attached to the bunkhouse and scooted around Ethan. "Dark sneaks up fast this time of year." His eyes scanned the motionless man on the bed, and he glanced up at Ethan. "You didn't leave much for me."

The small cabin didn't offer ample space for five grown men to maneuver comfortably around the bed, but they managed to give the doctor enough room to examine his patient.

Ramsey closed the distance between himself and the bed in two strides. "He lost a lot of blood, Doc, but otherwise, his wound wasn't fatal. Just the one bullet through the hand."

"You the one who shot him?"

"Possibly."

"Well, you leave me to him, and I'll let you know when he regains consciousness."

Ramsey shook his head. "Sorry, but someone has to stay with you. He's not much to look at now, but I'll not risk him waking up and you in here alone." Ramsey noticed the doctor's eyes shift quickly to the badge and nod sharply.

"One of you can stay."

Ben stepped forward. "I'll stay. You two have been at this long enough."

Ethan studied the ranch hand. "You're sure about this, Ben?"

Ben nodded and moved around the others to stand next to Ramsey. "I'm sure."

Ramsey stepped away to make room for Ben. "Would you say he'll live, Doc?"

"Perhaps." Brody tilted his head from side to side while pulling bandages, sewing thread, scissors, and a needle out of his worn leather bag. "If he doesn't lose more blood, he may pull through." He glanced up at Ramsey. "But don't take that as a promise. He's as pale as I've seen them next to a dead man."

Ramsey withdrew from the room, stepping into the darkness. The cold welcomed him and his eyes immediately lifted to the star-filled night sky.

"These are rare nights." Ethan looked up and then stepped away from the cabin.

"Too rare." Ramsey stared up at the night sky. "Reminds us we're mere humans walking on land with a greater purpose."

"You want to talk about it?"

"About what?"

"I heard what you told Tom"

Shaking his head, Ramsey stepped away. "Appreciate it, but not yet."

Ethan stepped around him and walked toward the main house. His voice carried in the tranquil night. "Eliza's always been a good listener," he said and resumed his trek to the house.

Standing beneath the starry sky, Ramsey closed his eyes. He knew forgetting the past would be an impossible feat, but he'd hoped time would ease the memory.

8

"You've finally released me from the confines of the stifling bedroom, and now you want me to go back upstairs?" Eliza gaped at Ethan.

"I opened the window," Elizabeth said.

"That's lovely, thank you," Eliza said sweetly, then turned on her brother. "I'm not an invalid, Ethan. I promise I'm well enough to leave my bed, walk around, and eat in the kitchen. I imagine I can even ride a horse again. Standing outside didn't hurt me last night, and it's certainly not going to kill me today." Eliza stood and lifted her arms above her head to demonstrate. A searing pain shot through her side. "Damn it!"

Ramsey hid his smile behind a mug of coffee.

"Eliza Gallagher!" said Elizabeth.

Eliza flushed. "They say it all the time," she said, pointing to her brothers, "but for a second, I forgot you were there. Sorry."

Eliza's frustration grew every day she was asked to remain inside to allow her body the proper time to heal. Even though her family cared enough to act protectively, Eliza refused to linger indoors, feeling useless while her family toiled and fought for their lives.

After nearly a week in bed with only sponge baths, Eliza expressed great delight when Elizabeth had two of the men haul a large copper bathtub to her room, allowing her more privacy than if she used the family bathing room. Her aching body lavished in the steaming water, and the fragrant soap they'd made during the summer glided over her skin. She inhaled the flowery scent and regretted leaving the bath when the first shots had echoed through the sky.

Eliza recalled how the soapy water splashed in her face after she dropped the soap. She almost fell in her attempt to step from the tub, and she pulled Ethan's stitches in the process. Drops of blood swam in the soapy water. By the time she managed to pull her arms through the sleeves of a robe and walk into the hall, she'd lost enough blood to soak through the material. Brenna, holding Jacob, saw her first and called out to the other women, and Elizabeth and Isabelle managed to help Eliza back into bed. Elizabeth, having the most experience with wounds, stitched Eliza back up the best she could.

The aching pain in her heart rejected all of her attempts at ridding the unwelcome feeling. *Was someone shot? Did they live?* These and far worse imaginings had filled her mind. When Brenna finally brought her news of what had happened, Eliza's dread escalated. Until she'd seen for herself that Ramsey, Andrew, and her brothers were safe, she couldn't be calmed. Nor could she move without stretching the new stitches in her side.

When Ethan and Gabriel discovered what happened with her, they shifted their focus from the ranch to making sure she was never left alone until her body healed. She went from worrying about them to feeling extremely annoyed by their constant presence. Eliza couldn't decide which she should feel worse about. Considering the most recent events, she opted to keep her opinion to herself—for now.

Eliza looked up at Ethan from the bench in the kitchen. "All right, I can't ride a horse yet, but don't ask me to hide inside any longer, Ethan. Elizabeth checked the wound this morning." Eliza glanced at Elizabeth, silently pleading for help.

Elizabeth bustled around the stove for a moment before answering. "The wound appears to be closing."

Eliza smiled but only for a moment.

"But it will only remain closed if you take it easy." Elizabeth pointed to the covered wound. "That's no simple scratch on your side. That bullet nearly killed you."

The truthful words filled the air, silencing everyone. The severity of the wound was not unknown to Eliza, and she used brevity and grit in an attempt to lessen everyone's worry. "I promise, I'll be more careful until the wound heals properly."

Both Ethan and Ramsey settled doubtful eyes on her.

"I promise."

"I'll hold you to that," Ethan said. "I'm going to spend a little time with my son before supper." Reluctantly, Ethan walked toward the door where he paused, his eyes returning to Eliza.

"Good grief, I promise."

Ethan nodded, feeling temporarily satisfied, and exited the kitchen.

"This soup has a bit of time left to simmer." Elizabeth set the lid over the cast iron pot hanging over the stove. Her eyes darted from Eliza to Ramsey. "Enough for everyone tonight, so you tell those boys at the bunkhouse to fetch their supper here tonight."

"Yes, ma'am." Ramsey watched Elizabeth leave the room, conveniently leaving him alone with Eliza.

"I had hoped for more time alone to talk, but would you be more comfortable in the library?"

Eliza shook her head. "Probably, but I'd rather stay here. This hard bench is a welcome change from the feather bed upstairs. Sitting here convinces me I've made progress."

"I don't blame you for itching to get back out there, but I don't blame your brothers for wanting to keep you safe."

"I don't blame them, either. I hound them relentlessly whenever either of them is injured."

"You'd never actually admit that to them, would you?"

Eliza slowly raised her eyes to his. "Stop figuring me out. I imagine you have something else on your mind."

"I do, though the timing may be inappropriate."

"Out here, the time is always right for a conversation—and always wrong. Time is the one commodity we can't control, so it's best to live in that moment."

"You sound like Ethan."

The pained look forming on Eliza's pale skin pulled a soft chuckle from Ramsey. The sound affected Eliza and reminded her it was no simple attraction she and Ramsey shared.

"What conversation did you want to have?"

"Horses."

"A subject I'm happy to discuss."

"While in Kentucky, you expressed to Mallory your intent to purchase a few horses. Were you serious?"

Eliza tilted her head slightly at his question.

"Yes, I did, and yes, I was serious."

"How would you feel about breeding horses here at Hawk's Peak? Not just for your own stock, or the occasional sale, but a full breeding program?"

"And you thought of this now?"

Ramsey leaned back, sliding his hands onto his lap. "I told you—bad timing."

Eliza shook her head. "No, that's not it."

The smile forming on her full lips was unexpected, and Ramsey waited for to continue.

"My brothers don't want me leaving the house, you were nearly killed yesterday, and we all know why you're wearing that badge. Yet, you talk of breeding horses." She eyed him suspiciously. "Is this your attempt at distracting me from my boredom?"

Ramsey returned her smile and leaned forward once again. He

lifted one of her hands into his and held it comfortably like an old friend's. "There's a life to live on the other end of . . . everything."

"You believe that?"

"Why would you think I don't?"

Eliza fixed her eyes on his and soberly confessed. "Ethan may have mentioned a conversation you had with him and Gabriel about doing whatever it takes to end all of this."

"I meant it, Eliza."

"I know."

"That doesn't mean I don't believe in the possibility of a positive outcome." Ramsey leaned forward. "I'll do whatever is necessary, even if the cost is my life, but I won't seek death if it doesn't seek me."

"Good, because we will make it through these troubles and . . ." Eliza paused a moment.

Ramsey noticed that his fingers moved slowly back and forth over her soft skin.

". . .and I'd like to talk horses."

Ramsey had spent enough time cautioning himself about Eliza. *On second thought, to hell with caution.*

Ramsey slid off the bench, his eyes steady with hers, and closed the space between them. He leaned toward her, watching the cautious dart of her eyes and admiring the beauty of the blue depths. She allowed him to pull her forward, slowly.

"Oh, my!" The soft cry blasted them apart as effectively as a stampede.

Ramsey groaned. "Better come in, Brenna."

"No, I'm sorry, Eliza, Ramsey." Brenna moved to back out of the room but halted with her back to the couple when Eliza called out.

Ramsey quickly slipped away from Eliza.

"Please, Brenna, don't leave." Eliza smiled at Ramsey,

believing he needed a bit of encouragement at the moment, then turned and addressed her sister-in-law. "Thank goodness it was you and not Ethan or Gabriel."

Brenna hesitantly walked into the kitchen and said, "I expect Ethan will be down soon." She looked from Eliza to Ramsey and smiled. "A surprise it is, though a pleasant one."

Ramsey stood and looked curiously at his sister. "Ethan didn't tell you?"

"What would Ethan know?"

"Well, nothing exactly, except—"

"Except what?"

"Oh dear, I'd best leave you two alone." Brenna took a step toward the door.

"No, you're fine." Eliza waved her in, but her focus remained on Ramsey, studying him. "What would Ethan have to tell Brenna?"

"Tell Brenna what?" Ethan sauntered into the kitchen.

Ramsey dropped his head momentarily on the table. "Nothing."

"Then why would I tell Brenna?" Ethan slipped his arm around his wife's waist and met her smile with one of his own.

Eliza finally realized the ridiculous direction the conversation had taken but not before a red hue crept into her cheeks.

"Are you feeling well?" Ethan moved away from his wife, walked to his sister, and pressed his palm against her face. "You feel a little warm. Perhaps you should go—"

"I'm fine and if you say I should go to bed, I swear I'll sleep on this table."

Ethan stepped back and studied her. He contemplated his sister's mood, but when he spoke it was to Ramsey. "Do I want to know?"

Ramsey shook his head. "I said I'd let you know when there was something to tell."

"Perhaps it's time to cool down—"

"Enough!" Eliza stood abruptly, and it cost her a quick and sharp pain in her wounded side. She held her side and took a deep breath. "Ethan, whatever you think you know, you don't, and if you do, mind your own business." Eliza turned to look at Brenna with the thought of apologizing but scowled instead. "You don't have to be enjoying this so much."

Brenna's green eyes sparkled. "Oh, but I do, and I'll be telling you why in my own good time."

"What's the racket in here?" Elizabeth walked lightly into the room with baby Jacob in her arms.

Brenna stepped forward and retrieved her son from her grandmother's arms.

Eliza spared one look for each occupant of the room, her eyes lingering on Ramsey longer than the others. He met her stare, yet somehow, she managed to pull away. "I'm going to bed," she said unexpectedly, and left the room, leaving in her wake a sea of mixed expressions and emotions.

Elizabeth faced those left behind with hands on hips and a stern expression. "What exactly did I miss?"

9

The sun shone through heavy white clouds, skimming over the mountains and valley. Minimal snowpack remained on the ground to allow for safe travel to Briarwood, a task which Ramsey had willingly accepted. Eliza's growing frustration at remaining indoors prompted him to volunteer, if for no other reason than to facilitate her escape from the house. He smiled, remembering the conversation in the kitchen earlier that morning. When Ramsey conveniently mentioned he was taking the wagon into Briarwood for supplies, Eliza immediately announced she'd accompany him. The ensuing argument between sister and brothers about jostling wagons and cold weather lasted less than five minutes. He welcomed her presence beside him on the wagon bench.

Ramsey's eyes scanned the surrounding landscape. They had survived the first storm of the winter season, but the long months ahead would require all of them to be ready and able. Eliza's injury had stirred emotions in everyone at the ranch, affecting Ramsey as much as it had her brothers. Ramsey wished he could push back the fear that consumed him after he knew the boy was finally safe. He'd mourned the loss of friends before, but never had he suffered the extent of fear when one believes he might lose someone he loves.

Someone, somewhere, hated the Gallaghers, or Hawk's Peak,

so much he'd be willing to kill anyone—even a child—to accomplish his goals. Everyone, including Ramsey, believed it was Hunter. No one else hated them enough—at least to their knowledge. But no one knew for certain.

Ben rode alongside the wagon, and Ramsey was grateful for the company. As much as he'd prefer to spend more time alone with Eliza, he wasn't fool enough to risk anyone's safety. Eliza sat next to him, bundled in her warmest coat. Ethan had refused to let her leave without an extra blanket and a promise that she would use it. Ramsey smiled, remembering the expression on Eliza's face. He'd been back with the family long enough to recognize when one of them was keeping quiet rather than lashing out.

The small town slowly came into view, and it was a welcoming sight. The cold weather hadn't been inviting, but the mountain air invigorated Ramsey, no matter what temperature the season brought. The church and schoolhouse appeared first, standing solid in the meadow, inviting travelers to Briarwood. Though he'd ridden the same trail to and from the Double Bar hundreds of times in his youth, he never tired of it. Briarwood had certainly changed over the years, but growth was slow, thanks to a cold climate most folks couldn't handle. He'd seen city folks travel up to the Montana wilderness, thinking they'd make a life for themselves on the wild frontier. Most didn't last their first winter before heading to Helena or Butte or back to from wherever they hailed.

He recalled meeting a young couple in Georgia who thought to strike it rich at the mines in Butte, but one year later they returned home. *Montana isn't the last best place for everyone,* he mused, *but it just might be mine.*

They approached town slowly, careful of ice that may have formed in ruts created by wagons. Ethan told him that morning that they were going to begin rebuilding the barn, but they needed to place a supply order with Loren at the general store. Ramsey had helped build a barn once during the winter at a Wyoming ranch, his first job after he left the Double Bar—not an easy feat, but not impossible either. He knew Ethan to be a practical man, and the smaller stable wouldn't accommodate the animals comfortably for long. Ramsey had been in Kentucky when the fire burned, he remembered Mabel and her kindness.

The general store and livery were open, as was the saloon, but the streets were bare, most folks seeking the warmth of home.

"We'll head over to the doc's first and have him give that wound of yours a look."

"I don't need the doctor." Eliza folded the blanket and set it under the seat when the wagon turned the corner. "I'm healing nicely; otherwise, my guards wouldn't have let me out of the house today."

Ramsey smiled at her. "The doc can take a look and give you a clean bill for your brothers, or they can keep hounding you. I would think you'd rather—"

"All right, you've made your point." Eliza smiled at Ramsey. "Doctor first. Ben, would you please—"

A ruckus broke out at the saloon, interrupting the quiet in the streets and Eliza's request. The saloon owners generally kept fights and too much drinking under control—one of the conditions of allowing the establishment in Briarwood—but that didn't stop the occasional over-imbibing or brawl between rowdy ranch hands and traveling cowboys. This particular ruckus included whistling, which meant there was a chance a lady had become involved. Ramsey had not stepped across the threshold of that particular building since returning to Montana. He didn't care to drink with the usual patrons who frequented saloons, nor did he enjoy watching the scantily dressed women subjected to the stares and wandering hands of the men.

Ben changed direction at the sound of the woman's scream.

"Sorry, Eliza, but I'd like to take a look."

"Of course, go." She turned to Ramsey, but he was already stepping down from the wagon.

Ben jumped down from his bay horse, tied him to the hitching post, and followed Ramsey to the entrance. A man came through the set of swinging doors and landed on his backside in the snow. The drunk looked up at them for a moment, smiled, and then passed out. Ben ignored the man and went through the doors first, and Ramsey followed.

Ramsey's eyes slowly adjusted to the din of the interior, smoke suffocating what little clean air might find a way in from outside. The large room held a small number of patrons, all men. The only woman Ramsey saw was Millie, the proprietor's sister, whom he remembered from his wilder days. The scowl and worried look on her face, coupled with the shotgun she pulled from behind the bar, spurred Ramsey into action. His eyes quickly scanned the room, falling on a group of men in the corner. Another shout from a woman and more movement caused the group to break up.

Ben rushed toward the corner, pushing drunks aside as he went. Millie came up beside Ramsey with the shotgun, but he stopped her and shook his head.

"Use that gun only if you have to."

Millie nodded.

Ramsey saw the young woman struggling on the man's lap and watched as Ben reached over, slammed a fist into the man's face, and pulled the woman away.

"Hey! You hit Buck!"

"Now, Ben, we wasn't plannin' to hurt the gal," said another more sober man, one who recognized Ben.

"Didn't appear that way to me, Stanley, or to Millie." Ben looked toward Millie holding the shotgun. Buck, the man he hit, remained unconscious.

"You can't just do that and leave 'im there." A man pulled his gun, pointing it with a wobbly grip at Ben.

"I wouldn't do that." Ben pulled the hammer back on his pistol. The room quieted.

Ben also recognized the man holding the gun on him. "I can and I did, Jim. Best you sober up and head back to the Rocking Creek." He then added to the men who appeared to be Buck's friends. "And you let Buck know that if I hear about him fooling around with another woman who isn't looking for his attentions that I'll come looking for him."

They holstered their guns and picked up an unconscious Buck, and one of the men said, "Let's get Buck on out of here."

Ramsey nodded to the only one of the men seeming to understand the situation. He felt semi-confident that the few men who managed to remain sober would clear out before Millie ended up using that shotgun of hers. Barely sparing the young woman Ben had rescued a glance, Ramsey addressed Millie. "Where's your brother?"

"Harvey rode down Butte way yesterday." Millie kept a careful watch on the rowdy group as they slowly made their way from the saloon.

"Are you going to be all right here alone?"

Millie offered him a look that answered his question. Her drab brown hair stuck out in disarray, and her equally drab brown eyes offered a man no encouragement. The bodice of her dress rose up to her neck, and the skirt swished along the floor. Her appearance certainly wasn't meant to entice anyone. Ramsey suspected that's why Harvey left his sister alone to watch over the saloon.

"We'll be taking . . ." Ramsey finally spoke to the young woman.

"Mandy is her name," Millie said and then added, "You'd best get her out of here. Harvey wanted a pretty one to serve the men, but she's caused nothing but trouble since she walked in that door." Millie turned to Mandy and said, "I am sorry, but—"

"I understand," Mandy assured her. "I'll be fine."

Ramsey nodded to Millie, and with one more study of the room, he slowly guided Ben and the woman to the entrance. "Wait, do you have any belongings here you'll need to collect?"

Mandy shook her head. "Just my coat there on the hook. I'm renting a room from Mr. Baker at the general store."

"Let's go, then." Ben pulled her coat down and helped her into it. Taking her arm, Ben walked beside her out the door and onto the boardwalk in front of the saloon. She stopped before he could walk any farther.

"Who are you?"

Ramsey turned to face her when Ben didn't immediately respond. Her light brown hair fell over one side of a face covered in smooth, pale skin. She lifted golden eyes to meet theirs, and her clothes, though fine, appeared worn.

"Ramsey, ma'am, and this is Ben. I'd feel more comfortable getting you away from the saloon in the event Buck wakes up." Mandy hesitated a moment and then presented them with a lovely, if somewhat apprehensive smile.

"Thank you for what you did in there," she said. "And the name is Amanda Warren. Millie took to calling me Mandy right off. I'm certain she would have stepped in, though I do feel better knowing she didn't have to shoot anyone."

Ramsey smiled. "So do I."

Ben offered his hand, and she allowed him to help her down the saloon steps and into the snow. "Pleasure to meet you, Miss Warren, but it seems to me we've lost you your job."

Amanda glanced back at the saloon and then looked forward toward the store. "You didn't lose me anything. They were bound to let me go anyway."

"If you don't mind my asking, how'd you end up working

there?" Ben clarified the question when he noticed her embarrassment. "I mean no disrespect, but you don't look the type to find employment in a saloon."

Ramsey watched her face brighten another shade at Ben's remark.

"I've just arrived and with jobs being scarce in town, I took what I could find."

Ramsey nodded. Unfortunately, that was likely true. Few businesses in town required additional help beyond the proprietors themselves, and those who did, tended to hire family or friends when the need arose.

"Ben, why don't you escort Miss Warren to the general store while I get Eliza to the doc?"

"I'm not certain if that's a—"

Buck chose that inopportune moment to saunter out of the doctor's office. "You there! I know you, don't I?"

Ramsey closed his eyes a moment and watched Ben motion Amanda toward the store.

"You that fella that knocked me in the head." Buck was obviously addressing Ben.

"Buck, come on now." Another man came up behind him and pulled him away.

"I wanna talk to this cowboy, Stanley." Buck nearly tripped.

Still drunk. Wonderful. "Best listen to your friend there, Buck."

"I ain't gotta listen to no one."

Stanley grabbed Buck and pulled him close to tell him something quietly. Buck paled. "He won't bother you none, Ben. We'll just be headed out now."

Ben nodded and watched the men head across the street to the saloon where they'd left their horses.

Ramsey motioned to Stanley. "Friends of yours?"

"They work on a small spread about an hour's ride south. An

easterner came out here a few years ago and thought he'd try ranching. Unfortunately, he doesn't know a thing about cattle, or how to keep his men under control."

Ramsey and Ben watched the men ride out of town and walked toward the wagon.

Ramsey saw Eliza standing next to the wagon rather than on it. "I wish you would have stayed up there."

"You're beginning to sound like my brothers."

Ramsey cringed. "All right, I'll ease up, but only after the doc confirms you've healed."

Ben lifted himself and grabbed the reins. "I'll take care of the wagon. And then I'll meet you at Loren's. I'd like to check on Amanda."

Ramsey waited patiently while Brody examined Eliza on the other side of the curtain. He heard them talking softly to one another. The doctor asked her to lift her arms, bend to the side, and then the room was silent. Ramsey imagined the doctor examining the wound and cursed himself for wishing it was he in there with her.

The doctor finally came around the curtain and smiled at Ramsey. "You may tell her brothers that she's healed nicely."

"I'll do that." Ramsey smiled when Eliza pulled back the curtain and walked across the room.

"Fit and ready for anything."

"Not quite." The doctor shook his head at Eliza. "No lifting or roping for another week."

"But I can ride?"

The doctor slowly smiled. "You can ride."

"You're not one for causing excitement around here," Loren said, coming around the counter when Ben walked into the store.

"I suppose I was due." Ben looked around the store but didn't see Amanda.

"She's gone up to her room."

Ben stepped closer to Loren and nodded toward the stairs. "How long has she been in town?"

"I guess it has been a spell since you've been in here. She rode in on the back of a traveler's wagon three days back. They got themselves into a bit of trouble during that storm. The lot of them didn't look good when they managed to drag themselves into town."

"Did she say where she'd been before here?"

Loren shook his head. "I asked but that one doesn't tell you much."

"She took a job at the saloon."

"Now, that's not my doing." Loren defended himself. "I offered her a job right here, but she told me she's better suited for the saloon. Don't look the type, though."

"No, she doesn't." Ben stepped toward the window in the door and watched the soft flakes begin to fall. The clouds had parted in the sky long enough to allow the sun to sneak through, the rays lighting up each flake as it fluttered to the ground.

Loren moved a few things around the counter, glancing up at Ben every few seconds. Then he closed his account book. "What's your interest in Amanda? You don't know the girl."

"Neither did you when you offered her a room." Ben stepped back when Ramsey and Eliza opened the door.

"Loren." Ramsey acknowledged the storekeeper and brushed a few flakes from his coat.

"I hear you've had a bit of commotion at the ranch." Loren nodded toward Eliza. "How are you, child? I'm sorry to hear about what happened to you."

"I've pulled through," Eliza said and turned a curious look to Ben, who only shook his head.

"How'd you hear about the trouble at the ranch?" Ramsey

leaned on the edge of the counter. "Except to fetch the doc, no one from Hawk's Peak has been into town."

Confused, Loren responded carefully. "Your new man stopped in here yesterday, told us all about it."

Ramsey looked down at Eliza and then up at Ben. "Did he give you a name?"

"Sure, it was Tyre, but I don't recall a last name."

Eliza stiffened next to him, and Ben's eyes narrowed. Ramsey managed to appear calm in front of Loren. "You didn't recognize the name or the man?"

"I would have remembered this fella. Long, dark hair and soulless blue eyes; he didn't look like a man you'd hire, but he knew all about it." Loren rubbed his clean-shaven face. "Are you saying he doesn't work for you?"

Eliza shook her head. "No, he doesn't." She turned and faced Ramsey. "Let's do what has to be done and get back to the ranch."

Ramsey nodded, placed his hands on her shoulders, and addressed the storekeeper. "Ben has a list for you, if you wouldn't mind filling that order. We'll be on our way."

Loren scanned the list Ben handed him. "I'll have to order most of this. You planning to rebuild the barn?"

"If we can get a break in the weather before the worst of winter hits," Ramsey said. Eliza stood to the side, focused on something out the window.

"I'd like to check in on Miss Warren," Ben said.

Eliza pulled herself from the window. "Is she the woman who left the saloon with you?"

Ramsey nodded and turned to Loren. "Does she have any family you know of?"

"I told Ben here that she has no one as far as I can tell."

They all turned their attention toward the door when a woman and child stepped inside.

Loren quickly stepped from behind the counter. "Can I help you with anything, Mrs. Pickett?"

"Oh, I can wait. We'll be buying material for a new Christmas dress for Daisy this year."

"You go on and look at those fabrics, and I'll be right with you." Loren turned back to them, lowering his voice. "I've had some complaints about having that young woman staying at the store."

Ben raised a brow. "Never thought you cared much what people thought."

"Don't look at me that way, Ben Stuart. I don't care what gossip goes around, but people aren't taking to the girl for some reason. Too bad really. She's a nice girl."

"She can come back to the ranch with us."

All three men looked at Eliza.

"You don't know anything about her."

"I know that, Ramsey, but she's welcome," Eliza said. Ramsey was right that she knew little about Amanda Warren, except what she had learned in the distance between the saloon and the store, which admittedly wasn't much. Amanda was from someplace east and may or may not be passing through Briarwood.

Loren scrubbed a hand over his chin. "That's mighty kind of you. You sure your brothers and their wives won't mind?"

"I'm sure." Eliza walked toward the stairs, but paused at the base, her eyes on Loren. "Do you mind?"

"You go right on up. Last door on the left."

Ramsey watched Eliza ascend the stairs, the boots she wore with her heavy skirt echoing softly on the wooden steps.

"Might be for the best." Loren leaned toward Ramsey. "I'll just help Mrs. Pickett and then get to that order. You tell Ethan I'll have everything in a few weeks." Loren walked to the other side of the store and began sorting through fabrics with Mrs. Pickett and her daughter.

After only a fifteen-minute wait, soft footfalls on the stairs regained the men's attention. Amanda stepped down onto the main floor and walked toward them. Eliza followed, but she wore an expression Ramsey had seen only once before—when she heard about the bullets aimed at Andrew.

"I didn't expect you'd still be here," Amanda said to the men and then looked briefly at Eliza. "But then I wasn't given much of a choice when offered a new job."

Loren looked at her kindly. "The Gallaghers are good people."

"I know my living here hasn't been good for you."

"Don't you fret about that," Loren said. "You're welcome back."

Ramsey peeked at Eliza over Amanda's head, though her expression hadn't changed. "Then you'll be coming with us."

Ben stepped forward. "Is there anything else you'd like me to get from upstairs?"

Amanda's bearing stiffened slightly. "This is everything I need."

"If you'll allow me, I'll escort you to the wagon."

Amanda focused her eyes directly on Ben and nodded. She gave no one else in the store a second look. Once she and Ben exited, Ramsey gave his full attention to Eliza.

"New job?"

Eliza watched Ben help Amanda into the back of the wagon and hoped he found a way to make her comfortable back there. "I imagine your grandmother won't take kindly if she ever heard me say this, but she can't keep up with everything she's taken on, and no matter how much we try to ease her away from chores, she becomes blustery."

"Blustery?" Ramsey smiled.

"She needs to slow down." Eliza's tone turned serious. "Not completely, of course—she has a lot of years left—but she won't.

I figure the only to make her is to bring someone else in."

Ramsey studied her for a moment. "You mean to make her feel guilty. A young woman in need of work; and of course if there isn't work for Miss Warren, then she ceases to be useful."

"That's about it."

"That's horrible on many levels, and I'm behind you completely."

"Let's hope everyone else shares your enthusiasm."

"We'd better get going." Ramsey reached out to stop Eliza when she would have passed. "First, what did Miss Warren tell you?"

Eliza raised her eyes to Ramsey. "Tell me when?"

"I saw the look you wore when you walked down those stairs." Ramsey's quiet voice reached only her.

Eliza studied Ramsey. "I'll tell you, but not here and not now."

"I can handle that. I have something else to discuss with you at any rate."

"Yes, the horses. We didn't have a chance to finish—"

"Not horses." Ramsey wrapped his fingers gently around her arm and looked across the store to address Mr. Baker, who was presently wrapping fabric in brown paper. "Two weeks on that order, Loren?"

"Yes, but maybe less." Loren excused himself from Mrs. Pickett's company and rushed over to Ramsey and Eliza. "About that other matter you asked me—"

"Yes, please let me know." He sensed Eliza's eyes on him, but he didn't meet her stare. "Send word out to the ranch if it's before I return."

Loren nodded, casting a brief glance at Eliza, then returned to finish with Mrs. Pickett.

Once outside, Eliza leaned back enough to lock eyes with Ramsey. "You know I'll ask."

"You won't have to ask." Ramsey placed his hand gently on her back and guided her to the wagon.

"I have to stop at the livery," Ben told them. "If you want to head out, I'll catch up."

Ramsey nodded. "That'll be best. We'll have a slow ride back."

"I shouldn't be long."

A shock of cold air hit Ramsey's face. Dark clouds now fully covered the sun, and the wind was determined to make the return ride miserable. He watched Ben walk back to the saloon where he'd left his bay tied. Rather than ride, he walked the animal across the snow-covered dirt street and around the large corner building to the livery.

Ramsey helped Eliza onto the seat of the buckboard and walked around to check on Amanda. "Are you comfortable enough back here?"

"I'm fine, thank you."

"I'll keep the ride as smooth as the road will allow." Ramsey turned around at the sound of his name.

"You've been a stranger, Ramsey." Otis walked toward them, his burly blacksmith's body clothed in only light clothing.

"Been busy. Ben just headed over to your place."

"On my way there now." Otis pulled the cap from his head and scratched his nearly bald head. "Heard you were back in town. You sticking this time?"

Aware that Eliza's focus centered on him, Ramsey said, "That's the plan."

Otis nodded. "You planning to rebuild that barn?" Otis directed his question to Eliza.

"We are."

"Tell me when. I'll spare time to help."

"I appreciate that, Otis."

The Gallaghers kept their private matters as private as

possible, and the townspeople let them believe they didn't know, but from what Ramsey had been told, almost everyone in the area knew of the Gallaghers' troubles and those who knew were relieved when his grandfather had disappeared. Nathan Hunter's men disrupted the town, and the Double Bar did nothing to help the community or the region. The Gallagher family put the land and people before themselves, bringing their business to the small town when they could simply procure what they needed directly from Bozeman. They cared about the well-being of the town and the people who worked to make their dream of carving out a life in the frontier a reality. Ramsey had envied the family their bond. *Perhaps I still do.* The wind increased, and Ramsey was mindful of his passengers.

"You just watch yourself going back." Otis ran a hand over the horses' necks and then walked in the direction of the livery.

Ramsey nodded and climbed up next to Eliza. "I regret we'll have a bit of discomfort heading out, Miss Warren."

"Perhaps it would be best if—"

"I promise you'll be safe, Amanda. I know this may have happened a little fast and be somewhat confusing, but it's a good option." Eliza handed the blanket back to Amanda. "Here, wrap this around you to keep the wind and snow off."

Amanda nodded but said nothing, already wrapping her body in a wool cocoon. Waving to Mr. Baker, Ramsey set the team in motion. Halfway through their drive, Ben caught up to them and the wind subsided enough for Amanda to lower the blanket from around her face.

"Miss Gallagher?"

"Please, it's Eliza."

"I've found myself in odd situations of late, but I do say this is the most ridiculous."

Surprised, Eliza turned and looked at her. The worn wool bonnet Amanda wore shielded her eyes. Eliza could see nothing else of her except smooth skin and stray brown hair fallen loose from the bonnet. "Ridiculous how?"

"You're taking a stranger home with you."

"You accepted the invitation."

Ramsey listened intently to the conversation. If he'd turned around, he might have wondered about the small scowl forming on Amanda's lips.

"Why?"

Eliza delayed her response to Amanda because, in truth, she lacked a good answer. Many reasons filled her mind, but none of them stood out as the truth, and none was likely to be believed.

Ramsey sensed Eliza's hesitation but was just as curious about the answer.

"I'm keeping a promise."

The blanket slipped a little down her shoulder, and Amanda quickly lifted it, covering every inch of clothing she wore. "A promise to whom?"

"An old friend," Eliza said, "I suppose you might say you're doing us a favor as much as I am you."

"I don't know that I understand."

Eliza looked away from Amanda. Her eyes scanned the familiar landscape and then sought out the buildings she knew would soon be within sight. "You will, Amanda."

Ramsey heard Eliza's sharp breathing against the cold and slid closer, his arms and legs pressed up against hers.

10

"We're here, Miss Warren." Eliza heard Ben from his seat on the bay. He rode up alongside the wagon when it slowed in front of the house, and Eliza turned to see how Amanda had fared.

Ben dismounted and handed the reins to Tom, who looked on curiously while Ben assisted the new guest. The front door of the main house opened, and Ethan stepped across the threshold. Eliza watched him look her over as though assuring himself that she had befallen no injury. She shook her head before Ethan could ask anything about their company, then placed her hand in Ramsey's when he offered her help down. The action felt comfortable, natural, and completely out of character for Eliza. Eliza had spent years endeavoring to make a place for herself in what many considered a world inappropriate for women.

She'd learned to ride like a man, shoot like a man, and to her mother's, and later Mabel's dismay, dress like a man. The men at the ranch accepted her in the beginning because she had been the boss's daughter. That acceptance had eventually shifted after years of witnessing her abilities—she'd earned their respect. The drawback of that had come when she reached womanhood and the only male company she kept was that of her brothers and the men at the ranch. With the exception of the occasional drive into town, few opportunities arose for her to socialize, and when the chance presented itself, not a single man interested her.

Her blue eyes lifted the few inches to meet Ramsey's, and she held onto him a moment longer than necessary. Mindful of their growing audience, Eliza pulled her hand slowly away and walked around the wagon to stand beside Amanda.

"They don't make men better than my brothers," she said, but thinking of Ramsey, she silently amended that.

"You're certain they won't mind?" Amanda whispered back, completely aware of curious glances.

"Let's find out," Eliza replied. She pulled Amanda to the front steps and looked at her brother. "Ethan, if you don't mind, I'd rather take this inside. It was a dreadfully cold ride."

Eliza saw Ethan raise what she termed the "infernal Gallagher brow," knowing Eliza rarely minded the cold. But he remained silent.

Eliza had not yet refined her reasons for bringing Amanda to the ranch or how she would convince the family to accept the stranger and offer her a job. She sneaked one more look at Ramsey, but he was already halfway to the corrals with the horse and wagon, Ben walking alongside him.

Eliza walked through the front door and nearly walked into Elizabeth. "Perfect! Would you mind getting Miss Warren something hot to drink? It's a cold day for traveling."

"Of course," Elizabeth replied and addressed Amanda. "There's a nice fire in the kitchen hearth and a fresh pot of coffee."

Amanda's eyes conveyed uncertainty, but she followed Elizabeth down the hall and into the kitchen.

"Now do you mind explaining?"

Eliza turned around and faced Ethan. "Yes, but I'd prefer to only do it once. Where's Gabriel?"

"He relieved me an hour ago."

"Brenna? Isabelle?"

Ethan looked her over curiously. "Brenna's feeding Jacob and Isabelle is giving Andrew his lessons. Do they need to be here?"

Eliza considered. "You'll do for now," she said and walked into the library.

Ethan followed and closed the door behind him. "All right, who is she?"

"Our new housekeeper."

Ethan sat down on the corner of the large oak desk and crossed his arms. Eliza recognized the stance—he looked comfortable but was all business.

"This comes with a long story, and one I may eventually tell you, but I need you to trust me," Eliza said. "Besides, we all know Elizabeth needs help, and Amanda needs a job."

Ethan nodded. "Trusting you is never an issue, but do you know anything about her?"

Eliza moved to sit next to her brother on the desk. "This wasn't meant for sitting," she remarked casually before explaining. "I know she's had it rough, but I don't know the details—yet. She speaks like someone who has been educated, and if I had to guess, she hasn't been in this situation for too long."

"Where'd you find her?"

"Ramsey and Ben broke up a ruckus at the saloon. I didn't see what happened, but they went in and came out with her." Eliza shifted and moved to one of the leather chairs facing the desk. "She'd been renting a room from Loren the last few days."

"And she just agreed to go with you?"

Eliza bore the slightest twinge of guilt about how she managed to convince Amanda to come with her. "I may not have given her much of a choice." She saw Ethan's eyes studying her, counting on the good heart beating in her brother's chest. She wasn't disappointed.

"Does Amanda have a last name?"

"Warren."

Always quick with a decision, Ethan said, "I don't think anyone else is going to have a problem with this. I know everyone would appreciate the help." He stood straight and took a step closer to her. "However, she's your responsibility, and Elizabeth will have to agree since she's claimed domain over operating the household."

"She will," Eliza said. "Speaking of which, this is Brenna and Isabelle's home, too. From what I hear, women don't generally like to share the running of a home."

"You hear?" Ethan smiled.

Eliza shrugged. "I never had to worry about that. We always had Mother and then Mabel—"

Ethan pulled her against him in a gentle hug. "It will take time."

"I know." Eliza stepped away and cleared her throat. "I'll see to Amanda. Would you mind telling Brenna?"

Ethan nodded, but she sensed he wasn't finished.

"Eliza, I know your intentions are always good, but sometimes . . . just make sure this is what Amanda wants."

She agreed and left the room, replaying in her mind the conversation she had with Amanda at the general store.

Eliza walked into the kitchen to find that Isabelle had joined Elizabeth and Amanda. Certain now that she'd made the right decision, Eliza smiled at the three women, grateful they all appeared to be getting on like old friends.

"Ah, Eliza, come and join us." Elizabeth motioned her to the table, and she gratefully sat down. Her body might be healed, but she wasn't back to full strength. "You've brought us a wonderful new friend in Miss Warren," Elizabeth said.

"Please, it's Amanda."

"Of course it is, dear." Elizabeth patted Amanda on the arm

and returned to stirring batter.

"Amanda will be staying with us for a while," Eliza said casually. "Isabelle, could I ask you to show her to the spare room near mine?"

Isabelle sent a wondering look to Eliza but set her tea down and kindly said, "Of course I will, and how wonderful it will be to have another woman at the ranch."

Eliza watched Amanda turn to Elizabeth and offer her thanks. She then followed Isabelle from the kitchen, which gave Eliza a chance to speak with Elizabeth. The older woman spoke first.

"You're forgetting I remember you as a child, Eliza Gallagher." Elizabeth set down her batter and sat in the chair Amanda had vacated. "Your mother would tell me the stories of how you wanted to bring home children from the school who you thought needed help. If you'd had your way, the Gallaghers would number more than three siblings."

Eliza spent a moment with her own memories before responding. "She needs the work, and if you're willing, I'd like her stay on and help out around here."

"We have four women under this roof. It doesn't take even that many to manage a household."

"This isn't about me or about us needing extra help. She needs this."

"I'm not arguing that point, dear. The poor thing is too skinny and in need of some rest. Looks strong, though." Elizabeth looked askance at Eliza. "If you're set on keeping her, I'll keep her busy."

Eliza promised her brothers a few more days before she went riding or worked the cattle. Unused to idle time, Eliza found little enjoyment within the walls of the ranch. Elizabeth had warmly accepted Amanda, and the two had remained in the kitchen talking after breakfast two days later. She caught the curious looks of both Ethan and Gabriel during the meal that morning, knowing they hoped for a better explanation about Amanda. Aware that Ramsey had also kept looking her way made her slightly less comfortable. Not because he made her uncomfortable but because she wanted to tell him. She needed to tell someone.

After the morning meal, Ethan and Gabriel both went out to join the ranch hands. Ramsey offered to relive them and work with the men later in the day, allowing the Gallaghers to take the afternoon meal with their family. Eliza knew her brothers appreciated Ramsey's presence, but she also sensed their growing frustration. Life on the ranch couldn't be put on hold because of personal vendettas. They wanted progress, and to be on the offense if—when—Hunter returned. If Ramsey was taking any action at all, as Eliza suspected, he had yet to enlighten them.

"You have the look of someone who'd rather be out there."

Ramsey stood in the doorway of the library, where she had set out her books and paper in effort to relieve the tedium. She held great respect for women who enjoyed caring for a home—but she was never trained for that. Her mother and Mabel had made a few attempts to teach her the basics of managing a home and cooking, but they released her from those lessons when it became glaringly apparent she was meant for something else.

"I'm holding my end of the bargain. I can't imagine you're happy indoors any more than I am."

Ramsey shrugged. "Not usually. I'm heading out with the men later, but I prefer to ride. Care to join me?"

She narrowed her eyes at him. "You're not playing fair, when you know I promised my brothers two more days."

"I was thinking more of you riding with me."

"They won't buy it."

He crossed the room and filled one of the leather chairs with his tall frame. "I suppose I've been on my own for so long, worrying about what others say or think hasn't been a priority. I envy you that."

Eliza looked up from her notes. "You can have that if you look at your return as a permanent choice. Your family is here, and I know they're waiting to annoy and love you."

"It takes time to change a certain way of thinking," Ramsey said. "Speaking of family, yours accepted Miss Warren well enough."

"She prefers Amanda, and yes they did," she replied. "Does that surprise you?"

"With your family—no, it doesn't—but I've wanted to ask you about that promise you mentioned." Ramsey vacated the chair and stood in front of the desk.

Eliza closed the book and set aside her paper and pencil. "It's not a pleasant story, and one I'd rather not share here." She pushed the chair away from the desk and looked around at the task she was attempting to begin, and then said, "How about a walk?"

The cattle had settled into the beginnings of winter and accepted that their expansive grazing ground had been reduced to the enclosed pastures close to the ranch. The practice of open range ended for the Gallaghers after their first altercation with Nathan Hunter. Eliza walked alongside Ramsey, passing the corrals and walking toward the small pond west of where the barn once stood.

"You certain you're warm enough?"

Eliza looked down at the wool skirt she had donned that morning, knowing she wouldn't be on the range with the men. She smiled because Ramsey had no way of knowing that beneath her wool skirt, she wore heavy bloomers she had made especially to wear under skirts while at the ranch. "Warm enough," she said.

Eliza stopped at the edge of the pond, now partially frozen

over. Geese and ducks often used the small body of water as a resting spot when traveling to and from wherever they ventured during the colder months. Her body and mind were aware of Ramsey's nearness, and the awareness offered her the courage she needed.

"I used to come here often with Mary." Eliza smiled. "I remember the first summer I met her. Her family had moved to Montana from Philadelphia, and she knew nothing of life in a place like this. She always worried about Indian attacks after a close encounter on her stage journey north. She soon learned to appreciate the land, but I still believe she was always afraid. I taught her how to fish on this pond, the same way my father taught me and my brothers not long after we learned to walk." Eliza slid her boot along the frozen edge.

Ramsey tensed when she began speaking of Mary. Ramsey waited patiently, not pushing or expecting, and he hoped that the silent reassurance gave her the courage to press forward—to share a story he imagined she had kept suppressed these past years.

"I watched Mary struggle and saw the terrified look in her eyes as they dragged me away. Two of them held onto me as I fought, but I couldn't break free from their firm grip. I lay there, listening to her screams, burying my face to hide the tears and my own helplessness. Then everything went quiet—I feared her dead and struggled to get up and run to her. One of the men hit me, and I blacked out, uncertain what happened." Eliza kept her eyes focused on the mountains, fully cognizant of Ramsey's presence and of the space closing between them.

"I woke up in my bedroom. Ethan and Gabriel had found us both, but my father and brothers wouldn't allow me to see Mary that first night. They tried to explain that she was badly beaten and in a bad state. They warned me about what to expect when I did see her, but I refused to believe them. In the morning, I quietly went to her room. Her mangled body and still somewhat bloodied face showed the black and blue bruises the men had left. It was much worse than I had expected, and I held back the bile that rose up. What agony she must have endured, and to know her innocence was brutally taken from her . . . I held her and cried, trying not to wake her."

Ramsey stopped her from continuing. "You don't have to relive this, Eliza."

She turned to face him. "I relive it every day because that is the moment when I first truly hated another human being." She looked back to the mountains and continued. "As Mary lay on the bed in our home, she cried for two days. Then on the third day she stopped and asked for me. I knew her body was too damaged, and her spirit too broken. I knelt beside the bed, asking her to forgive me for not helping her."

"You couldn't have stopped it," Ramsey said, stepping closer to her.

"That's what Mary told me, but the guilt didn't go away. She died and I lived because I was a Gallagher"

"I'm so sorry," Ramsey said softly and stepped forward to wrap his arms around her. "It wasn't your fault, and there's nothing you could have done."

Her eyes now closed against the mountains and the land, Eliza leaned back against Ramsey and raised her arms to cover his. She felt his breath on her hair and the strength of his body. "I swore if I ever believed anyone needed help, and it was in my power to do so, no matter how small or great the challenge, I would come to his or her aid. I won't make the same mistake again."

Eliza allowed Ramsey to slowly turn her until she faced him. "You're forgetting I've kept in touch with Loren. From the stories I've heard, you've been helping people ever since your friend's passing."

Eliza nodded. "I'm not naïve enough to believe I can help

everyone, but I've known more could be done."

"What is it about Amanda Warren that made her different?"

Surprised, Eliza raised dry eyes to Ramsey. His gaze intimated that he read her so effortlessly.

"Amanda reminded you of Mary—why?"

"I can't explain what I don't know." Eliza absently toyed with the long braid in her hair. "I sensed sadness and that she needed help from something or someone."

Ramsey's gloved finger raised her chin until she looked directly at him. His next words eased the worry and inner ache clouding her mind.

"I'm here, you know; I'm not walking away."

"But it's not your burden."

He smiled at her and brushed back a loose strand of her hair. "I'll be here anyway."

The shout broke them apart, and they turned to watch Henry riding toward them.

Ramsey instinctively reached for Eliza and waited for Henry to reach them. "What's wrong?"

"We went to the upper pasture searching for strays—it's not good," Henry said, then promptly turned and rode back.

Ramsey faced her, a hand on her arm.

"I can't run, not yet. Go." She watched Ramsey run across the snow-covered ground as quickly as he could without slipping. She attempted to do the same, but at the first hard impact, a sharp pain raced up through her side. One of the men saddled her horse, but by the time she reached the higher pasture, she immediately saw the devastation every rancher dreads. Half a dozen steers lay lifeless on the red-stained snow.

"Damn it, Eliza, what are you doing out here? You shouldn't be riding yet!"

Ethan was shouting at her, but she saw the worry in his eyes.

"Are you all right?"

"I'm fine, I promise." Eliza's eyes scanned the bloody scene, narrowing in on the steers' necks. "Are their throats slit?"

Ethan didn't take his eyes off the mess. "Every one of them."

"Looks to have happened yesterday or at least, last night." Gabriel set his boot against the back of one of the steers. "The blood and carcasses are nearly frozen."

Henry leaned over the horn on his saddle. "We should have pulled them in yesterday."

Ethan shook his head. "No changing what's happened, but I sure as hell want to know who's responsible for this senseless brutality!"

Eliza followed the conversation, but she closely watched Ramsey. He'd dismounted nearly two hundred feet from where they sat on their horses and studied the ground intently, circling a small area. Eliza guided her horse around the others and slowly approached Ramsey.

"What is it?"

"It's what I'm not seeing." He glanced up at her. "The tracks stop about fifty feet away from the steers and then pick up again here."

Eliza tried to see what he was seeing. "Whoever did this, had to have known someone would notice, wouldn't they?"

Ramsey nodded. "Perhaps, or perhaps they thought it expedient to leave quickly."

"Find something, Ramsey?" Ethan asked. He and Gabriel rode up and stopped next to Eliza.

"The missing tracks you noticed back there pick up again here." Ramsey knelt down and pushed against the snow with his gloved fingers. "But another set of tracks from another horse and rider took off to the west."

"The Double Bar is east," Eliza said. "It had to have been—"

"It could still be them," Gabriel said. "We presumed this happened at their hands, but let's not forget the extent to which the Double Bar has gone to attack us. Killing a few head is senseless—it won't ruin us."

Eliza said, "There's no one else. Rustlers would steal them, and Indians wouldn't kill animals this way."

"It feels a lot more personal," Ramsey said. "Someone's taunting us. It may not be Hunter directly, but it's someone who knows about the feud."

A piercing whistle carried over the land, and they all turned to see Henry waving at them from where he stood. Ramsey remounted and the group returned to the slaughtered cattle. Henry and Colton had turned one over to find it gutted, and the meat of the animal removed.

"I ain't never seen anything like it," Henry said.

Ramsey looked closely at the smooth edges of the skin. "Have you had any problems with the natives up here?"

Gabriel shook his head. "Nothing in the last few years."

"And nothing ever like this," Ethan said. "Eliza, I'd appreciate if you'd head back to the ranch. Send Ben and Kevin out this way and tell them to bring the makings for a fire and some food. We'll be here for a while."

Ethan stared out over his family's land, his body worn and his heart angry. They'd moved the carcasses into a pile and burned them until nothing remained except a black circle in the snow. He looked up when the door opened and attempted a smile for his wife.

"I won't ask how you're doing," she said in the soft lyrical voice he loved.

"Wouldn't have an answer for you if you did." Ethan patted the seat on the bench next to him.

"Eliza told me what happened out there." Brenna looped her arm through his and leaned into him. Ethan slid his arm around her shoulders, holding her close. She smelled of flowers and their son.

"For too long now we've focused our efforts on ending the trouble, believing it could only be—"

"Hunter," Brenna said softly. "It's all right. No matter my blood relation to him, I understand the type of man he is, and what he's done—and what's he probably still doing."

"Except this time something is different," Ethan said. "Hunter has always had a purpose driving him, no matter how misguided, but this slaughter makes no sense. No cattleman, including Hunter, would ever brutally harm an animal that way. He's depraved, but I can't credit him this barbarism."

"You're certain of that?"

Ethan looked at his wife's upturned face. "To be honest, I'm not certain of anything anymore—at least when it comes to these latest incidences."

"Perhaps it's time to speak with my grandmother."

"About what exactly?"

Brenna's green eyes studied her husband's face. "No one knows him better."

"Asking Elizabeth about Hunter could force her to relive memories she doesn't want to face."

Brenna gently covered his hand with hers. "Do we have a choice?"

Everyone had returned from the snowy fields where they'd burned the butchered cattle, except a few ranch hands to keep watch over the herd. Supper long past, Eliza found herself alone on the front porch, welcoming the quiet. The air smelled of winter, with a promise of more snow. Wrapped in the wool blanket she'd carried with her outside, she looked out into the night. Her blue eyes adjusted to the darkness as the bright moon shone on the mountains. She listened to the river as it flowed over rocks. It was deep and swift enough to flow year round, ensuring their stock never wanted for water. When other ranches struggled to keep their stock alive, Hawk's Peak managed to build a spread that was strong and secure. After tonight's slaughter, she nearly questioned that security, but she believed in the strength of her family. Hunter could burn them out, slaughter a few cows, and keep coming with more trouble, and they would keep fighting.

Eliza slowly scanned their land until her eyes touched upon the piece of earth where the barn had once stood. The ruins had not yet been removed, and though they planned to rebuild soon, she knew the pain that they all held onto had prevented the complete demolition of the ruins. Voices from the house faded, and Eliza imagined her brothers retiring to spend time with their families. Ramsey left immediately after supper to join the ranch hands in the bunkhouse for a card game, but she saw only the dim light from lanterns within. She didn't consider herself to be lonely, nor did she wish for a life other than one she'd spent years living, but tonight she felt the pangs of emptiness.

Pulling the edges of the blanket together, Eliza stepped off the porch and walked under the moonlit sky. Passing the corrals and stable, she crossed the frozen earth to the charred remains of the barn.

"I don't have to tell you how much we miss you, Mabel," she said softly. Tears filled her eyes without warning and flowed freely. "I never thought you wouldn't be here to meet the husband you tried to convince me I needed."

Eliza wiped away the tears and smiled. "I remember how difficult I was when you and Mother tried to teach me how to keep a home. I was so stubborn, and you loved me anyway. I didn't know how to go on after Mother and Father died, but you were there for us, for me. I know you're up there with them looking down, so I hope you're not too disappointed with what you see." She touched the charred earth and whispered, "Give them a kiss for me."

She slowly turned at the sound of boot steps behind her and wiped away the remaining tears. "How long have you been there?"

"Only a moment." Ramsey slowly closed the distance between them and stood beside her. He carefully looked over the boards protruding from mounds of snow and the ash still visible under sections where the snow had melted before freezing. "You miss her."

"I failed her."

Surprised, Ramsey turned her toward him. "How do you figure that?"

"We've had more than one chance to end this, but we didn't, and this happened."

"You couldn't have done anything to stop what happened."

"There's been more than one chance to kill him."

"No, you're not going to do this," Ramsey said forcefully. "Don't blame yourself for being more human than Hunter. He's *my* grandfather. If there is anyone guilty, it's me—I'm the one who left, knowing the kind of man he is."

Eliza lifted brightened blue eyes to look at Ramsey. "You came back."

"Not nearly soon enough, and I can't change that, just as you can't change what happened here. You know Mabel doesn't blame you, and she would not want you to feel this way."

"This wasn't her fight." Eliza choked the words out and leaned into Ramsey, welcoming the comfort of his arms encircling her. "Can we end this? Really end it or is our determination for naught?"

Ramsey released his arms enough to pull back, studying her. "We will end this," he promised. "Whether that means finding a way to keep him locked up or—"

"Or killing him? I've thought many times about killing him and ending this mess."

"But could you kill a man?"

"I don't know, to defend my family, probably," she said quickly and truthfully. "You?"

Ramsey now placed a few steps between them. "I already have."

Eliza studied him patiently to see if he wanted to say more, if he trusted her enough. She'd witnessed death, but despite the terrors her family had faced, she had never taken a life. She shuddered, considering the possibility because, above all else, she never wanted to be like Hunter.

"People talk of taking a life as though it's something they do every day. Fighting in a battle of any kind allows a person to justify death because war means someone will die. A man is justified if he's defending his home, life, and family. Planning to kill a man—that does something to you."

"And you're saying you've killed a man with the intention of killing him?" Eliza stayed her ground, believing that she couldn't have been wrong about Ramsey. She sensed his hesitation in telling her everything, but she was willing to wait for as long it took.

Ramsey watched her closely, but when he saw the determined stance and questioning eyes, he knew it was time for the secret to emerge.

"When I left Montana, I only got as far as Wyoming. I hired on at small ranch outside of Cheyenne and spent a few months working cattle. I shouldn't have remained there long since it was still too close to here, but I wanted to stay near. A few years after I arrived, the rancher hired on a few more men to help with the drive, and I recognized one of them."

"From where?"

"The Double Bar. They didn't work there, but Hunter hired men from outside for odd jobs. He was with the men who raped Mary Preston."

The shocking rush should have forced Eliza to step farther away, but she held her ground.

"How did you find out?" she whispered. "You'd be gone for years before that happened."

"I had. I promise you, I didn't know until he showed up at the ranch in Wyoming. We were in the bunkhouse playing cards. He was drunk and started talking. When he described—when he bragged about what he'd done—it sickened me. The hired hand became more intoxicated and carried on that it happened while he was at the Double Bar, and how—"

Ramsey faltered as he relived the nightmare of thinking it was Eliza. It wasn't until he had heard "Mary" and "dead" that he found some measure of relief. He was then stricken with guilt because his relief came at the expense of a young woman's death.

"How what, Ramsey? How he'd raped a girl and beat her so badly that she died just a few days later?" Her heart raced. "You killed him?"

Ramsey nodded, his eyes pained, but honest. "I wired Loren, asking if it was true—I had to be certain, and I needed to know you weren't—that he hadn't—"

"I was spared the raping and beating because I'm a Gallagher. Whatever his reasons, Hunter didn't want me harmed."

"I have no regrets for pulling that trigger. I forced the man into a situation where he'd have to draw, and I didn't hesitate."

"And no one ever questioned the shooting?" Eliza once again closed the space between them. Her eyes met his and her hands found a hold on his coat. "You could have told me, should have told me."

"When you showed up at the Tremaines' farm, the memories followed you. I had to believe that I'd come beyond the man who did that, and the incident was in the past."

"Have you?" Eliza pushed down the mounting fear while she waited for his response.

"I know I have." Ramsey brushed her hair back with a gloved hand. "But it stays with a person. I have no love for Hunter, and his death would not affect me. But I can't simply walk up to *my grandfather*, no matter how evil a man he is, and take his life."

"I didn't stop to consider that you may not be as bloodthirsty as I've been."

"I have. Understand that I've thought of killing him so often, ever since I learned what happened to you and to Mary. And I will give my life, or take his, if necessary—but it has to be me."

Eliza shook her head. "No, it doesn't."

"This all began with me and Brenna, and she's not getting near this. I'm the only one left."

Eliza closed the last of the space between them. "Kiss me."

"Eliza, I—"

"Kiss me."

Ramsey hesitated for the briefest moment and then leaned into her, lowering his lips to meet hers, pulling her body slowly forward.

His soft lips warmed her, the sensation reaching every nerve ending of her body. The kiss awakened Eliza, unleashing without exception, the feelings she'd kept hidden. So much of her life had been about loss, and yet the memories of a happier time unexpectedly woke within her. She released those memories, allowing emotions to fuel her passion.

Unwilling to release him too soon, Eliza joined Ramsey as he deepened the kiss. When they gradually eased apart, she raised her dark eyes to meet his and quietly said, "You're not the only one, and you're not in this alone."

With his forehead pressed against hers, his warm breath caressed her skin. The smile in his voice was unmistakable when he spoke. "Do you have any idea what you've done?"

"No," Eliza said honestly. "But I'm willing to do it again."

"I can't promise—"

"I'm not asking for any promises. I'm asking you to trust me—to trust all of us." Eliza stepped away but kept her hand in his.

She watched Ramsey hesitate, and then slowly he raised his eyes to meet hers.

"There's something I need to show you."

The sound of shuffling papers filled the silence. After Ramsey and Eliza returned to the house, Ramsey asked the others to join them in the library. Brenna and Isabelle were busy putting the children to sleep but promised to join them shortly. Ramsey discerned the curious energy around him. He'd remained silent when Eliza first asked what he needed to show them, but he wished to tell them only once. He believed Eliza spoke the truth when she told him he wasn't in this alone—that responsibility to end this was not solely his—but believing it didn't erase the guilt that clouded his thoughts. Regardless of what Eliza thought, he still believed the burden to bring his grandfather to justice was undeniably his. He's the one who left when he should have stayed to protect his grandmother. He couldn't change the course of events already passed, but he could accept the consequences of leaving and do what was in his power to make it right.

Ethan finally spoke, asking the one question for which Ramsey had no good answer. "Why didn't you tell us? From the condition of these papers, you've had them for at least as long as you've been here."

Ramsey said, "I obtained those documents before my arrival. The sheriff in Wyoming was quite adamant about handing them over in person."

"Your reason for the delay?" Gabriel asked.

Ramsey shook his head. "No, that was the weather as I told you. I spent three nights too long as a guest of the sheriff and his family until the winds subsided enough for travel."

"That doesn't answer why you didn't say anything."

Ramsey met Ethan's stare. "I wasn't planning to tell you—at least, not yet."

He quickly became the focus of three pairs of deep blue eyes. "Eliza made me realize that this fight isn't mine alone, but this doesn't change anything."

"You're still going after him alone?" Eliza stepped closer to Ramsey.

"No, I won't do that." He looked at Ethan and Gabriel now. "But when it comes time to end this—whatever has to be done—you have to step aside."

"That's not how family works," Gabriel said.

"I wouldn't know about that." Ramsey walked around the desk where Ethan stood, half-bent over the documents. Ramsey noticed him focus on one paper more than the others. "This information doesn't prove Hunter's guilt. I still have to find him and either hope he confesses or force it."

Ethan interrupted, not bothering to glance up from the desk. "There's a note here from Sheriff Carver about further investigation and a Buxley Whit from Texas written beside it." Ethan finally looked up at him. "Do you know what this means?"

Ramsey said, "Not yet. I sent a telegram when Eliza and I went into town."

"Sheriff Carver didn't say anything when he gave you the information?"

"He handed me that last letter before I rode out of town." Ramsey reached over and with a nod, Ethan handed him the paper. "This was nothing more than a communication between Tyre and Carver during the sheriff's unfortunate days as a gunslinger. I didn't have a chance to study it until after I'd arrived at the ranch. That's when I noticed the newly scrawled note at the bottom."

A soft knock sounded at the door. It opened, and Brenna walked in. "Andrew talked Isabelle into an extra story tonight. Am I interrupting?" Ramsey often wondered if his voice would have sounded like the Scottish Highlands met British refinement had his life turned out differently.

"Please, come in," Ramsey told her. He watched her walk into the room and stand near Eliza.

Brenna glanced around the room at each of them. "If your expressions are any indication, I've missed quite a lot."

"I'll catch you up tonight," Ethan said absently, but he still managed a smile for his wife before turning back to Ramsey. "With winter heading in strong and fast, there won't be many opportunities to find Hunter or Tyre Burton."

"Which is why I'll ride into town tomorrow—perhaps my telegram received a response."

Eliza studied Ramsey. "What aren't you saying?" She surprised him and her brothers. "I don't know why, or what, but you're not telling us something."

Ramsey exhaled slowly and fixed his eyes on Eliza.

"Perhaps you're wrong about this, Eliza," Brenna said.

"No, she's not wrong," Ramsey said to Brenna. To the others he said, "But I owe it to Brenna and our grandmother to tell them first."

"Tell us what? If it's about what's happening—"

"It's not—at least not directly. Is Grandmother still awake?"

Brenna shook her head. "She retired while you were outside. Amanda offered to close up the kitchen."

"Then it will have to wait until tomorrow."

"We may as well follow Elizabeth's example and retire early," Ethan said. "The coming days won't get easier."

Ethan stacked the documents and handed them to Ramsey with a glance and a firm nod.

He'll be patient—for tonight. Ramsey watched Ethan walk to his wife, but Brenna stepped toward Ramsey instead.

"I know it doesn't yet feel like we're family, but please do not give up on us," she said to him softly. "You do have a family here—one who loves you, who trusts you, and who will stand beside you always. They don't give up on their own."

Brenna didn't wait for a response. She leaned over and gently hugged him, then walked to her husband.

Ramsey watched his sister leave the room, protected by Ethan's strength and lasting devotion.

When she was alone with Ramsey, Eliza walked to the window, staring at the darkness through the glass. Not a single star shone through the black clouds. She listened to the familiar wind gather strength, and her eyes automatically followed the barely visible fence to the pasture beyond, where she knew the cattle would pass the night and coming winter. Eliza felt Ramsey's presence behind her and wished for wisdom. She had heard Brenna's softly spoken words, but she wondered if Ramsey believed his sister. She sensed his doubt.

When Ramsey did speak, he stood close enough for her to hear his soft words above the sound of the wind through the glass.

"You all embraced Brenna so easily," Ramsey said. "I owe your family a lot of gratitude for that. When I learned I had a sister, I didn't know if I would ever meet her, but I thought of Brenna often. I couldn't have imagined a better life for her. With Ethan and your family, I know she's loved."

"There is no debt to pay for loving Brenna—loving our sister."

Ramsey joined her at the window, both of them staring into the blackness.

"I have so many questions to ask her and our grandmother about, but I'm not certain I should."

Eliza turned her head, watching Ramsey, though he was focused on the black landscape outside. She said, "You have a right to know what happened and find out why you were separated from your family."

Ramsey said, "It's possible my parents had a reason to send me away as a baby, but I may never have the answers." Ramsey recalled how he felt when he learned of his parents and that he had a sister. Anger and rejection consumed him for weeks, but then he remembered only sadness because he'd been robbed of a life with his family. Eventually he accepted it, but he never stopped hoping.

"That shouldn't stop you from asking the difficult questions," Eliza said.

Ramsey faced her. "I will when the time is right."

"What were you told as a child?"

Ramsey hesitated, but he knew she wanted to understand how deeply he'd been hurt. "Hunter told me that my parents gave me up and died soon after. He said they were killed in a fire, which is why there wasn't a funeral. He told me they died in Texas, so that's where I began the search for any record of them, but I didn't even have their real names. I kept searching for Davis and Lacy Crawley. I was in the kitchen when he told me. My grandmother was preparing supper, and she overheard me asking about parents. She looked sad and defeated, but she said nothing. I know now that Elizabeth feared Hunter too much to tell me the truth."

Eliza had known the pain of those she loved and cherished, as though it were her own, but never before like this. Her connection with Ramsey was greater than even she realized, and her heart ached for the child in him and longed to heal the man he'd become.

"Ask her the questions, Ramsey. She is stronger than you think."

"When the time is right," was all he murmured.

Minutes passed, and the howling wind subsided. The dark clouds parted, allowing the moon's light to touch the ground and the stars to softly blanket the sky. The weather changed so quickly in Montana, similar to a person's life—one minute safe and warm, and the next like a tempestuous storm.

"I don't intend to give up on anyone," Ramsey said quietly.

"I know." Eliza still faced the window but reached toward him, holding out her hand. After a moment, she welcomed the warmth of Ramsey's skin as his hand slid into hers. She closed her eyes while the raging storm abated.

12

He stood beneath the doorway, watching her move quietly and efficiently around the spacious kitchen. The fragrant scent of bread rose from the oven while cuts of meat sat in a bowl on the table, waiting for their turn on the cookstove. His desire to learn of his family's hidden secrets competed with his desire to never see his grandmother in pain. He had no wish to cause her to feel guilty about the choices she had made, but he'd made his own decision to leave her behind all those years ago, and right or wrong, those choices led them both to be here.

"I'm not so old I can't hear someone standing in my doorway." Elizabeth glanced over her shoulder. She wiped her hands on the white apron tied around her waist. She picked up a wooden board covered with vegetables and slid them into a large iron pot that hung on the swinging crane.

"No one could accuse you of being too old for anything," Ramsey said and walked into the kitchen. "Need any help?"

He smiled at the once-familiar look she sent his way. "All right, no help. Mind a little company?"

"I would love some." Elizabeth motioned him to sit at the table.

He hesitated before pulling out a chair.

"And I know my limitations, regardless of what all of you think. I won't pretend that Amanda wasn't brought here in part to help out. I'd be indignant about it, but I like the girl. Eliza always was a smart one—that young woman she rescued could use a break. Brenna and Isabelle both offered to help in the kitchen, but they have enough to do with the little ones, and Eliza is wise enough not to come near my stove."

Ramsey smiled to hear her speaking like this was her home. He leaned forward, curious about what Elizabeth knew about Amanda Warren. He asked, "What do you mean Amanda was rescued?"

"She puts on a good show, but I'd be willing to bet the winter vegetables that Amanda has a few sad stories. She's been overdoing since she arrived. I fear she worries we'll turn her out if she doesn't work extra hard. She doesn't feel secure yet, but we'll get her there."

"She told you that?"

"Of course not, and she won't either," Elizabeth said. "But you didn't search me out this early in the morning to talk about Amanda. The sun won't be up for at least another hour."

"I'm joining the men for the first shift with the cattle, and then I have to ride into town this afternoon."

Elizabeth set down the long wooden spoon she'd been using to stir a light batter. "Is everything all right?"

"I'm waiting for a telegram, and I'm not the most patient man." Ramsey moved from his chair to another one closer to the hearth where Elizabeth worked. "Do you mind if we talk before the others come down?"

He scooted out a chair for his grandmother and ignored her curious scrutiny.

"Are you sure you're all right?"

Ramsey nodded and said, "It's not always easy to catch you alone these days, and I have a few questions." He heard the sound of boots meeting wood floor. "But it seems this conversation will have to wait until later."

Elizabeth watched Ramsey stand. "If you're certain—"

"I'll find you later, but whatever is on that stove smells wonderful."

She stood agilely. "Don't wait too long." Elizabeth raised her eyes to look directly at him and said, "I can't answer all your questions, but I hope I can fill in some of the gaps."

Ramsey nodded and walked toward the hall.

"You haven't had breakfast," he heard behind him. Elizabeth walked forward and handed him biscuits wrapped in white cloth. "They're from last night but still soft."

Ramsey smiled and said, "Thank you, Grandmother." He gently kissed her cheek, but he missed her easy smile and the tears filling her bright eyes.

The crisp winter morning brought a mixture of sun and snow. Thick clouds covered the landscape in shades of gray, allowing rays of sun access to the earth intermittently. Snow covered the peaks making up the Belt Mountain Range that spanned part of the north and west ends of the land. Eliza wrapped the wool scarf around her neck once more in an effort to keep the chill away from her skin. Andrew had woken multiple times from nightmares, and he'd kept Gabriel and Isabelle up most of the night. When she met Gabriel in the hallway earlier, she offered to join the morning shift so that he could sleep. She doubted he would manage to rest for more than an hour or two, but his face told her that he was in desperate need of sleep.

"Didn't expect you out here this morning."

Eliza pulled up and waited for Ramsey to ride up alongside her. "Gabriel didn't get much sleep. Andrew kept them awake most of the night."

"Is he all right?"

"Gabriel said it was a bad dream, but it was bad enough to keep both him and Isabelle awake."

"I'll be riding into town later. Do you want me to bring the doctor back?"

Eliza said, "If Andrew was bad off, Gabe would have sent for the doc last night." She looked at Ramsey. "Another trip to town so soon?"

Ramsey smiled at her. "Not everyone is as opposed to being around people as you are."

"I don't mind it." Eliza smiled. "But I do prefer human contact in moderation."

"I'm still amazed that you traveled to Kentucky by yourself."

Eliza felt Ramsey watching her and knew he waited for a response. They'd not spoken in detail about the days she was in Kentucky or of her real reasons for going. She had told him the same thing she'd told everyone else—that they needed Ramsey to help settle issues at the ranch, but she often asked herself if that was her only reason. She certainly hadn't thought of him much over the years, and they'd never spent any time alone together while he lived at the Double Bar. She'd gladly share her reasons—once she knew exactly what those were.

"It got you back here."

"Yes, it did. Would you like to ride into town?"

Eliza wondered at the abrupt change in conversation. "The supplies wouldn't have arrived yet, so what takes you into Briarwood?"

"I'm expecting a telegram."

Eliza had been waiting for Ramsey or one of her brothers to broach the subject of Hunter again, but work on the ranch had to come first. Their families were a greater priority, and they didn't exactly have any leads. According to the hands riding fences the past two days, the Double Bar had been vacated. This should have pleased everyone. Instead, a mounting frustration plagued the household. No one at the Double Bar meant they had no clues as to Nathan Hunter's whereabouts. Their desire for justice and to end the fighting increased every day, but they remained on guard and on edge. Eliza's thoughts returned to the question. Ramsey's inaction had confused her, but perhaps he'd not been as idle with the situation as she assumed.

"From whom?"

Ramsey faced her. "Sheriff in Bozeman."

Eliza pressed her back teeth firmly together. She eased the tension in her face before speaking. "You found him?"

Ramsey shook his head. "I only know where he's been, but right now that's all we have. If I can find someone who knows where he's going, we might be able to track him down."

"You're sure he was in Bozeman?"

"Not sure. It's just a hunch—a hopeful one—but a hunch anyway."

"Will you go there?"

"Depends on what the sheriff has to say."

Eliza said, "It doesn't appear we have a storm on the horizon. They've already put the hay out for the cattle, and we don't all need to sit out here in the cold watching the herd."

Ramsey said, "Doesn't stop you from coming out here."

"I come out here for the fresh air and quiet. Most ranches don't keep this many hands on through the winter months, but with everything that's happened over the last year and in recent weeks, Ethan wasn't willing to do without the extra men. Besides, most of them have been here since my father passed away, and they're family."

Ramsey said, "I may ride into town early—if you're sure I won't be needed for a few hours."

"I don't think I'm actually needed today either, but a Gallagher has always worked with the men—no matter how simple the tasks. Gabe and Ethan haven't been able to spend much time with their families, so today I'm that Gallagher."

"I'll hurry back."

Eliza called out to him. "Ramsey, be careful out there."

He smiled at her. "Always am."

She watched him leave, not bothering to stop at the house. Instead he turned south in the direction of Briarwood. Eliza heard one the ranch hands, Colton, yelling something about a blockage in the river. She cast another look at Ramsey's retreating form and sighed, then rode toward the ruckus.

By the time Ramsey reached Briarwood, the sun had managed to find an opening in the clouds large enough to cover the town in the illusion of warmth. However, the bitter cold mocked the sun's efforts, and Ramsey slowed his horse to a sedate walk as they approached the road through town—unusually well-traveled for this time of morning. Ramsey watched a group of cowboys mount their horses and ride away from the general store. He stopped in front of the store and dismounted. He saw no other customers. He looked around the deserted town. Smoke slowly rose from Otis Lincoln's forge at the blacksmith's shop, and he smelled something fresh in Tilly's ovens, but little other sign of life met him on the steps of Mr. Baker's general store.

Ramsey opened the door and called out Loren's name. Silence met his calls. Carefully, he moved through the storefront; the only item out of place was the overturned money box he knew Loren kept under the counter. *Damn it to hell.* "Loren!" Ramsey rushed to the back storeroom and nearly tripped over the storekeeper's still body. He lowered himself down enough to place his fingers on Loren's neck. A faint pulse gave him a small measure of hope. The small pool of dark blood seeping from underneath Loren's head did not.

He pulled a fancy fabric from the nearest shelf and set it under the storekeeper's head to help stem the flow of blood. "Hold on for me, Loren." Ramsey rushed from the store and almost ran over a young woman and small child.

"Loren's been hurt, and the store robbed. Don't take the boy inside. I'm going for the doctor."

He left the startled woman and ran over snow and ice to the residence he knew Doc Brody kept behind his office. He'd left the ranch shortly after 6:00 a.m., which meant the pounding on the doctor's door was likely to wake the man. Ramsey stepped back when the large Irishman yanked open the door.

"You'd best have a bloody good reason for waking—"

"It's Loren."

Brody, clad in only his union suit undergarment, slipped into a long heavy coat, picked up his medical bag from a chair set next to the door, and followed Ramsey to the general store. They rushed passed a small crowd of concerned citizens, including Tilly, who told them that Otis was inside with Loren. Otis quickly moved aside when he saw the doctor.

Ramsey looked around Otis's burly form at Loren. "Is he still alive?"

Otis nodded. "Bleeding stopped, but he don't look good."

"Quiet down so I can hear if the man has a bloody heartbeat." Seconds passed and then minutes while the doctor examined, shifted, and finally lifted Loren's head to examine the wound. "He's lost a lot of blood."

"Will he live?"

"Don't know yet." Brody's experienced eyes studied what he could see of the wound. "Give me a hand. I need to get him on my table."

Otis and Ramsey each lifted an arm and braced Loren under the shoulders. Once Otis had a good grip, Ramsey released one of his hands and held a fresh section of cloth under Loren's head wound. Being the largest of the three men, the doctor lifted Loren from the center and kept his legs stable as possible while they moved him from the storeroom, past the growing number of onlookers, and down the street to the small medical clinic.

Ramsey carefully opened the back door of the clinic and followed the doctor's instructions.

"Set him down—slowly—that's right."

Brody shrugged out of his coat and walked to a nearby basin to wash his hands.

"Otis, start a fire going in that stove. There's a pot of water that needs boiling. Ramsey, I've a store of bandages in the cupboard by the stove. I'll need a good stack of them." Brody hovered over Loren and shifted the man slightly to see his wound from a better angle. "Come here, Ramsey. I need you to hold him up so I can see what those bastards did to his head."

Ramsey braced Loren, careful not to let the body move while the doctor examined the head wound, and thought how grateful he was that Eliza hadn't come with him.

"How bad is it?"

"The wound can be fixed well enough, so long as nothing was damaged on the inside, but he's lost too much blood. Too soon to tell if he'll live. I need to turn him so I can stitch up that gash."

Brody and Ramsey carefully turned the body until Loren lay face down on the table. "Grateful for the help, lads, but there's nothing more you can do here."

Otis peered around the doctor's stocky body for a better look at Loren's exposed wound. "You'll let us know?"

"Aye," Brody said and gestured toward the door. "Now let me alone with him."

Ramsey remained behind.

Brody stared at him. "I work better alone."

"I'll keep out of your way, but there has to be something I can do."

The doctor carefully cut the hair around the wound and then looked up at Ramsey. "Blood is what he needs."

"Can you do that? Put blood into him?"

Brody shook his head. "I've heard of doctors who do it. The

procedure sometimes works, but more often than not, it doesn't, so I avoid the risk. Once I have him stitched, we'll try to get water down him. He needs fluids. I'll call you in when I'm done."

He stepped outside to where Otis waited.

"Will he make it?"

Ramsey hated to feel useless. "The doc doesn't know yet. May not know for a while. I saw a group of men leave before I found Loren, and I'd wager they're the ones who robbed the place. I'm riding out to see if I can find their trail. Will you close up the store? If Loren pulls through this, we don't want him left with an empty shop."

Otis nodded. "Mr. Simmons at the newspaper office sometimes fills in for Loren."

"Thanks. If Doc finishes up before I'm back, tell him I'll check in when I return."

"You're going to look for those men alone?"

"Better one man who is hard to see than a posse of men," Ramsey said. He walked back to the general store with Otis and found Mr. Simmons already behind the counter. Most of the townspeople standing outside appeared to be more concerned about satisfying their curiosity than moving out of the way. Ramsey stepped in front of the door and slid his coat to the side, revealing the marshal badge pinned to his vest.

"Nothing more to see here, folks. Go about your business."

The young woman with the small boy, who was outside the store earlier, approached Ramsey. "How is Mr. Baker?"

"Doc is working on him now, but we don't know yet." To the crowd he said, "Mr. Simmons is running the store until further notice. Don't give him any trouble, or you'll have trouble with me. Now, unless you have business here, go about your morning." He watched the dispersing crowd and then walked into the store.

Ramsey said to Mr. Simmons, "You're certain you can cover

the store?"

Mr. Simmons nodded. "I'll keep the place open for a few hours, and then I'll be back again later after I put out the paper."

Ramsey nodded and left. He mounted and rode east out of town, slowly so as not to alarm anyone. Once he cleared the last of the buildings, he increased their speed as much as the ice and snow would allow. Enough time had passed for the suspected robbers to travel a fair distance from Briarwood, but without fresh snow to cover their tracks, their burgeoned horses left behind a trail easy to follow—too easy. Either the men didn't know any better, or they were too arrogant to care if anyone followed them. Ramsey suspected the latter, which made them dangerous. Only two of the men had come out of the store, and those were the only two he cared about right now—one of them was responsible for hurting Loren.

Nearly an hour later, Ramsey noticed the stride between the horses' hooves shortened, evidence that the men he chased had slowed down. Ramsey slowed his stallion. A mere two inches of snow covered the ground, safe enough for his horse to move off the trail, closer to the tree line. He soon crossed tracks with what he could only assume were the robbers—they had also moved off the trail. Ramsey continued to follow the heavy indents in the snow. When he finally heard the voices of men, he dismounted and tossed the reins onto a low-hanging branch. Crouching low to the ground, Ramsey moved to where he could see them but not close enough to see their faces. His horse warned him of company before he saw the riders. Turning, careful not to alert the thieves, Ramsey faced the direction of the trail. Two men, walking their horses, came around the copse of trees.

Ramsey lowered his gun and motioned them over. Quietly, he said, "How in the hell did you know where I went?"

Gabriel said, "Otis rode out to the ranch, nearly broke his horse's leg. He told us what happened."

"And what you were planning?" Ethan said. "That badge won't stop bullets. You really thought to bring them in alone?"

Ramsey said, "I didn't plan to take them all in. How did you get here so quickly?"

Gabriel said, "Otis saw the direction you went. There's an access from the ranch to the main trail, and thankfully, you didn't travel far."

Ethan shifted. "Did you see which one hurt Loren?"

"Two men walked out of that store—I saw them both. The tall one on the far right and the stocky one kneeling over the bag. I don't know the others."

"We can try and surround them," Gabriel said.

Ramsey said, "They should go down easy enough. Those aren't gunslinger rigs they're wearing. The women back at the ranch would have my hide if one of you got shot, so be careful."

Ethan and Gabriel looked at each other, one smiling, the other grim. Gabriel said, "This isn't our first gunfight."

"Then I hereby deputize you both."

"What, no badge?" Gabriel smiled, then slipped away to cover the men from the north.

Ramsey watched Gabriel disappear behind the trees. "Since when does he enjoy a fight?"

"He seems to enjoy everything more these days. Marriage will do that to a man." Ethan moved quietly away to cover the men from the south.

Ramsey watched Ethan and wondered if he'd feel the same way. He shifted his focus back to the task at hand and watched the men huddled in the trees. Ramsey couldn't understand the words, but he definitely understood the tone—the men were arguing. Ramsey watched as the stocky man drew his gun on the tall man and pulled the trigger. Trusting that Ethan and Gabriel knew when to act, Ramsey moved quickly forward; his gun on the robbers.

"U.S. Marshal, drop whatever you're carrying."

"Won't happen, Marshal!" The stocky man turned his gun on Ramsey, but a shot from the trees hit the man's arm and the pistol fell from his grasp. Gabriel stepped from the trees on one side, and Ethan entered the clearing from the other while the other three men assessed the situation. They were evenly matched, but the other two wisely chose to lay down their weapons.

Ramsey said, "Glad to see you have more sense than when you robbed the general store. Step away from the guns and put your hands behind your backs." Ramsey tossed Gabriel a rope. "Do you mind stringing them together?"

Gabriel holstered his gun. "I hope you boys are ready for a long walk back to town."

One of the men spoke. "Hugh there done hit that storekeep over the head. We was just waiting outside."

Ramsey stepped closer. "Your name?"

The man shook his head.

"It's in your best interest to cooperate if what you say is true." Ramsey knew the man wasn't one of the two who had walked from the store. One of them was bleeding on the ground, and the other was dead.

"Tobias Peeler."

"Shut your mouth!" Hugh reached out to hit Tobias but hit only the cold air. "I'm dying here!"

"Wait." Ethan stepped toward Tobias. "You have a ranch ten miles south of here. Peeler Cattle Company."

Tobias nodded. "Ranch went under a few months back. We lost too many of our herd last winter."

Ramsey said, "And now you're a thief."

"We didn't mean for no one to get hurt," Tobias said. "I swear we didn't."

Gabriel finished tying the men together and wrapped Hugh's

arms with a section of the man's own shirt. "We offered to buy you out when news of your troubles reached us."

"I want a doctor!" Hugh said.

Gabriel leaned down and spoke to him quietly. Hugh quieted after that.

Tobias said, "We didn't want no big outfit like yours taking away our land. My daddy built that ranch. It was meant to go to my sons."

Ramsey said, "Now you've lost your ranch, and you're going to prison." He looked at the others. "Who are you two?"

"They don't matter," Tobias said, but he spoke too quickly.

Ramsey studied the other two men, younger than Tobias, but both bearing a passing resemblance. "Your sons? Brothers?"

After a moment of indecision, the older of the two spoke. "His sons, sir. I'm Byron, and this here is Grant."

"Say nothing more, boys."

"You do your sons an injustice, Tobias Peeler," Ethan said.

"I know, Mr. Gallagher, but if the marshal here could let my boys go, I'll do their time."

Ramsey holstered his gun. "The law doesn't work that way, but you cooperate and things will go easier for them."

Ethan said, "In light of circumstances, we'll let you ride instead of walking back to town, but you'll have to stay tied together."

"I understand. Appreciate it." Tobias lowered his head in regret, though Ramsey doubted he cared what they thought of him. He'd lost his home, his way of life, his pride, and now his freedom. The man had a lot of reasons to feel disgraced, but Ramsey understood desperation, and he knew Tobias Peeler wasn't alone. Small ranching operations rarely survived in the northern lands. They were either bought out or taken by larger operations like Hawk's Peak, or they struggled until nothing remained but a dwindling memory of a dream to carve out a legacy.

They helped the men onto the horses, and while Ethan kept watch, Gabriel and Ramsey looped a longer rope around their waists, connecting each one to the next. Ramsey mounted and Gabriel handed him the end of the rope. Ramsey leaned back and said, "This is going to be an uncomfortable ride. I'll take it as slow as I can, but we have a friend to check on."

13

Ramsey left Hugh and the Peelers with Ethan and Gabriel at the jailhouse. He then stopped at the telegraph office before riding to Doc Brody's, where he dismounted and entered the clinic without knocking.

Brody looked up from his desk, a desk too small for a man his size. "You catch the vile miscreants?"

"We did. Is he still alive?"

"Aye, he is, but I don't know yet if he'll stay that way. He hasn't woke up yet."

Ramsey said, "Let's hope he does."

"Who were they? Professionals?"

"Two of them looked to be. You ever hear of the Peeler Cattle Company?"

"Sure. Small outfit south of here somewhere. Patched up one of Peeler's hands a couple of years back. Don't tell me they were there."

"Tobias Peeler and his two sons," Ramsey said. "I've got one of the two men who went into the store over at the jail. He took a bullet in the arm and needs patching."

"Times like this I'd as soon ignore the oath and let the dastardly riffraff get their comeuppance." Brody shrugged into his coat, not bothering with the closures, and picked up his medical bag. "Let us go and patch him up before he bleeds all over the jail."

Brody followed Ramsey into the cold winter air. The sun had once again disappeared behind darkened clouds. The air smelled of pine and pending snow, and the wind whipped open the front of their coats.

"Will you stay in town tonight?"

Ramsey pushed open the door of the jailhouse. "I will. Without a sheriff or deputy in town, someone needs to watch these men."

Ethan stepped from around the desk. "How's Loren, Doc?"

"Still breathing. I'm told you have vermin in need of care."

"In the back cell. Gabriel's back there now with the prisoners. Hugh hasn't shut his mouth since we locked him up."

"You know where I'll be." Without ceremony, Brody opened the wooden door separating the cells from the front of the jailhouse.

When he was alone with Ramsey, Ethan said, "Will you keep them here?"

Ramsey walked over to the small stove and filled a tin cup with hot coffee. "Appreciate this," he said, raising the cup before bringing the edge to his lips for a long swallow. He closed his eyes a moment and then faced Ethan. "I'll wire the district judge, but there's no telling how long it will take for a trial."

"You didn't sign on for this when you became a marshal."

"No, but it's only a temporary appointment."

"Exactly how temporary?"

"I have one more month until an official appointment is made."

Ethan crossed him arms and stared at Ramsey. "You forgot to mention that deadline."

Hugh's shouting from the back room grew louder. They all ignored him.

"I didn't think it would take me that long to find the old

man."

Ethan sat on the edge of the desk. "Then we need a sheriff. If our time is that limited, dealing with local matters will only bring us closer to the deadline without hope of doing what needs to be done."

Ramsey set his empty cup on the desk and walked to the window. The late afternoon clouds hovered over the mountains. Ramsey imagined a warm hearth and a hearty meal at Hawk's Peak, knowing he wouldn't be there to enjoy either. In the past, his meals were more often than not prepared at a small café like Tilly's. "Without a mayor or town council, who organizes the elections?"

"Loren usually convened as many people as he could in the church. Gabriel's been talking for years about forming a council, but truth is, we're not in town often enough."

"Then it's time to hold an election."

"You speak like a man planning to do more than arrest someone and disappear again."

"I have no intention of disappearing." Ramsey knew the words he spoke to be true. "In the meantime, the prisoners need to remain here."

"You'll need a temporary sheriff or at least a deputy."

Ramsey looked at Ethan. "You have someone in mind?"

Ethan nodded. "It so happens that Jake and Tom were both deputies before coming to the ranch."

"Lawmen to cowpokes. The stories in the bunkhouse must have been interesting back then." Ramsey listened for more shouts from the cells, but Hugh finally quieted down. A moment later, both Gabriel and Brody emerged.

"The thief will live. Now, I'd better get back to Loren. I'll return in the morning to change his bandages." Brody nodded to the men and left the jailhouse.

Ethan turned to his brother. "How do you feel about asking

Jake or Tom to help out at the jail?"

"They're both qualified, but it would have to be their choice." Gabriel set down his rifle. "We need a sheriff."

"You need a mayor," Ramsey said, "but that's not my concern right now. This badge comes with a time limit, and I didn't ask for it to referee local squabbles."

"I hardly think—"

"It's not," Ramsey said, interrupting Gabriel. "It's not minor what happened to Loren or that three otherwise good men are going to prison because they fell on desperate times and made some poor choices."

Ethan leaned forward, his arms bracing his weight against the desk. It was a stance Ramsey remembered from times past, and it generally indicated someone was about to have a talking down.

"What aren't you telling us?"

Ramsey reached inside his coat and pulled out a slip of paper from his shirt pocket. "I trust Doc, but I wanted to wait until he'd left. Some matters aren't the concern of locals." He handed the paper to Ethan. "This was waiting at the telegraph office."

Gabriel looked over Ethan's shoulder and read the few sentences, printed out finely by the telegraph operator. Ramsey saw the expected surprise in their expressions.

Ethan set the telegram on the desk. "Do you believe him?"

Ramsey studied them both. "No, I don't believe him."

"We go after him," Ethan said.

Ramsey nodded.

"I'll watch over things here." Gabriel turned to Ramsey. "If Jake and Tom agree, can you deputize?"

"Not officially, no, but if you pin a badge on them and post a notice, I imagine that will suffice until something more official can be arranged."

Ethan pushed away from the desk. "I'll stop at the newspaper and ask Mr. Simmons to post the public notice."

"That's not all." Ethan stopped his departure at Ramsey's words. "Buxley Whit in Texas also contacted him."

Gabriel said, "The mysterious note on the papers. What did Whit know about Tyre?"

"Apparently Tyre killed Whit's brother, and he's been looking for him ever since. It seems the only witness came forward after Tyre had disappeared. This is the first lead Whit's had in years."

"Will he come after Tyre?"

Ramsey shook his head. "He's sick, and from the sound of it doesn't have much time, but he wants to see Tyre hang before he goes, and he has proof. If we can't get Tyre on charges up here, Whit promised he could in Texas."

Gabriel asked, "Will Texas let us jail him here?"

"Well, we'll find out. Authorities down there have been notified, so we may not have much time. They'll have to deal with extradition and that might buy us a few more days."

"Then we're wasting time."

"I'll meet you outside the livery, Ethan." Ramsey picked up his hat and left the jailhouse.

Gabriel made himself comfortable at the chair behind the sheriff's desk. "He's a lot like you."

Ethan looked at his brother. "Ramsey?"

Gabriel nodded. "Don't deny it either. You keep the anger boiling inside until at some point it explodes. You look calm, and you're certainly in control, but that doesn't mean you feel calm."

"And you believe he's on the edge of something?"

"I'm just saying you're a lot alike. Whatever you might think of doing, he'd probably think of it, too."

Ethan slipped into his coat and lifted his hat off the iron peg by the door. "I'd go after Hunter alone."

"Yes, you would. We all would."

"Ramsey won't."

"I'm inclined to agree, but he'll think about it. We all know this isn't his fight alone, but that won't stop him from wondering if he can save us."

Ethan paused at the door. "There's something between him and Eliza—something real."

"Yes." Gabriel laced his fingers behind his head. "Does that worry you?"

"Ask me when this is over."

14

Eliza watched the sky darken. Something wild cried out in the night, most likely a mountain lion. The cattle were surprisingly quiet. Silence would allow her to hear riders approaching—a sound she'd been waiting to hear for the last several hours—although she wouldn't admit it to the others in the house. Eliza preferred to remain optimistic, but she tended to expect trouble these days. Brenna and Isabelle were up, waiting for their husbands, but they'd grown accustomed to the long and odd hours ranchers kept.

Eliza knew better than they how much of a day was consumed by hard backbreaking labor, and that sometimes this meant not sleeping in your own bed for a night or two, but roughing it beside a campfire with a bedroll on the hard ground. Eliza wasn't waiting because she expected Ramsey and her brothers to return at any moment. Concern for each other's safety was a constant worry whenever one of them left the ranch, but rarely did the disquiet consume her or her brothers. It was the way of their lives and the need to live life, trusting that each of them would be as careful as possible when leaving the safety of the ranch. Yet, something felt different this time.

Listening for the sound of hooves on snowy ground was a fruitless task, but it was a chore Eliza had assigned herself from the moment her brothers rode away. Hours passed, and she took the time to work with a colt born that spring. It was time to begin halter-breaking what she believed would be a magnificent stallion. She watched from the corral as Kevin and Henry hitched the hay wagon and filled it from a temporary hay shelter. Everyone had a turn at feeding the cattle during the long winter, all the while longing for the warm days of spring when the grass would begin to cover the range. At breakfast that morning, Andrew had enthusiastically asked Gabriel if he could help feed the cattle. Everyone in the room smiled and knew Gabriel wouldn't turn down Andrew's request. Her nephew, as she now thought of Andrew since he'd become so much a part of their lives, had the heart of a rancher.

Pete, Jake, and Colton had spent the morning clearing debris from the burned-down barn. The snow left over from the last storm was no longer too deep to move the wagons to and from the barn. It was time to rebuild before the worst of winter set in. Ben, having helped with more than a few barn raisings, would eventually be in charge of the supplies arriving from town and would assist Ethan with the final layout. For now they cleared away the debris—and with it some of the memories. Eliza led Koda, the young colt named by Andrew.

The sun made an appearance once more before disappearing behind the mountains while Eliza secured Koda in the stall next to his mother. When the latch on the door scraped against metal, she finally heard the sound of riders—one of the men shouted out to warn them of someone approaching. Eliza slipped the halter and lead rope onto a metal hook and walked out of the stable into the cold evening air.

Comfortable with Gabriel overseeing the prisoners at the jail, Ramsey returned to the ranch for the evening but promised to return early the following morning. Riding over the final hill, Ramsey saw Hawk's Peak. A rush of peace he couldn't explain coursed through him—like coming home after a long absence. Darkness had descended upon them, but their horses managed to bring them home as the moon's meager light replaced the sun's rays.

They stopped a short distance from the house and both men dismounted. Brenna and Isabelle stepped outside a moment later. He watched as Ethan embraced Brenna and then turned to Isabelle, he imagined, to explain why Gabriel was not with them. Ramsey waited, but no one else emerged from the house. With a twinge of regret, he untied the reins of Ethan's stallion from the hitching post and started for the barn.

"You don't need to see to my horse, Ramsey," Ethan said.

"I don't mind. Go, I'll be in shortly."

Ramsey saw Ethan hesitate before he nodded and followed the women into the house. Colton walked toward him, his clothes and face covered in soot from the burned, wet timbers. He looked like someone had brushed paint over him. Pete and Jake weren't far behind him and were in the same condition.

"What happened to you?"

Colton removed a glove to wipe a hand over his face. "Clearing the barn debris."

Ramsey looked past Colton to where the rubble once covered the ground. Soft moonlight touched the earth, but nothing remained of the barn remnants. "Can you raise a barn right now?"

"If we can get the frame up soon," Colton said. "You ever raise a barn?"

"Yes, but Kentucky in the summer is a mite different."

"You catch 'em, Ramsey?" Pete walked up behind Colton with Jake.

"We did."

"Can't believe they shot Loren," Jake said. "He never hurt anyone."

"How is Loren?" Colton asked.

Ramsey said, "The doc won't know until Loren wakes up—if he wakes up."

"Sorry to hear that. You'll let us know if you need any help," Colton said. He and Pete continued to the bunkhouse, but Jake remained behind. Once the others had moved away, Jake said, "I didn't see Gabriel ride in with you."

"He volunteered to stay over at the jail for the night." Ramsey studied Jake carefully. He was a kind man, and from what Ramsey had observed, a hard worker who got the job done. "Ethan mentioned you used to be a sheriff."

Jake nodded. "Started back in '73 out in Butte, but rustling cattle is easier than trying to keep miners under control. Some days I still miss the badge, but I ain't never worked for better people than the Gallaghers, so I stayed. Listen, about that help Colton mentioned. Will you be needing it?"

"Ethan wanted to speak with you directly, but we could use a temporary sheriff. Tom was a lawman, too?"

"He was, and I can't speak for him, but I'll do it." Jake rubbed his gloved hands together. "I'll talk with Ethan in the morning. Loren's a good man, and he sure didn't deserve what happened to him. Who did it?"

"A couple of amateur gunslingers—never heard of them. But Tobias Peeler and his boys were there."

Jake's eyes narrowed. "That's a tough one to swallow. I know Tobias—always thought him an honest man."

"Good men make mistakes. He and his boys didn't go into the store—they didn't shoot Loren."

"Time was, a man stood by watching, they strung him up alongside the killer."

"I can't condone what they did, and they should be held accountable."

"With a hanging?" Jake shook his head. "Don't seem right

somehow."

"I'll speak with the judge." Ramsey caught a movement by the stable and saw a light flicker. He said to Jake, "You'll speak with Ethan?"

Jake nodded. "First chance tomorrow." Jake walked away, his movements easy in the darkness.

Ramsey led the horses to the stable and through the open door. Eliza stood with her back against the door of an empty stall. Ramsey met her eyes, but they said nothing. She shifted forward and opened the stall door. Taking the reins of Ethan's horse, she tossed them over the edge and removed the saddle and tack before guiding the stallion into the stall.

Ramsey walked his horse to an empty stall at the other end of the stable. When his horse was brushed down and secure, he walked back and hung his horse's bridle on a hook next to the saddle and other tack. He turned toward Eliza, allowing his eyes to follow her movements. "How long have you been out? Temperature's dropping fast."

Eliza smiled and said, "You've spent too much time in the South. Your blood will thicken after a long winter, and I'm tougher than I look."

"That I know," Ramsey said quietly. "I should be a gentleman and not ask, but I'm going to—were you waiting for me?"

"Yes." Her honesty surprised him. "You and my brothers."

"Any trouble today?"

She shook her head. "Quiet as it's ever been. Reminds me of life before—"

"Before Hunter," Ramsey finished for her.

Eliza slowly nodded. "When there's a quiet moment, of which there are few on this ranch anymore, but when it's quiet, I remember those days." Ethan's stallion leaned his head over the stall door and nickered. Eliza obliged him by smoothing her bare hand over his muzzle. "Life has never been easy here. The work is hard, the weather can be brutal, and we never know what will happen from one year to the next, but life was simpler back then. Open-range neighbors getting along for the most part—the work was still hard, but emotionally, it was easier."

Ramsey didn't want her to stop and wondered what she was trying to tell him.

"This morning at breakfast, after you had gone, Andrew told Gabriel that he wanted to help feed the cattle. After Brenna finished feeding Jacob, he smiled at everyone who walked into the room. He can't speak, but somehow you know what he's thinking." Eliza looked up at him. "I feel a change coming, Ramsey."

"I never imagined you as someone frightened of change?"

"It's not fear of change I have. I've had a hatred burning for your grandfather for too long. I never imagined I would say this, but I wish I didn't feel this way. There's new life here, and I don't want Andrew and Jacob to grow up in a home where hate exists. Montana is changing faster than I ever imagined. Soon the railroad will reach nearly every corner of the territory, and with talk from people fighting for statehood, I don't know how long this way of life will last. I want to leave behind a legacy that goes beyond a feud, but I don't know how."

Ramsey placed his hands on her arms, turned her to face him, and met her eyes. "You speak as someone who is taking responsibility for everything that's happened. You're not the only one here who has hated, who has believed death would be the only possible outcome. This fight isn't one of your making."

"I wish I could believe that," she whispered. "I spent most of the afternoon with the new colt and watched the men clear away the debris from the barn. Little by little they piled memories into the back of the wagon. We were all still young when our parents passed, and we hadn't yet earned the respect our father managed to garner—that came later. Had my father lived, I imagine life would have turned out quite different."

"Perhaps, but you can't know what would have happened, just as I can't know how different my life would have been had I spent it with my parents and Brenna. There's always more to know, another story or possible outcome." He rubbed his hands up and down her arms.

She leaned into him. "What's the other story?"

"Had my parents kept me, Brenna would have no cause to find me, to come here. She wouldn't have met Ethan, and Jacob wouldn't be here. I wouldn't be here. I would have lived my life in Scotland, been raised as a country gentleman, and I would have a family." Ramsey lifted her chin so he could look at her eyes. "I know you would rather have your father alive, but it's possible that this has always been the right story."

"You believe that?"

"I have to. This is where I am—it's where we all are. We can change our story, our futures, but we can't change the path that brought us to this point in our lives."

Slowly, Eliza leaned into him, and he slid his arms around her. She released the tense hold she had on her body.

The fresh scent of a day outside wafted from her hair when she laid her head on his shoulder and took a few deep breaths. He leaned his cheek against her soft hair and closed his eyes. The animals seemed to sense their need for a moment of peace because the stable was quiet.

Remaining in his embrace, she said, "How do we end this? How do we find the peace we need and keep our family safe without becoming like him?"

Ramsey opened his eyes. *Our family*, she had said. *Not mine, not yours, but ours.* "Will you trust me?"

She pulled away from him, surprised enough to look up. "You know I trust you. You've known it all along—you only need to believe it."

"I do know, but I need you to trust that I can end this." He felt her tense again. "Please, Eliza. Trust me and your brothers to finish what I helped start when I left Montana."

"My brothers?"

"I'll need them, and I'll need you, but we need to know you're safe."

She tried to pull away, but he held fast. She said, "I have the right to see it end. I have bled on this land as much as my brothers. Why—"

"Because worrying about you can get one of us killed."

She stilled, and her body went limp in his arms. He watched her eyes widen and tears form, but she was strong, always too strong.

"No one denies what you're capable of doing, Eliza. You have more strength than any of us—you're fearless. You know your brothers worry, but in the end, they would let you win. Of course you want to be involved in the end, but having their minds distracted even a little bit would be dangerous."

Ramsey finally released her and stepped back. She stared at him, but her eyes told him nothing—until a tear fell from bright blue eyes. "I should beat you, and I would if I could. You have no right—except you are right." She swiped the tear from her cheek. "It really is bitter cold out here."

He watched her struggle, and then what he had only hoped for happened. She turned back to him, and looking directly at him said, "I trust you, and our family puts its trust and faith in what you are about to do."

15

They'd made a start. Ramsey and Eliza walked slowly and quietly from the stable to the main house, their path illuminated by a rare, starry, winter night. Clear nights brought freezing temperatures, and Ramsey found himself looking across the pastures to the herd. No one would sit with the cattle, even bundled up, on the long nights of winter. Despite everyone's fear of another attack, forcing men to remain outdoors in bitter winds and snow was not an option they would consider. Ramsey asked himself why Hunter or Tyre Burton hadn't attacked again, though he suspected they watched Hawk's Peak. He should be grateful, but unless they knew where to find Hunter, searching for him would leave the ranch unprotected and vulnerable to further attack.

Ramsey opened the front door for Eliza. She paused in the doorway, held onto the frame, and stared into his eyes. They'd reached an understanding, and Ramsey knew she would do just as he had asked—trust him—even as she struggled with the promise. They entered the house to the warm smell of dinner simmering on the stove and the sound of laughter coming from the kitchen. They removed their coats, hats, and winter layers and walked into the kitchen, Ramsey behind Eliza. Ramsey expected there would be concern shown by her brothers and questions from everyone. Instead, they were welcomed with warm smiles.

Elizabeth handed him a cup of hot coffee and told him to wash up and sit at the table. Amused, he set down the cup and moved to the basin Eliza had finished using.

"Is it as cold as it looks out there?" Isabelle helped Amanda set the last of the food down the center of the long table and then took a seat next to Brenna.

Eliza smiled at her sister-in-law. "Your blood is still thin. Give yourself the winter, Isabelle. Come summer, you'll be praying for winter again."

Isabelle shuddered. "Not likely, although it is beautiful. I was young when we lived in the North, but I still remember how much I enjoyed the snow. I don't, however, remember the cold."

Brenna laughed. "That's why womankind was wise enough to create catalogs. Your warmer clothes will be here any day."

"So should the extra lumber. We'll be able to start on the barn and get it up as quickly as possible," Ethan said.

Ramsey listened to the easy camaraderie and then stood to pull out his grandmother's chair. He stepped around to the other side of the table and pulled out another chair for Amanda. She stared at him, appearing uncertain.

Eliza said, "We sit together, at least when we can manage it." Eliza motioned for Amanda to take the offered seat next to her. Amanda hesitated a moment, smiled at Eliza, and walked around the table to sit in the seat. The conversation continued.

"I thought Loren was still abed," Brenna said.

Ethan tweaked Jacob's chin and nodded. "He is, but Otis handles lumber orders, Loren accepts payment, and then pays Otis. I don't like to think about practicalities with Loren held up, but we have to think about getting the new barn raised before we're too deep into winter."

"I get to help!" Andrew chimed in. "Gabriel said so."

"Don't speak with your mouth full," Isabelle whispered.

Ethan smiled and ruffled Andrew's hair. "Yes, you can help. We'll need everyone's help."

Eliza drew Ramsey's attention. "How long will it take?"

"Once the ground is cleared, we'll put in the foundation," Ethan said. "How long it takes will depend on how many men we get—a few days in this weather."

Ramsey said, "Otis wanted you to know that he'll pull together every available working body he can from the town. Just tell him when."

Ethan nodded. "I appreciate that, and I know it's expected, but I also know some of the men in town can use jobs right now."

Eliza looked up from her plate. "You want to hire?"

"I know it's a lot of men, but only for a few days—I wanted to speak with all of you about it first. The books can handle it."

Ramsey appreciated that Ethan respected everyone's opinions on the matter. He wasn't used to sharing ideas before making a decision, a practice he understood had to change if he chose to remain. As the family patriarch, Ethan's decision was final, but that didn't stop him from considering his family's opinions. Ramsey thought of the papers tucked away in one of his saddlebags; the information they contained offered no promise of finding Hunter or Tyre Burton, but the others deserved to know about them. Ramsey worried they would spend too much time searching, but they had to find Hunter. He hadn't spoken yet with Brenna or their grandmother—he knew they understood that this fight might not end well for Hunter, but he owed them the chance to share their own thoughts and concerns.

Eliza said, "I'm not opposed to it, and I don't believe Gabriel will be either. It's what Father would have done. You're more like him than you may ever want to admit." Eliza lifted a glass of water to her mouth, but paused as though realizing what she had said. Her eyes met Ethan's.

"That's about the nicest thing a person could ever say. We

had our differences, but I always held him in the highest admiration." They shared a smile and the kind of warm look reserved for siblings who love each other. Ramsey hoped someday he allowed himself to open enough to have that kind of relationship with Brenna.

Ramsey glanced at his grandmother and Amanda, neither of whom had said anything since they sat down. He noticed his grandmother smile once or twice at something that was said, but she seemed content to listen. Elizabeth resembled someone now at peace living with the Gallaghers, Brenna, and him—here she was safe. Amanda was stonily quiet and avoided eye contact with anyone, but he was certain she was listening.

Ramsey said, "So, how old are you going to be Andrew? Ten? Eleven?"

Andrew's big grin had everyone at the table smiling. "No, Uncle Ramsey! I'm gonna be six!"

"Going to be." Isabelle automatically corrected.

"I thought for certain you were at least ten." Ramsey smiled at the young boy. "I'm pretty sure you have to be a few years older to have a party."

"No, Uncle Ramsey!" Andrew's light laughter told Ramsey he liked the teasing.

"Oh, I think Ramsey is right," Eliza said. "You can't possibly be old enough for a party."

Andrew was having none of it. "Will you come to my party, Aunt Eliza?"

"Face it, the kid is too smart for any of us," Ethan said.

Isabelle set her napkin down. "Smart or not, it's time for a bath and then to bed with you."

"Can't I stay up a little longer, Ibby?"

"You may read in bed."

"Can I take a bath in the new house?"

Isabelle laughed. "The new bathhouse isn't ready yet, and

that's for the men when they come in from work."

"Ben didn't have a chance to tell you earlier, but he said it would be finished up tomorrow," Eliza said. The new structure was an expansion of the existing washroom attached to the bunkhouse, allowing the men more privacy and comfort.

Ethan nodded. "I'll help them tomorrow. It will give me a chance to talk with Jake and Tom."

"I mentioned something to Jake when we crossed paths tonight. Actually, he guessed that's what you wanted to speak with him about," Ramsey said.

"Pardon the interruption. Andrew, please say good-night to everyone," Isabelle said.

Andrew went around the table and gave each person a quick hug. When he leaned over and hugged Amanda, everyone saw how it startled her, but her smile told them she didn't mind. Andrew waved to everyone and followed Isabelle out of the kitchen and into an adjoining bathing room. Though the sound of laughter could be heard by those still in the kitchen, it was far more convenient to heat water over the kitchen hearth and carry into the next room, rather than carry it upstairs.

The family was still at the table when Isabelle and a cleaner Andrew emerged later.

"I'll be putting Andrew down, but if either of you ladies would like to join me, I believe I'll begin work on a new quilt," Isabelle said.

"You quilt?" Brenna asked.

"Not well, but my mother insisted I attend her quilting circles. I'm attempting to remember."

"I'd enjoy that," Brenna said. "Jacob is ready to go down."

Eliza looked at Brenna. "You know how to quilt?"

Brenna nodded. "Some, though it's been ages."

Eliza sighed and said, "Elizabeth, that leaves me in the kitchen with you."

Elizabeth stood and waved Eliza away. "Nonsense. You've been working outside all day. There's not much to it, and Amanda and I are perfectly capable."

"I suddenly feel inadequate." Eliza quiet words didn't go unheard.

"Inadequate isn't a word I would use for you," Ramsey whispered.

Ethan pushed his chair away. "That leaves me with the little man." Ethan held his hands out for Jacob. "Hand him over."

"You wish to put him to sleep?"

"I've handled tougher jobs."

Brenna smiled and transferred their son to Ethan's arms. "Of course you have, dear." Ethan bent down and kissed his wife and left the room, all the while talking to his tired son.

Isabelle and Brenna left the room together, and for a moment Eliza wondered what it would be like to know how to do what they did. She never thought of herself as a tomboy, but she had to wonder if others thought of her that way—if men thought of her that way. She leaned over to ask Ramsey, "How will you occupy your evening?"

"I'd as soon go out and work, but I'd forgotten how short the winter days are up here."

Eliza watched Ramsey watching Elizabeth.

Ramsey said, "She looks tired."

Eliza nodded. "It won't do much good to say anything. We've tried, but she won't slow down. Amanda has helped, though. You haven't spoken to her yet?"

Ramsey shook his head.

"Waiting won't get you answers."

"I know that."

Eliza stood up from the table and helped Amanda clear the remaining dishes. On her way out of the kitchen, she stopped and said quietly to Ramsey, "Don't wait too long."

He reached his arm out. "Do you have a few minutes?"

She met his eyes briefly and nodded. "We could talk in the library."

"I was thinking the front porch."

Eliza raised her brow in the same manner he'd seen Ethan and Gabriel raise theirs when they were amused. "I guarantee it's not any warmer out there than it was an hour ago."

Ramsey smiled. "I won't keep you long."

Eliza nodded and preceded Ramsey from the kitchen. At the front door, she allowed him to help her into her coat. She waited while he slipped into his coat, but he didn't bother to close the buttons. He opened the front door for her, and the cold air rushed to surround her. Eliza walked directly to one of the rocking chairs and sat down, waiting for Ramsey to decide where to stand. He finally turned and looked at her, though he didn't speak immediately.

"What didn't you want to talk about inside?"

"Horses."

"The breeding program you mentioned before."

Ramsey nodded. "You said there was never a good or bad time for these things, and I find myself with a few minutes to spare this evening."

"I told you I was interested, and I know Gabriel would be on board. He tried telling us about the quality of horses bred on some of those Kentucky horse farms. I saw it for myself, and I agree with him."

"It wouldn't be easy, and it would require a long-term commitment," Ramsey said.

Eliza wrapped her scarf comfortably around her neck. "You've decided to make that commitment to Montana?"

"Yes, but I still can't promise how circumstances will play out."

"Then why do it? Why make the investment?"

"To leave something substantial behind. You and your brothers—you have this place—you have Hawk's Peak. It will pass through the generations. My sister is a part of that now, and I'd like to add something to the legacy."

Eliza studied him, her mind filled with too many questions and yet one that stood out. "I don't know how much of an inheritance you have, but I do know what starting an operation costs. And don't get me wrong, we do well here, and we'll welcome it, but even we couldn't front this type of business right now. If you have that kind of capital, why not start a ranch of your own?"

Ramsey hesitated. "Just in case."

Eliza wouldn't let him get away with that vague of an answer. "Just in case of what?"

"You know exactly what, Eliza."

She stood. "I'm unclear on the details." She wasn't, and she knew he knew that.

"Yes, it's in part because something could happen when I finally do find Hunter."

"In part?"

"That's all you get for now."

"All right, but can you tell me something?" The warm fog of her breath hit the cold air. "Why can't we talk inside where it's warm?"

"I'm acclimating myself."

Eliza couldn't prevent the smile her lips formed, though the cold didn't make smiling an easy task. "You're not used to spending long hours indoors, are you?"

"No, but neither are you."

"I'm used to it when I'm not working."

Ramsey leaned against the railing. "I have spent more nights under the stars than under a roof, and sometimes I need the open air."

The slow howl of a wolf echoed through the mountains. Ramsey stood straight and looked out over the dark pastures. "It sounds close."

Eliza stepped up beside him. "We've lost a few head to the wolves over the years but usually the strays. I remember a few winters back when the pack came closer than usual to the herd and caused a stampede. When we finally got them under control, we'd lost a few head, but the wolves lost two of their own. If it's the same pack, they've likely learned to wait until a stray separates from the herd."

Ramsey listened to the howls fade one into the next. "I remember losing a few from the Double Bar stock but that was when the herd was still in high country."

"Connor doesn't sleep well—never has. He's usually the first one to hear anything amiss and warn the others. If the pack comes too close, we'll put a couple men on watch."

"A little cold out here for that."

Eliza laughed. "You don't remember nighthawk duty when you were at the Double Bar?"

"Yes, but we kept watch from the porch off the bunkhouse."

Another howl broke the evening silence. Eliza's eyes shifted to look at the outline of the herd in the pasture. "It's still a ways out there and could be alone."

Ramsey continued to look out over the land, though at what, Eliza couldn't be certain. "I want to talk about the horses, but let's move this to the library please—I've acclimated enough."

Ramsey smiled and left his place against the railing to open the door for her.

Eliza led the way back into the house where she shrugged out of her coat and immediately walked to the library. Thankfully, the fire still burned. She set a couple more logs on the low-burning flames and turned when she heard Ramsey.

Amanda stepped quietly under the doorway carrying a small

tray. "I don't mean to interrupt, but I heard you come back in and thought you might like something hot."

"Bless you, Amanda." Ramsey lifted the tray from her hands.

"I didn't expect you to still be down here," Eliza said.

"I told Elizabeth to retire early. I was preparing dough for tomorrow's bread."

"You told her, and she listened?" Eliza set the fire iron back in the stand. "Someday you'll have to tell us how you managed that. Thank you for the coffee—I'll clean up when we're finished in here."

"Have a good night," Amanda said and quietly left the room.

Eliza took the hot cup of coffee that Ramsey held out to her. "What do you think of her?"

Ramsey glanced at the empty doorway and then back to Eliza. "I like her. She's quiet, but bright and intuitive. If you watch her, you can see how she's listening to everything going on around her."

"I agree. I'd like to know her story." Eliza closed her eyes when she drank from the steaming cup. "And I'd like to know how she manages to make a superb pot of coffee using the same tools and beans I use."

Ramsey laughed. "Your coffee isn't good?"

"It's hot," Eliza replied. "Tell me what you have in mind for the horses."

Eliza sat in one of the leather chairs because she knew Ramsey wouldn't sit until she did. Once they were comfortable and settled, Ramsey apparently changed his mind about comfort and sat forward.

"One stallion, three mares to start. Then there's additional men trained to work with horses, expanding the stables and bunkhouse, and extra tack and supplies. Nathan Tremaine would deliver the horses. This idea would require rounding up some of the mustangs, assuming it can be done."

"It can." Eliza also leaned forward and set her cup back on the tray. "I see the appeal of breeding the thoroughbreds with the mustangs—you'll end up with a powerful horse that could easily handle these climates and terrain, but why do you believe it will work?"

"I don't know that it will, which is why I'm going to recommend the mares we bring up are covered by the stallion. Then bring in some of the mares from the mustang herd and let the stallion cover them."

"And you don't think there will be a problem cutting out the mares?"

"I didn't say it would be easy." Ramsey finished his coffee and set the cup down next to Eliza's. "It's a substantial operation and one that would require the use of land and expanding existing buildings."

"We have more than enough land, but why would Nathaniel be willing to part with some of his best stock, because I'm assuming that's what he'd be doing?"

Ramsey said, "The stock is his, and he's not interested in remaining in the horse business."

Curious, Eliza inched forward another inch on the chair. "Why not?"

"For reasons that escape understanding, he prefers politics and plans to run for local office. His father passed away, and his sister is marrying someone who already has an impressive horse farm. They're splitting the stock, and he wants to sell his share."

"I saw their operation—they have more than a dozen mares," Eliza said.

"They have double that, along with half a dozen geldings, and of course the two stallions."

"You only wanted the four horses?"

"I'd rather take them all, but again, more horses would require more land and expansions. Once you begin breeding, your stock will soon double, and of course you have the mustangs to consider."

Eliza had to ask the question, regardless of her own desire to send for the horses immediately. "I've seen his stock, and if Ethan and Gabe agree to this, we'll find a place for the horses. The question is, are you absolutely certain you want to use your inheritance in this way?"

Ramsey looked down at his hands and rubbed them together as he worked up a way to tell her something he didn't want to reveal. He finally looked up at her and leaned back into the chair.

"I haven't used any of the money, not a cent or dollar. I still don't know my parents' reasons for leaving it the way they did, but it's there, and I want to put it to use, doing something they would have liked. Brenna told me they loved horses." He scooted forward again, as though he couldn't get comfortable. "This is what I want to do with it—invest in the ranch."

Eliza considered what he was giving up and admired the commitment he was making. If the money was hers, she would do the same thing, and she didn't doubt Ethan and Gabriel would accept Ramsey's plan. However, she also knew they would have a difficult time accepting that Ramsey would be using his own inheritance to expand their ranch. Her brothers would expect to give Ramsey something in return, and ownership in Hawk's Peak would be the most likely solution. Eliza didn't know if Ramsey would accept. She believed she had a solution to that issue, but it wasn't something she could mention to them— or to Ramsey—at least not yet.

"I'll make a deal with you, but it's not one you'll like."

Ramsey's green eyes flashed with a bit of amusement. "You have my attention."

"We talk to my brothers, first chance." She paused. "But first, you have that talk with Elizabeth and Brenna."

Ramsey studied Eliza carefully. He should have known the

deal came with strings. To her credit, she was only calling him out on something he should have done within a few days of his arrival. She was strong, stubborn, and he'd learned since his arrival, someone who demanded authority, even if she wasn't entirely aware of it. Her brothers had taught her well—she knew exactly when to play each card. He still had a few plays of his own, but in this instance, it was time to fold.

He'd caught glances from Brenna and his grandmother during the past weeks, but they continued to wait patiently.

"I expect I'll get an early start tomorrow," Ramsey said.

"Elizabeth is usually in the kitchen before the sun rises. We can't seem to stop her."

Ramsey stood and offered a hand to Eliza. She took it, though it wasn't necessary. He wasn't willing to admit this to anyone yet, but he enjoyed touching her, even if it was only the briefest meeting of hands. Eliza released his hand and picked up the tray. He moved to take it from her, but she shook her head at him.

"I'll worry about cleanup. You have an early morning."

Her slow smile warmed him. He watched her leave the room and then doused the lanterns, checked the fire, and walked into the hallway. The parlor, where Brenna and Isabelle had been quilting earlier, was now dark. The only illumination was a dimmed light from an oil lamp on the hall table and a soft glow coming from the kitchen. Ramsey picked up the lantern and walked quietly down the hall, stopping at the doorway of the kitchen.

Ramsey watched Eliza for a moment. She never wasted a movement. Each step, reach, and touch was deliberate. His eyes settled on a lantern sitting on the table, and before he was caught staring, Ramsey backed away, turned the lamp down a little more, and made his way down the rest of the hallway and up the staircase. In the upstairs hallway, he paused at Eliza's door and looked into her room. No frills like most women had. No fancy adornments or racks filled with complicated gowns. And yet, he'd never met a more beautiful woman, more appealing to him than the young debutantes who had been forced in his path through the years.

He heard her footfalls below and moved quickly past her room to his own farther down the hallway. Distracted, Ramsey set the lamp on the dresser next to the bed and stripped. He splashed cold water on his face, chest, and arms, and then rubbed the water away with a towel he didn't remember seeing there that morning. It smelled fresh, though he couldn't imagine how. No one was hanging laundry outside in this weather.

Ramsey opened the large bedroom window a crack, and exhausted in body, he slipped beneath the heavy quilts. It took his naked body a moment to adjust to the cool linens, but with his thoughts hovering just below improper, he welcomed the cold from the blankets and the air seeping through from the window. He watched the night sky change, the clouds gray and tumultuous, much like his thoughts. His mind registered the howl of a wolf, and then another, but reassured by Eliza that the wolf or wolves were far enough away, he settled into sleep.

Ramsey woke earlier than he'd planned. Sometime during the night, he'd kicked away one of the quilts, and despite the freezing air coming in through the open window, his body was covered in moisture. Whether it was the lustful dream, or the nightmare that followed, he couldn't be certain, but since he was awake, it was time he fulfilled his end of the deal. Ramsey had ultimately decided to speak with Elizabeth alone, rather than ask Brenna to join them. He wasn't certain what would be said, and he preferred not to cause his sister pain. He would get his answers and then speak with Brenna.

Ramsey pushed away the remaining bed linens and walked barefoot across the room to close the window. He moved to the wash basin, and with what was left, he bathed himself the best he could, using the icy water and a large cloth, but he knew he'd need a hot bath later. Reasonably certain he'd washed away the sweat and whatever dirt remained from yesterday, he dressed and made his way downstairs.

As reliable as a sunrise, Elizabeth bustled around the kitchen. It was too early for coffee, but the kettle of water on the stove told him he might be able to talk her into a cup of tea. He preferred coffee, but he'd grown accustomed to tea during his time in the South.

"Do you ever tire?"

Elizabeth turned abruptly. "Goodness, Ramsey, you startled me." She pulled a cloth-covered bowl off a shelf and dropped a large round of dough onto a floured cloth set out on the table. "Whatever are you doing awake this early? After what I heard happened yesterday, I didn't expect any of you to be up at this hour."

"Unfortunately I have to ride back into town early to relieve Gabriel. It's important for him to be here."

"He wouldn't have volunteered if he minded," Elizabeth said.

"I know, but this is his ranch and temporary or not, I asked for the badge."

Elizabeth paused with her hands deep in the dough. She covered it with a white cloth and wiped the flour from her hands. "The coffee isn't quite ready, but would you like some strong tea?"

"I'd appreciate that."

Ramsey sensed the shift in her mood and was sorry for it. They all knew why he had asked for the badge, but the more time he spent here, and the more time that passed, he had to ask himself why he thought it necessary.

Hunter had been quiet since the last incident. He knew the danger was far from over, but his thirst for revenge waned with each new sunrise. Ramsey had wondered how the Gallaghers had gone on living their lives. After his sister's kidnapping was bungled, she and Ethan found time to be in Scotland, have a baby, and marry. Nearly losing Andrew certainly angered Gabriel and frightened Isabelle, but he'd never spent time with two more hopeful people, despite the seriousness of current unknowns.

Ranchers always had worries, but Ramsey didn't want those worries to be about whether or not their families were safe from his grandfather because, regardless of Hunter's absence from their lives, Ramsey believed it was short-lived.

Elizabeth was an innocent bystander in this long-lasting feud. He didn't want to hurt her by raising the past, but she was the only person who had the answers he sought.

She motioned for him to sit down, but he waited until she was ready to join him. Her eyes moved back and forth between her tea and the covered dough. He almost hesitated in broaching the discussion, but remembered what Eliza said. The delay wasn't fair to his grandmother either, but it was Elizabeth who spoke first.

"I've wondered how long it would take for this talk to come."

Ramsey rested his arms on the table. "I wanted to spare you the pain of having to answer my inquiries about my past, but there's no one else I can ask."

"When did you learn of your parents?"

"I received a letter from a Boston lawyer when my father died."

"That was an unkind and sad way for you to learn of them," Elizabeth said quietly. "When you found out, you didn't try to find your sister?"

Ramsey leaned back in the chair and shook his head. "I considered it, but the letter said that Brenna would come here, though it didn't say when."

Elizabeth's confused expression was understandable, and

Ramsey remembered he'd had part of this conversation with Eliza and part with Brenna but not his grandmother.

"A note from my father was enclosed with the letter. I didn't know what to think or to believe. Suddenly I had a father, or would have, but by then it was too late. I felt betrayed, hurt, and angry."

Elizabeth reached across the table and set her hand on Ramsey's. "We all did everything wrong when it came to you. I'm so sorry for my part."

"How long did you know?"

Elizabeth breathed deeply, perhaps to give herself more time. "From the moment it happened," she said.

Ramsey leaned forward and slipped his hand out from underneath hers. "When I left the ranch, why not tell me then?"

"I made a promise to your mother, my daughter." Elizabeth's eyes shone with unshed tears.

"I could have had years with them." Carefully, Ramsey asked, "Why did they send me away? There were ways to protect you. Even later you proved that by disappearing. With their help, you would have been safe."

"They didn't send you away." Elizabeth wiped a tear away. "You were taken."

Had Elizabeth told Ramsey that she was the one who stole him away from his parents, he couldn't have been more surprised.

"I don't even know how to respond to that."

Elizabeth hesitantly reached out. "Please, Ramsey, let me explain."

Cameron Manor in the Countryside of Borthwick, Edinburghshire, Scotland—June 1859

Anne Murphy loved Scotland, and she loved Ramsey and Brenna Cameron. She had always desired to see places beyond the shores of Ireland, and she believed the best chance for her to visit America would be as a nanny, caring for children of wealthy parents. When a friend of her grandfather's, who was a solicitor in Edinburgh, was tasked with locating a caregiver for two young children outside of the city, he recommended Anne for the position. Scotland wasn't a grand adventure, but it was a start.

Anne came from Dublin and had never ventured beyond the city. She was in awe of Cameron Manor and Scotland—the beauty, the people, and the great expanse of land owned by one family. Her first meeting wasn't with Mr. Cameron but with his wife, Rebecca, as she preferred to be called. They weren't a family of noble birth, but Anne had no one with whom to compare, and so to her, they were the noblest people she'd ever known. The Camerons doted on their twins—one boy and one girl—and spent nearly as much time with them as Anne did.

A truly exciting moment in Anne's life came three months after she began working at Cameron Manor. Rebecca informed her that they would be traveling to America to visit her mother, and they would need her to accompany them to help with the children. Anne readily showed her enthusiasm—her dream for adventure and to see America was coming true.

Much was to be done in preparation for their journey, but the Camerons assured her that the staff would manage all of the packing. Anne's priority was to continue looking after the children—a job she enjoyed immensely. When the weather permitted, a maid or footman would help Anne carry the children and their bassinets outside where she would lay a blanket on the grass and tell them stories of Ireland and her family. They couldn't understand her, but her voice and the fresh air soothed them, and it wasn't long before they were napping.

Anne was careful to stay a close distance to the house in case she had need of immediate assistance from another staff member. The Camerons traveled often to Edinburgh, and so Rebecca had a bed large enough for a single person placed in the nursery, which Anne made use of whenever her employers were out of town. On a gloriously sunny day in July, Anne followed her routine of laying out a large wool blanket and moving the children's bassinets, with the help of a footman today, on the blanket. She was well into a story about the time Anne and her younger sister pretended they were princesses who would soon be rescued by the handsome American cowboys. She couldn't be certain, but she swore Ramsey and Brenna both laughed at her story.

Anne reached over to adjust the blanket covering Brenna. "There you are, dear one. Might you be hungry already? We enjoyed our lunch only an hour ago, but I suppose we best be getting you inside now." Whenever the Camerons were at home, Rebecca made a point to check on Anne and the children every few minutes, either from one of the windows in the manor or by walking nearby on the grounds. When they were gone, Anne decided that the best way to gain the attention of a passing servant was to wave a piece of red cloth tied to the end of a stick. It might take a few minutes, but eventually someone would come outside to help her.

She reached for the homemade flag, but a friendly voice caught her attention.

"I'm sorry, miss," the gentleman said, "but I seem to be lost."

Anne smiled. "I reckon so, sir. You've ventured onto the Cameron estate. Where might you be going?"

"The Gordon farm," the stranger said.

"Hmm, there's a family by the name of Gordon north of the village. Perhaps it is them you seek." Anne stood, this time holding the flag.

"That must be them, miss. I hope to be hired on in their stables."

Anne understood all too well how difficult it could be to find work. She was truly blessed to have found the Camerons. "Your horse appears tired. Perhaps I could ask at the stables if they might drive you."

"That would be mighty kind of you."

"My name is Anne, if you please."

"Lovely name, Anne," the man said. "Are these your children?"

"Oh, heaven's no." Anne laughed. "I merely care for them. They are the children of this house."

"It looks like a fine place to work."

"It certainly is!" Anne said in her lyrical Irish brogue, then titled her head at the man. "You have a most unusual accent, sir."

"You can call me Frank. I'm from America, visiting with kinfolk here in Scotland. I have to earn enough to pay my way back, though."

"America! It has always been my dream to visit. It would be lovely to hear more about your home, if you're not in too much of a hurry."

"I could spare a little time," Frank said.

"Wonderful! I'll settle the children inside, and I will ask Maggie, the housekeeper, if she'd allow you in the kitchen for a spot of tea." Anne turned to face the house and started to raise her hand holding the flag. She said over her shoulder, "Perhaps Maggie will have pastr—"

The knife sliced across her neck smoothly and swiftly. Anne's limp body dropped to the ground, blood rushing from her throat, slowly seeping onto the blanket. Ramsey's soft cry began the moment he was roughly picked up. Awkwardly, Frank mounted his horse and set the bassinet in front of him. A shout from someone up the hill spurred Frank into quick motion.

When he reached Edinburgh, the baby was delivered into the hands of the woman who made the journey with Frank. He left the horse at the docks, and together with the woman, boarded a ship bound for America.

The Double Bar Ranch Outside of Briarwood, Montana Territory—August 1859

"How is this possible, Nathan?" Elizabeth wiped her hands on the edge of her white apron and lifted the baby from his bassinet. "Where is Rebecca?" She cradled Ramsey in her arms, her smile bright and her eyes soaking in the beauty of her grandson.

"He's come to live with us."

Elizabeth raised her head so she could look into her husband's eyes, and her smile vanished. "Where are Rebecca and Duncan? And Brenna?"

"You just worry about that boy and mind yourself!"

Elizabeth clutched Ramsey closer to her body, unable to quiet his cries. A deep-rooted sense of terror filled her heart. "What have you done?"

"Rebecca cost us a fortune when she married her Scotsman.

She'll pay with her son, and you'll say nothing against it!"

Elizabeth set Ramsey back down in the bassinet. "With her child? You stole their son!" Elizabeth tore her apron and lifted the bassinet. "He's going back, Nathan! You cannot expect me—"

The force of her husband's fist against the side of her face knocked her down, her hands losing their grip on the baby. Nathan picked the crying baby up, bassinet and all, and set him on the table, then stood over Elizabeth. Her eyes opened despite the pain. "You're mad! You can't do this!"

"Rebecca betrayed her family and she will pay, so will that Scotsman. He took my daughter, and I will take his son." Hunter pulled her roughly to her feet, his face barely an inch from hers when he said, "You will do as I say . . . if you want to live—if you want him to live." Hunter shoved her aside and left the kitchen.

Elizabeth stumbled back to the table and lifted Ramsey into her arms. Sitting down, she cradled him in her arms. "There now, little one, he won't be hurting you again." Elizabeth rocked her body, whispering soft words to the baby until he quieted and closed his eyes. "Rebecca, my darling child," Elizabeth whispered to the air. "I pray you and Duncan find your way here and back to your son."

What Duncan meant to be a reuniting of his son with his family quickly became a bloodbath, leaving four of his hired men dead, and two of Hunter's men seriously injured. Rebecca had pleaded to accompany him to America, but he refused to risk her life or to leave Brenna unattended. He'd foolishly assumed that a dozen men would be able to break through, giving Duncan time to find his son, but he hadn't counted on Hunter's determination to thwart him.

Neither he nor Rebecca ever imagined her father would go to

such lengths for revenge. When a messenger had arrived at their house in Edinburgh out of breath, carrying an urgent message, Duncan had feared the worst, but the news was even more devastating. They had immediately returned to Cameron Manor to find Maggie in mourning for the young nanny and distraught over the loss of Ramsey. Duncan had called upon every police force he could, including the local guards and constables. It took them almost a week to discover what had happened, only to learn that the kidnapper sailed for America with the children. Nearly one month later, they received an urgent telegram from Rebecca's mother with four words: *Your son is here.*

"You'll not get him back!" Hunter cowardly stood behind a line of men.

"He's not yours! I will not rest until you give me my son! The laws of these lands will not allow this!"

"I'll kill him first!"

Duncan paled and his horse danced beneath him. He looked down at the men on the ground, dead in the fight to save his son. The remaining men kept their guns raised, but they no longer advanced or fought—Duncan knew no amount of money would convince them to risk their lives again. Duncan walked his horse a few paces closer to Hunter. "Do ye hate Rebecca so much?"

Hunter remained behind his men. "You took my daughter away, and now you'll have to live without your son. I'll kill them both if you come again, Cameron!"

"Both?" Understanding came, and Duncan stared at Hunter in disbelief. "You would kill your own wife?"

Tears threatened to fall, but Duncan would not show such a weakness to Hunter. He then made the only choice a father could make—his son would live.

17

Hawk's Peak Outside of Briarwood, Montana Territory
October 1883

"They tried, Ramsey, they tried." Elizabeth wiped a tear away. "Women rarely speak against their husbands and live to tell of it. Your grandfather nearly killed me when I tried to escape with you. Your father managed to get me a message, and I was to meet someone he was sending to secretly fetch us, but one of his workers saw me try to leave and told Nathan. He beat me so hard—every punch to my body and my face . . . I was lucky to have survived. I feared too much to try and leave with you again."

"Why did no one ever tell me? Or Brenna?"

"They didn't know how to tell Brenna about you, or about what happened, and your grandfather forbade me from ever telling you," Elizabeth said. "I couldn't risk what might happen if I did. We all did wrong by you, but we couldn't risk your life."

Ramsey leaned back again. "You spoke with them again after that?"

Elizabeth slowly shook her head. "He did allow letters through, for a time, at least."

It wasn't anger that burned within him, at least, not anger at his grandmother. He could find a way to forgive his parents for what they had done. Ramsey preferred to believe that no set of circumstances would force him to leave a child, but he couldn't know—not with certainty.

Elizabeth's silent tears tore through his thoughts. He reached across the table and lifted her small and capable hands. Moments passed before her eyes met his.

"I can't imagine what you went through with him, and I berate myself for leaving you as I did."

Elizabeth gasped. "You didn't—"

"I did. I left you to fend for yourself. If I had known the extent of his madness, I would have taken you away from him long ago," Ramsey said. "Life is difficult enough for women now, let alone twenty-six years ago." Ramsey brushed his fingers across his grandmother's cheek and wiped away another tear. "I've had a good life, and it's turned out as it should have. There is no blame to carry on your shoulders."

When Elizabeth began to weep, Ramsey slid off the chair and onto the floor beside her. He bundled her in his arms and let her cry. She gained control of her emotions quickly and pulled away so she could look at him.

"Please don't stop learning about your parents. I know for a fact that Brenna would like to share the memories with you. Their pain was the greatest of all, knowing they had a son they would never see again. They would have been proud of the man you've become."

Ramsey smiled and embraced his grandmother before returning to the chair. "I'm glad you found your way to Brenna, to the Gallaghers, and that you're safe."

"You said it yourself; life has turned out as it should have."

"I do believe that, but what I came to do isn't over."

"You're going to hunt him down?"

Ramsey sensed her worry but couldn't reassure her of the unknown. "I've questioned whether or not it's still necessary, but I believe it is. If we're all going to move forward, we need to close this chapter and find a way to move on. Ethan and Gabriel have married, Brenna is happy and has a son—they're doing their best to live their lives, but I can see that this hangs over them. I don't need to tell you how much pain Hunter has caused."

Elizabeth wiped away a fallen tear. "Whatever you have to do, promise me you won't let what he did to me, or to us, affect your judgment."

"He was this man before he did those things," Ramsey said evasively, but then added, "I won't do anything outside of the law—I promise."

Ramsey heard movement in the hallway and stood. A glance at the small clock on the sideboard told him more time had passed than he had planned. It would take him a while to ride into town, but he needed to relieve Gabriel and stop in at the telegraph office. He expected word from the judge out of Helena today. He reminded himself to ask Ethan to send Jake and Tom to town once he had a chance to speak further with them about handling temporary deputy duties in town.

He said to Elizabeth, "I have to be going now, but I'll keep in mind what you said about letting Brenna share her stories."

"Thank you for . . . understanding," Elizabeth said.

Ramsey leaned over to kiss her cheek. He stood straight when Ethan walked into the kitchen.

"And I thought I was the only one crazy enough to be up this early," Ethan said. "What are you doing up right now, Elizabeth? You promised Brenna to rest more."

"I did rest, young man, and I woke when my mind wanted to wake." Elizabeth stood, whipped a towel in the air as though shooing away Ethan's objections, and returned to her dough.

Ethan smiled. "I'll just pretend I didn't see you." Ethan turned to face Ramsey. "You're going back to town this morning?"

"Yes, as soon as I—"

"Not without something to eat." Elizabeth motioned to the table. "I have a chunk of bread from yesterday, and I'll fry up some eggs. Coffee will be ready shortly. Sit."

Amused, Ramsey tipped his head. "Yes, ma'am. Mind if I have a word with you, Ethan? Here's fine," he said and glanced at Elizabeth.

"Of course it's fine," she said. "Have a seat."

Ethan was obviously used to women directing him because he sat at the table without argument. He said, "I'll rouse Jake and Tom this morning; they can ride in with you."

"No need for that," Ramsey said and paused to thank Elizabeth for the coffee she set in front of him. "I want to check in with the doc before I take over for Gabriel at the jail."

Ethan nodded. "Then I'll send Ben with the wagon. He can pick up any supplies that have come in and ride back with Gabe."

"Chances are good that I'll be transporting the prisoners. I'll be gone a few days but that will free the men from jail duty to help with the barn."

Ethan thanked Elizabeth for the plate of toast, fried eggs, and warm ham, and then turned his attention to Ramsey. "Where will you take them?"

"Bozeman most likely," Ramsey said between bites of food. Conversations with Eliza floated through his thoughts. He told her he wouldn't go alone. "I thought I'd ask around about Hunter."

Ethan set his fork down slowly and wiped his mouth with a cloth. "You're going alone?"

"I planned to, but I promised Eliza I wouldn't," Ramsey said.

Ethan smiled. "She has a way of making a man do what she wants."

Ramsey nodded. "I know there's a lot to do around here, but to be honest, I could sure use your or Gabriel's help."

"I'll go. It will give Gabe time with his family. Besides, he's a better builder than I am," Ethan said with a smile. "They can handle the barn."

Ramsey finished off his meal and then carried his plate and utensils to the wash basin. He said a quiet thank you to Elizabeth, who stood at the stove, having listened intently to the conversation. To Ethan he said, "I'll be heading out. I should have a wire waiting from the judge; we may have to head out early as tomorrow."

Ethan nodded and cleared his plate. "I'll be ready."

Eliza walked back and forth across the length of her room. The dawn began to color the mountain peaks and light up the corners of an unusually clear sky. Eliza never tired of watching a beautiful sunrise. Normally she would be in the kitchen or already out with the horses, but she had delayed going downstairs until she thought enough time had passed for Ramsey to speak with Elizabeth.

Sleep had not come easily the previous night, though it should have considering her mind had been emotionally taxed. Her body was used to long days of hard work, but she was rarely plagued with emotional exhaustion. Questions had kept her awake, and she heard both Elizabeth and Ramsey walk down the hall earlier, Ramsey nearly thirty minutes later than Elizabeth. She had confirmed it by opening her door enough to see each of them. Her actions felt juvenile, but she had been more concerned about someone else not interrupting the two of them. Elizabeth had a habit of being the first to rise, but Eliza had noticed the evenings were becoming a little more difficult for her.

The most pressing of the questions keeping her awake was, "Would Ramsey stay in Montana when this was over?" No matter how many times they had a conversation, the question arose in one form or another, and yet he never gave her a direct "yes" or "no."

Perhaps she shouldn't expect an absolute. Life on the rugged land had already proven that the only absolute was death.

Two hours later the morning sun blanketed the snow-covered ground. When Eliza walked into the kitchen, she noticed that Ramsey was no longer there.

Elizabeth glanced up when Eliza walked into the room. She moved to stand from her place at the table, but Eliza waved her back down.

"I'm not much in the kitchen, but I can manage to get my own breakfast," Eliza said. The task was made easy because Elizabeth had covered pans with hot food on the sideboard.

"Did you not sleep well?"

Eliza set her plate down and sat down next to Elizabeth. "Well enough, I suppose. Do I look tired?"

"You're not one for lagging behind the others. Ramsey and Ethan breakfasted nearly an hour ago."

Eliza inwardly chastised herself. An hour ago is about the time boredom crept up on her, proven by the almost sure wear pattern on her bedroom rug.

Unexpectedly, Elizabeth said, "Ramsey spoke with me this morning."

Eliza kept her eyes on her food and said, "You must have both enjoyed that."

"Thank you, Eliza."

This time Eliza set down her fork and looked up at Elizabeth. "For what?"

Elizabeth smiled. "These old eyes see more than people realize. You've spent more time with Ramsey than anyone, and I have a feeling you may have nudged him a little."

"Meddled is the word you want," Eliza said.

"It's not meddling when you act from love."

"I know he had questions, and when the two of you were in a room together, you avoided everything except casual niceties."

"I thought he would come to me when he was ready."

Eliza shifted in her chair. "May I ask how it went?"

"It won't be easy to forgive myself, but we've made a start," Elizabeth said. "Would you like to know—"

Eliza shook her head. "The details aren't my business. If Ramsey chooses to tell me later, he will, but for now I'll enjoy knowing you've both found some peace." She finished her meal and cleared the plate. "Elizabeth, why don't you rest today? Amanda can take care of whatever it is you do around here."

Elizabeth looked up at her, and to Eliza, it appeared as though the woman wanted to laugh. "Eliza Gallagher, do you truly know nothing of running a household?"

Eliza shrugged. "I should, but no. I can handle the books and anything outside these walls, but otherwise I'm hopeless. My mother and Mabel both tried, but Mabel wouldn't let anyone else do the work anyway."

"I told Amanda to rest in this morning. I don't think she's been sleeping well."

"Is she all right?"

"I believe she is, but I'll be sure to ask her later. She's been rushing to get all of the housework done before I have a chance, though I can't imagine why."

Because I may have told her to in so many words, Eliza thought. *Great, now I'm the reason why Amanda's not feeling well. How much work could the inside of a house possibly need every day? Never mind, someone might not feed me again if I ask that.*

"I'll visit with Amanda later," Eliza said.

"Don't concern yourself too much. She most likely wants to impress everyone."

"I'm impressed, but I will ask her to slow down a little," Eliza said and started for the hall.

"Will you be keeping her on?"

Surprised, Eliza turned back. "I planned to. Is there a reason why we shouldn't?"

Elizabeth shook her head. "Not that I've seen. I'm quite fond of her."

Eliza hadn't spent much time with Amanda since she encouraged her to work at the ranch. It was probably time to get to know her a little better. "I'm happy for that. I'll find her later today for a talk."

The frigid air hit Eliza when she stepped outside. She took a moment and stood at the edge of the porch as the sun brought warmth to the exposed skin of her face. Her eyes closed, and she enjoyed the few minutes of rare winter sunshine. The sound of a horse approaching brought her out of the temporary solace, and she opened her eyes to see Ramsey and his horse walking toward her.

"You looked so peaceful, I almost didn't want to bother you," he said.

"Please, bother me. I'm getting a late start, and by the sound of things, the men are already at work."

Ramsey nodded. "Ethan and Ben are stringing the barn layout. I have to get to town so Gabriel can come back to the ranch."

Eliza stepped off the porch, automatically reaching for the horse. "Will you stay in town tonight?"

"Ethan spoke with Jake and Tom this morning. I'm hoping the judge sent a wire confirming that I can take the prisoners to Bozeman, but if there's a delay, Jake and Tom will remain in town. They're gathering a few items together now. If not, they'll help bring back the rest of the supplies for the barn." Ramsey shifted from one foot to another and then said, "I spoke with Elizabeth this morning."

Eliza nodded. "She told me but only that you'd spoken."

"You can ask," he told her.

"I know, but it's not time for that. What's important is that your questions were answered." Eliza paused. "Were they answered?"

"Yes, though not as I expected," Ramsey said. "The truth turned out to be more shocking than I had expected."

"Will the two of you be all right?"

"We will; we're family. You've taught me about that since I've been here." Ramsey mounted his horse and looked down to Eliza. "Enjoy the sunshine, beautiful lady, and be safe," he said and rode away from the ranch.

Eliza kept her eyes on him as she walked toward the stables. Jake and Tom emerged with their horses when she approached.

"He's already left," she told them both.

"Thought he might," Jake said, "We're waiting for Colton; he's bringing around the wagon to haul back supplies for the barn."

Eliza nodded absently and looked past them to the site of the old barn. Nothing remained except patches of charred earth. "Good luck in town. I'll see you both later," she said and walked toward Ethan.

On approach, Eliza noticed one distinct difference between the old structure and the layout of the new—the size. They'd all talked about expanding both the barn and the stable, and practicality told her that they'd have no better time than during the rebuild. Eliza found herself curious about Ethan's plans and curious even more that he hadn't told her about them.

Her boots crunched on the hard-packed snow, alerting Ethan and Ben to her arrival. They both turned to look, Ethan standing up from the small marking post he'd placed in the ground.

Eliza stopped next to her brother. "When did stringing out a barn become a two-man job?"

"This is the easy part," Ethan said. "Besides, I've had an idea and wanted to see if it would work with the lumber we have in the shed and with what's coming."

Eliza eyes scanned the carefully sectioned off square outlining what would be a structure half again as large as the original. "You just thought of this?"

Ethan said, "I promise, I would have spoken with you and Gabe before doing anything. We had to make the measurements, and we have enough lumber to put up the main structure, but the interior stalls will have to wait until I place another order."

"Why do we need more stalls in the new barn?"

"Ben, would you mind giving us a few minutes?"

Ben looked at both her and Ethan, and Eliza wondered if there was something he knew that she didn't.

"I'll pull Connor and Jackson off duty, and we'll bring the timbers over," Ben said. He nodded to Eliza and walked off in the direction of the herd.

Eliza faced her brother. "What's going on?"

"Ramsey talked to me about breeding horses here at the ranch."

"I see. When?"

"It was after he spoke with you the first time, I believe. I didn't have a chance to work through the details with him or even think about the cost and the extra work for everyone."

"Did you know he wants to use his own money?"

"His and Brenna's."

"No, only his. He says he wants to leave something substantial behind—a legacy—for his sister and your children."

"What about his own children?"

Eliza shrugged. "He doesn't give a straightforward answer about his future, but I believe he wants to stay."

"He's welcome to stay. He's family. Hell, we'll build him a house on the ranch if he wants."

Surprised, Eliza studied her brother but saw that he meant what he said. He truly cared for Ramsey and it warmed her heart.

"I'm sure he would appreciate that."

"It's not only out of kindness," Ethan said. "Brenna would love to have him stay, and you know I'd do anything for her, but the more I've considered his idea for the horses, the more I think it would good for the ranch. Besides, I prefer to keep the ranch and everything on it in the family."

"And he's family," Eliza said, her voice trailing off. "He told me you'll be going with him to deliver the prisoners."

Ethan nodded. "I think he would have preferred going alone."

"He made a promise," Eliza said quietly. "Do you think it's odd that nothing has happened recently?"

"You're serious?"

Eliza quickly said, "I know, we've had enough, but it suddenly stopped. Like that time you were in Scotland, and I went to Kentucky. If Hunter is so intent on destroying us, why stop at all?"

"Interestingly enough, Brenna asked me that same question a few nights ago. I didn't have an answer for her, either."

"Is it possible that what we think he wants isn't really what he wants? He has to know we'll keep fighting, and by now, he must realize that he'll never get a hold of Brenna and Ramsey's money."

"I wish I knew, but I'm willing to agree with you that something else might be happening." Ethan turned his head at the sound of timbers being loaded onto the wagon. "I need to get over and help them load."

"Wait, are you serious about the horses?"

Ethan nodded. "I am. We'll build the larger barn either way, but I want to sit down with Ramsey to go over the details. I've been looking over the books, and we can manage to invest. This may be Ramsey's idea, but it's still our ranch, and we need to shoulder part of the costs. You should be there. He came to you first with this idea, and he must have had a reason for that."

"How does Brenna feel about it?"

Ethan smiled. "She didn't want to touch the extra money, either, but she loved the idea. She wants to bring her horse over from Scotland. I thought we might bring one over for Jacob as well."

"Did you ever want a different life from ranching?"

Ethan shook his head. "No, I always knew I wanted to raise cattle. Did you?"

"I never wanted to be anywhere else than Hawk's Peak, but I'll admit I'm more passionate about horses than cattle."

"We all know that," Ethan said. "Added to the advantage of expanding the family business, you'd have something more to do during the winter."

Eliza smiled. "I'll still be taking my shifts with the herd. They are, after all, the reason father built the ranch."

Turning wheels and horse hooves drew their attention. They moved aside to let the wagon pull up alongside the taut string and short posts.

Ben jumped down from the wagon seat. "A few of the beams we had stored rot, but by my calculations, we should still have enough."

Ethan examined the timber on top. "Let's get another load moved over, but we don't know what the weather is going to do, so we'll leave the rest under the lean-to until it's needed." He turned back to Eliza. "Will you be out here long?"

Eliza nodded. "I'd like to spend more time with the colt, and then I want to pull Amanda away later for a ride if she's willing."

"We don't even know where she's from," Ethan said. "A ride in this cold might be too much for her."

"We'll see." With a wave to the men, Eliza headed to the stable.

Despite the cold and the early hour, people walked the snowy streets of Briarwood. Ramsey rode past the general store but saw that it was closed. His horse walked slowly, and Ramsey guided him to the jail. He dismounted and walked inside the small building. Gabriel sat behind the desk, eating what looked like a hearty breakfast.

"You're here earlier than I expected," Gabriel said, taking another bite of a thick biscuit.

"Thought you'd like to get back to the ranch," Ramsey said and indicated the plate. "Did Tilly bring that over?"

Gabriel grinned. "She's fond of me. She also brought meals over for the others."

"That was thoughtful of her." Ramsey looked around. "They give you any trouble?"

"Hugh, still no last name, got vocal last night, but he shut up when I threatened not to feed him."

Ramsey nodded. "I probably wouldn't have. If you don't mind, while you're finishing up, I'd like to check on Loren."

Gabriel said, "Otis stopped by a short time ago after visiting the clinic. He said there was no change yet."

"All the same, I'd like to talk to the doc. I may need his testimony about Loren when these men go before the judge."

"Speaking of judge, Horace dropped this telegraph off last

night." Gabriel stood and Ramsey stepped forward to take the small envelope from Gabriel. A clerk for the judge had responded with two simple lines.

Judge Baldwin's docket is full for three weeks.
Suggest holding or transporting prisoners to Deer Lodge to await trial.

"Did you read this?" Ramsey handed the paper back to Gabriel before he could respond. "As much as I'd like to see Hugh at Deer Lodge, I'm not sending the Peelers there without a trial first. Damn it."

Gabriel said, "What did you hope would happen."

"I would have preferred taking them to Bozeman immediately for trial."

Gabriel inched his empty plate away and leaned back. "This morning, Otis asked me if we'd had any more incidents at the ranch, which had me asking why we hadn't."

Ramsey exhaled deeply. "Because Hunter has something bigger planned. Though at this point, I don't know why he'd bother with any of us. He's not getting the land, he's not getting the money, and the family isn't getting any smaller."

"Isabelle has asked me if it's safe enough for her to teach again at the school. I didn't want to tell her 'no,' but I wasn't going to lie and tell her everything is safe. I just don't know." Gabriel stood and walked around the desk, then sat on the edge. "We move on, we get through each day, we enjoy our family, and we even find reasons to laugh, but none of us have forgotten what brought you here."

"I haven't forgotten either," Ramsey said quietly. "I'll be back soon."

Ramsey left his horse at the jail and walked the short distance to the clinic. He knocked but entered in the front door without waiting for a response. The main room was empty, which either meant Loren had died or was well enough to be moved. Brody walked through the door that led to the recovery room in the back.

"He'll live, though it will be a while yet before he can move around," Brody said. "He tried to yell at me this morning because I wouldn't let him open the store."

Ramsey was relieved that he didn't have to say good-bye to a friend, and now he wouldn't have to charge the Peelers with murder.

"That's excellent news, and I don't suspect he will make a model patient," Ramsey said. "If he wakes later, will you send for me? I have a few questions."

"Of course, though it's doubtful he remembers what happened."

"I still have to ask," Ramsey said. "And Doc, I appreciate what you did for him."

Ramsey returned to the jail to find that Jake and Tom had arrived. A familiar wagon waited around the corner by the livery. Gabriel was pulling on his coat when Ramsey walked inside. He hung his hat and coat on the iron hook Gabriel's coat had vacated.

Gabriel stepped back to allow room for Ramsey. "How's Loren?"

"Doc said he'll make it, but it will be a while before he's back at the store."

"Loren won't be cooperative," Jake said.

"The doc has already discovered that." Ramsey slipped out of his coat. "I saw the wagon at the livery."

Tom said, "Colton went there directly."

"I'm headed over there now," Gabriel said. "Will you be coming back to the ranch tonight?"

Ramsey looked over at Jake and Tom. Jake said, "We'll be fine for as long as we're needed. We brought supplies, and there's a small room off the back for sleeping. Besides, I hear Tilly has a soft spot for lawmen."

Ramsey smiled and said to Gabriel, "I'll head back later. I have to speak with Tobias, and then I want to check on things at the store."

"The reverend offered to watch the store for a few days since Otis is busy at the livery," Gabriel said. "I'll see you back at the ranch.

Ramsey turned back to the other men. "Unfortunately, the judge isn't available for a few weeks."

"It won't be a problem," Jake said. "I was a lawman for a lot of years, so was Tom here. We'll get along well enough, and a person can't beat Tilly's cooking."

"I haven't had the pleasure yet."

"Just one thing," Tom said. "When and if things come to a head with Hunter, we want in."

Ramsey hesitated because he couldn't make any guarantees about when and where resolve would come. "If we have warning, I'll make sure someone sends for you."

Jake said, "Good. Now don't worry about coming back to town every day. It's a long ride with the weather, and they'll need every hand available for building that new barn."

Ramsey nodded and walked into the back room that housed the cells. Tobias and his sons shared one cell, and Hugh shared the other. They had to bring in extra cots to accommodate three men in one cell, but it was preferable to putting any of them in with a man who'd likely find a way to kill a cellmate.

"You and I need to have a word, Tobias," Ramsey said.

Hugh moved quickly to the bars separating him from freedom. "I know more 'n that coward," Hugh said and spat through the bars.

"That's doubtful, Hugh."

Ramsey's sympathy extended to the Peelers. He'd bet Hugh hadn't shut his mouth since they were put in here together. "Now, quiet down or I'll find a nice tree to leave you tied to."

Hugh quieted, but Ramsey didn't believe it would last long. He turned back to the other cell. "I need to know how you came to ride with these boys, and don't tell me it was because your ranch went under. From what I've heard of your reputation, you aren't the type to break the law."

"You have to tell him, Pa."

Tobias kept his eyes forward, but Ramsey knew Tobias heard his son. Ramsey was patient, allowing the other man the time he needed to make the right decision. "We managed to hold onto a cabin on the north section of our property. Hugh and his men worked for the new owners, but they were fired a while back. They came one day while me and the boys were out hunting, and my wife Charlotte was alone. When we returned, they had a gun to my wife and said we were to go with them or they'd kill her. They left one of their men at the cabin with her."

Ramsey looked back at Tobias's sons and then over at Hugh, whose anger was evident. "I can understand your desperation, Tobias, but did you believe they'd let her go, or you for that matter, when you were done? Hugh didn't hesitate to kill his own partner."

Tobias looked directly at Ramsey and said, "I swear to you it's all the truth. I don't know what's happened to my Charlotte—I feared for her life."

"You should have told me when I brought you in," Ramsey said.

"I couldn't, Marshal. Their other man had orders to go back and kill Charlotte if anything happened to them."

Ramsey looked sideways at Hugh, then back to Tobias. "There wasn't another man."

Tobias frantically shook his head. "Hugh said—"

Hugh reached through the bars, but Tobias was well out of reach. "I knew we shoulda' killed ya jest for being stupid."

"Your first mistake was listening to Hugh. Where's the cabin?"

"I don't reckon they're still there, Marshal," Tobias said.

"At this point, I don't care what you reckon, Tobias, but I'll be going out there anyway. Where's the cabin?"

One of Tobias's sons answered. "The cabin sits on the northwest ten acres of our old ranch."

"That filthy whore of yours is dead, Peeler! Dead!" Hugh rattled the bars of his cell, but the exertion caused him to reach for his bandaged wound.

Ramsey yelled out for Jake, who a moment later walked through the door.

"Everything all right in here?"

Ramsey pointed to Hugh. "He says one thing you don't like, tie him to the tall pine outside."

"Yes, sir."

Ramsey left the jail, fuming and worried, and barely acknowledged Tom on the way out.

Gabriel was mounted and ready to ride out with Connor. Ramsey called out for him to wait, mounted his horse, and rode up alongside Gabriel.

"Do you know where to find the old Peeler ranch?"

Gabriel nodded. "What's wrong?"

"Tobias claims a man was holding his wife and that's why he went along with the robbery. I need to check it out, but if he's right, I'd rather have someone else there, and I prefer Tom and Jake remain here. Do you mind?"

Gabriel said to Connor, "Head back to the ranch. Tell Ethan we went to the old Peeler spread and to expect us back this afternoon."

"He'll want to ride out and help," Connor said.

"Only if we aren't back by sundown."

Connor nodded and flicked the reins, urging the team into motion.

Gabriel turned his horse around to face Ramsey. "The ranch isn't too far south of town."

"Let's go!"

With a combination of snow and ice on the road south, they had to ride slowly, but they eventually reached the section of land Tobias's son had told Ramsey about. The small cabin had been built in the center of the acreage, most likely as a line shack for ranch hands during the summer months. Smoke seeped from the small chimney, but they saw no movement outside of the cabin and were too far away to see through the small windows on either side of the door.

"I don't see a horse," Gabriel said. "If someone was holding Mrs. Peeler, they killed her or left her here when Hugh and the others didn't return."

Ramsey had no reply because if they went in there and found Tobias's wife dead, he'd have to tell Tobias that he played a part in his own wife's death.

Cautiously, they gave the cabin a wide berth, but without trees to obstruct their advance, they had to hope there was only one man inside and that he wasn't a good shot. When they were approximately fifty yards from the cabin, the front door inched open and the barrel of a rifle appeared. They quickly dismounted and pulled their guns, but a shout from the cabin stilled their movements.

"You drop those guns and do it now!"

A woman with a gun was no laughing matter, which is why Ramsey and Gabriel both holstered their guns slowly but wouldn't drop them.

"Mrs. Peeler? I'm U.S. Marshal Ramsey Hunter, and my companion is Gabriel Gallagher. We're here to help."

"A Gallagher you say? I met Eliza Gallagher—she your kin?"

Gabriel called back, "She's my sister, Mrs. Peeler."

"Let me see that badge, Marshal."

Ramsey pulled the flap of his coat back until he was certain the woman could see it from the distance between them. He breathed easier when he saw the gun barrel disappear and the door slowly open.

Gabriel and Ramsey walked their horses to the front of the cabin, where Mrs. Peeler looked them over until she was satisfied.

She looked at Gabriel and said, "You have the look of your family; otherwise, you wouldn't be standing here, young man."

"Yes, ma'am," Gabriel replied.

Ramsey looked past her into the cabin. "What happened to the man who was holding you?"

"That fool left when his idiot friends didn't return. Couldn't even tie a proper rope, and I finally got loose this morning." Mrs. Peeler set the rifle against the wall next to the door. "Is my husband all right? My sons?"

"Yes, ma'am, they're alive, but they're in jail." Ramsey rubbed a hand across his face in frustration. "They got themselves in a lot of trouble. Now I understand they wanted to keep you safe, but Loren Baker, the storekeeper, he was badly injured during the robbery."

Mrs. Peeler motioned them inside and moved to the center of the small room before she paced across the board floor. "Will they hang?"

"No, ma'am, they won't hang, but it will be up to a judge how long they go to prison." Ramsey offered no words of encouragement, and he didn't believe she expected them.

"Can I see them?"

Ramsey nodded. "You can, and it's best if you didn't stay out here alone."

"I have a sister who lives in town. She might put me up for a spell. How long before my husband and boys see the judge?"

"It will be a few weeks, so they'll have to stay in the jail until the judge says otherwise."

Ramsey waited for the expected ranting, but she appeared to be a woman without hysterics.

"I'll put together a bag. May I bring them a change of clothes? They don't have much, but a person stinks if they stay in the same clothes too long."

Mrs. Peeler's serious expression is the only reason Ramsey forced down the smile. "Yes, you may bring them a few items," he replied.

She nodded to them both and disappeared behind one of two doors. After a few minutes she came out and then went into the other room. Not fifteen minutes later, she emerged from the room with two small bags.

"Those fool thieves took our last horse, but I will saddle the donkey in the pen around back," she said and handed each of them a bag as she brushed past them.

Ramsey glanced at Gabriel and saw he was also amused. They carried the bags outside and tied them to the back of their horses. Ramsey waited with the horses while Gabriel walked around back to help Mrs. Peeler with the donkey.

"Is there something wrong with my work?" Amanda gripped the reins.

"Not in the least." Eliza guided her horse across a shallow section of the stream. "You don't enjoy riding?"

"I do, but I didn't expect . . . it's nice to get out. Thank you."

Eliza's eyes studied her riding companion while continually scanning the area for anything that shouldn't be there. Amanda appeared to tolerate the cold and snow like someone who'd spent recent years in the North. Eliza had put her on their most docile mare, and Amanda handled the horse with unexpected skill. Eliza knew the family would like to know more about her, but they were kind enough not to pester her with questions. Eliza understood the desire to keep one's life private, but that wouldn't stop her from learning something new about Amanda. One question had plagued her since the moment they brought Amanda back to the ranch.

"Why did you take the job? I know I can be convincing, and I made a good argument that an old lady needed help. Working in saloons was no way for a respectable woman to make a living, but why did you say yes?"

Amanda faced her, but Eliza couldn't tell whether or not the question bothered her. "You gave a compelling argument as to why I should accept."

What Eliza remembered most about the conversation was the overwhelming feeling that Amanda needed help, which is why she had insisted.

"Yes, but you made the choice to come—why?"

Amanda returned her gaze to the snowy landscape, but after a minute she quietly said, "It sounded like a way to get lost."

"Lost from what?"

Amanda faced her again, this time her eyes pleading with Eliza. "If it won't affect my employment, I prefer not to say right now."

"Are you running from the law?"

Amanda shook her head. "Nothing like that."

"Then I'll let it alone," Eliza said, "but if you ever want to talk about it . . ."

"Thank you." Amanda smiled at her, but the warmth didn't reach her eyes.

Amanda may not be ready to share her story, but there was a discussion Eliza had to have with her. The guilt she carried for not telling her about the feud had been magnified by Brenna's mention of their current situation this morning.

"Amanda, when I invited you to the ranch, I may have put you in danger."

Amanda looked at her curiously. "I knew about all that when I agreed to come."

Eliza pulled back on the reins to stop her horse. "What do you mean you knew?"

"About the shootings."

Eliza shook her head, unbelieving. "How? You arrived in town after those things happened, and only a few people knew about it."

Worry marred Amanda's features. "I heard two men speaking at the saloon, so I thought it was common knowledge."

"No, it wasn't," Eliza replied, her grip tense on the reins. "I need to know who you heard."

"I'm sorry, Eliza, I don't know his name," Amanda said, concern in her voice. "He was frightening, and I didn't want to stay too close."

"What did he look like?" Eliza reached out and touched Amanda's arm while trying to keep her horse calm beneath her. "It's important."

Amanda let out a deep breath. "He stood taller than a lot of the other men when he was at the bar. His eyes were pale blue and he looked like an Indian, but not—what did I say?"

Eliza released her grip on Amanda's arm and turned her horse around. "We have to get back, now!" They'd ridden far enough from the building so that all Eliza could see was a faint outline of the house and the mass of cattle in the field. Eliza's horse threw back her head and danced when the loud howl ripped through the air.

Amanda was able to keep her mare under control, but Eliza could hear the fear in her voice. "That sounded close."

Eliza nodded, but her eyes remained focused as they scanned everything in all directions. She finally spotted the wolves roaming between them and the herd. The pack seemed more intent on reaching the herd, but they were close to them. Eliza's only solace was that the animals hadn't caught their scent. Eliza was always armed, so their safety wasn't her biggest concern. If the pack got any closer to the cattle, the herd would spook and run.

"Amanda, how good are you on a horse?"

Amanda nodded and breathlessly said, "I can ride!"

Eliza pulled her pistol from the holster and handed it to Amanda. "Can you shoot?"

"I've never . . . no."

"The gun is ready; you just aim and shoot. If the wolves are close enough for you to see their eyes, they're close enough for the shots to scare them. You have five bullets, but I hope you don't have to use them. Make a wide berth and get back to the house, and tell whoever you see first what's happening."

"Won't they see the wolves?"

Eliza nodded, but that's when a shot rang out from the direction of the ranch. Whoever was on watch had spotted the pack, but now the wolves were headed in their direction.

"Amanda, I want you to go. Go now. There's enough of them to take down one of the horses."

But Amanda hesitated. "What are you going to do?"

"Go!" Eliza waited only a second after Amanda rode off and then rode directly toward the pack. She fired first in the air, but only one of the wolves broke away. She fired again, this time directly at the wolves and clipped one in the leg. The wolves finally veered off in the other direction, but her mare grew frantic and reared back. With Eliza's hands holding the rifle, she lost her grip on the reins and fell to the ground. The mare reared in terror and ran off, leaving Eliza alone. The injured wolf was joined by another and began to approach her. Before she had a chance to raise the rifle, a gunshot echoed through the air and hit the injured wolf. The remaining wolf ran into the trees to rejoin the pack.

Eliza shifted, but a pain shot up through her leg and lower back, and her body sank back into the snow.

19

"You get some fool notions, Tobias Peeler!"

Mrs. Peeler pulled the small bag from Gabriel's hand and dropped it in front of the cell.

"You can't know how we worried," Tobias said. He smiled at his wife and reached through the bars to clasp her hand. "How'd you get away, Charlotte?"

"That simpleton's friend got scared and left me tied up. He wasn't much good at it, though."

Hugh tried to reach for Mrs. Peeler, but Gabriel pulled her back and stepped between her and the other cell. "Sit down, Hugh."

"Brought you some clothes so you don't smell up the place. You best find a way to get that judge to let you go. I won't be left alone, you hear?" Charlotte said.

"I hear you." Tobias raised his eyes to look at Gabriel. "Might I have a word with the marshal?"

Gabriel nodded. "Mrs. Peeler, I'll have to ask you to come back out with me."

Mrs. Peeler stood a foot shorter than Gabriel, but small in stature didn't mean lacking in courage. "You'll take care of them?"

"We'll do what we can," Gabriel said, avoiding a guarantee.

Gabriel said to Tobias, "I'll see what can be done about some water for washing up."

"That's right kind of you, Mr. Gallagher."

"I got rights too!" Hugh shouted from his cell.

Gabriel walked over and motioned for Hugh to step forward. Gabriel reached between the bars and twisted the front of Hugh's shirt. Softly, so no one else could hear his words, he said, "Loren had rights, you miserable filth. You have a roof, a bed, and you'll get your three meals. Now shut your mouth." Gabriel released him and stepped back from the cell. He picked up the small bag Mrs. Peeler had dropped on the ground and guided her out of the room, but Hugh called out from his cell.

"I know something."

Gabriel ignored him.

"I know me Tyre Burton."

Gabriel stopped and looked up. Ramsey had heard him. Gabriel nudged Mrs. Peeler into the other room and turned back toward the cell. Ramsey passed him and walked directly up to Hugh.

"How do you know Tyre Burton?" Ramsey managed to keep his voice neutral, but his body tensed.

Hugh shook his head and sneered. "You tell that judge to let me go, and I'll tell you."

This time Ramsey lifted the keys and unlocked the cell door. Hugh's surprise was evident, but Ramsey advanced and pushed him up against the wall.

"You don't understand how this is going to work," Ramsey said in a calm voice which contradicted his rising emotions. "You will tell me what you know, and I won't find a tree to string you up."

Frightened now, but too stupid to know it, Hugh said, "You're the marshal. You can't kill me."

Ramsey reached up, unpinned his badge, and slipped it into his pocket. Hugh's eyes widened, but he started talking.

"Me and Hank, he's the one who threatened that Peeler lady, well me and Hank was down in Bozeman and heard Tyre talking about shootin' a woman. He was braggin' something good 'bout he nearly killed her."

Gabriel and Ramsey watched as Hugh pushed himself against the wall, but he ran out of space. He walked to the cell door. "How do you know it was Tyre?"

"Blue-eyed Comanche," Hugh said, breathing rapidly. "Everyone in these parts knows that crazy half-breed."

Ramsey backed out of the cell and locked the door. Without another word to the men in the cells, he walked from the room, followed by Gabriel who closed the door behind him. Ramsey walked around the desk and pulled two deputy badges from the drawer and handed them to Jake and Tom.

"The jail is yours."

Jake said, "Don't worry about anything here. Tom and I know what we're doing."

Ramsey nodded and turned his attention to Mrs. Peeler. "We need to get you out of here. Where does your sister live, ma'am?"

"My sister is married to Hal Stimpley."

Tom stepped forward. "I know where Hal lives. If you don't mind, I'll escort you over."

She squinted at Tom, but after a minute she gave a curt nod. "I reckon that's all right."

Gabriel handed Mrs. Peeler's bag to Tom and tipped his hat to the lady when they left the jail. He pivoted on his heel and shook his head.

"Tonight I'll be thanking my dear sweet Isabelle for taking a chance on me. I wouldn't be cut out for a local woman—tough stock!" Gabriel said.

Ramsey glanced at Gabriel, smirked, and then went back to studying the posters. "Careful, your sister's as local as they come."

"No, Eliza's definitely ten steps above, but that's what comes from having a mother from the East."

Surprised, Ramsey said, "I'd always thought your mother was from Texas."

Gabriel shrugged. "Most people did, but before she met our father, she lived with her family in Boston. She wanted to be a schoolteacher, so she came out west with a group of missionaries for safe travel and met our father."

"And that's the end of the story?"

"Not even close," Gabriel said with a chuckle, "but Eliza tells the stories better than I do. You should ask her."

"I will," Ramsey said absently. His focus was back on the posters. He pulled one from the stack and held it up to show Jake. "Take a look at this. Our friend Hugh is wanted for robbing a stage in Wyoming. There's a note here to contact the sheriff in Cheyenne." He handed the paper to Jake. "I'll send the wire before we head out." Ramsey was pulling on his coat and hat when Tom returned from delivering Mrs. Peeler to her sister.

"Did she settle in all right?"

"Seemed to," Tom said, "but I don't envy the man who crosses that woman."

The men laughed and then said their good-byes before Ramsey and Gabriel exited the jail. When they stepped outside and the door was closed behind them, Gabriel turned to his brother. "You avoided talking about Tyre for a reason—care to tell me why?"

"I know you trust the men at your ranch, but we don't know what this is yet. We won't know until I find Burton."

"You mean until *we* find Burton."

"Trust me, I won't cut you or Ethan out of this. Even if I wanted to, Eliza would raise hell."

Gabriel smiled. "Yes, and she does it well. Let's get moving before Ethan or someone else comes looking for us."

Ramsey nodded. "I have to send a telegram first."

20

Ramsey and Gabriel were only a few yards from the front porch of the main house when they heard the first gunshot. One of the men shouted, "Wolves!" Another gunshot rang out and then another. He and Gabriel raced past the men, Gabriel shouting for them to remain with the herd. Ramsey saw the rider running toward the wolves and then watched as the rider fell backward and the rider's hat flew off, revealing long dark hair.

He urged his horse to run faster, praying he kept his footing. When he was close enough, he fired off a shot, hitting one of the wolves as it descended on Eliza. The other wolf ran off, but Eliza wasn't standing. Ramsey dismounted before his horse fully stopped, and Gabriel followed. Panicked, he ran his hands over her quickly. "Are you all right?" Then he got a good look at her. "What the hell are you smiling about? Do you have any idea what a hungry wolf can do to a person?"

Eliza sobered and nodded. "I'm really happy to see you both. I seem to have lost my horse."

"Damn it, Eliza," Gabriel knelt down and helped pull her to her feet. "What were you thinking, riding into the pack that way?"

"Did you pass Amanda?"

Ramsey said, "We didn't notice."

Eliza bent over and brushed away some of the snow from her clothes. "It was the only thing I could think to do." She shrugged and attempted to take a step but had to lean against her brother. "If you wouldn't mind bringing one of those horses closer, I'll mount from here."

Gabriel put his hands on Eliza's shoulders and stepped in front of her. Ramsey saw clearly the concern he had for his sister and sympathized. Had he been around when Brenna was taken, he doubted his fear and anger could have been contained.

"You have to stop doing this to us."

Eliza smiled. "I might give in and let you and Ethan boss me around for a while. It will give me a chance to heal."

"I'm not amused, but I will hold you to that." Gabriel said to Ramsey, "Will you take her back and pass her off to Elizabeth? She makes a salve that should help with the soreness." Gabriel turned back to his sister. "You're sure you're okay?"

"It's only a few bruises, I promise."

Gabriel's skeptical look said he didn't quite believe her, but he let it go. "I'm going to take care of this wolf. We don't want it to attract other animals."

Ramsey walked his horse over to where Eliza stood and mounted. Gabriel half-lifted her and Ramsey helped the rest of the way, settling Eliza sideways in front of him.

Eliza settled herself and then said, "And to think Isabelle and Andrew almost joined us."

Gabriel turned back. "What do you mean?"

"Don't worry, Gabriel, they're safe at home," Eliza said, but Ramsey saw that Gabriel wasn't letting the subject drop. Eliza continued. "Andrew wanted to go for a ride, but I wanted to speak with Amanda alone. I did have to promise him a ride tomorrow if the weather holds."

"I'll take them out tomorrow. You rest." Gabriel patted the back of Ramsey's horse as they rode away.

"I'd complain about this position," Eliza said quietly to Ramsey, "but I don't think my body could handle direct contact with the saddle right now."

"You are hurt more than you claimed!" He nearly pulled the horse to a stop so he could examine her more closely, but she told him to keep riding. Ramsey resumed their ride. Concern was soon replaced with the comfort of knowing she was safe, and right now, in his arms.

"Nothing that won't heal after a hot bath and some of Elizabeth's salve."

"I'm of a mind to agree with your brothers that you should all be locked up in the house during the winter." Ramsey slowed the horse to a slower gait when he noticed Eliza wince.

"That will never happen, no matter how much my brothers strong-arm me. Besides, I know the others have felt cooped up lately." Eliza shifted again, but finally settled. Ramsey wished she wasn't in pain, but he welcomed the feel of her close to him. "Isabelle worries that if she lets Andrew out of the house that he'll end up shot, my brothers worry that Brenna or Isabelle will be shot or taken, and Elizabeth worries about everyone."

"Everyone has a right to worry. They nearly lost you and could have lost Andrew." Ramsey moved the reins to one hand and wrapped the other around Eliza's waist to shift her position.

She looked up at him and grinned. "Am I too heavy already?"

"Hardly," he said, laughing. "Lean in a little, though." She did so without question. Feeling her even closer against his body was certainly pleasant, but he preferred to have both hands completely free if something happened, and she'd been leaning primarily on his right arm. The front door of the main house came into view, and Ben ran up to help Eliza down.

Ramsey glanced around quickly. "Where's Ethan?"

"He and Connor are riding the northern pastures looking for any strays. We noticed a few head missing at feeding time.

They'd have heard all the shooting, but they'll have to ride back in some deeper snow."

Ramsey nodded and dismounted. Once on the ground, he slipped his arms around Eliza. Noticing that she was unsteady on her feet, he took the steps to the porch slowly and gently.

Eliza glanced at Ben. "Where is everyone else?"

"I told them not to come out until one of us told them it was safe. After Amanda came in waving a gun and yelling for help and then got done retelling the story, no one argued with me." Ben grinned. "But it looked like they wanted to."

"Thank you, Ben." Eliza attempted to stand straight and was able to if Ramsey held her. "Gabriel's out taking care of the wolf. Would you please send one of the men out to help?"

Ben said, "Kevin rode out after we were certain the cattle wouldn't spook from all that gunfire."

Ramsey ended the conversation by guiding Eliza into the house. Once they were through the door, four women came out of the kitchen and down the hall.

Eliza held up a hand to stop them. "I'm fine! Please let's not make a fuss."

"I can't believe you did that! If anything had happened to you, it would have been my fault."

Eliza wouldn't allow Amanda or anyone else to make her feel guilty for what she did.

"But nothing did happen, and what do you mean your fault? You only did what I told you to do." Eliza leaned back against Ramsey and said, "I'm okay to walk now if you want to go back out and help Gabriel."

Ramsey did want to help outside where he could, and he had to find Ethan. "You're sure?"

Eliza nodded but then touched his arm. "Wait. I need to speak with you and my brothers. It will keep until tonight, but I need to speak with you."

Ramsey, mindful of the other women looking on, simply nodded. He saw in her expression that whatever she wanted to tell them was important. With care, Ramsey released her, and when he was confident that she would be all right, he quickly left.

The afternoon quickly shifted to evening. The shortened days meant less time to do the work that was needed, and with Jake and Tom remaining in town for the foreseeable future, they were all going to have to work harder to ensure the barn went up before another snowfall.

The ride back from town with Gabriel had been one with productive conversation, but he'd forgotten everything the moment the first gunshots fired. The last thing he wanted to do while she was in pain was tell Eliza what Hugh said about Tyre. Eliza's requested meeting for that evening would be soon enough.

He and Gabriel had formulated what they believed to be a viable plan, but they would need everyone's cooperation. Gabriel had also expressed concern for Andrew, worrying that whatever they did would affect the boy. Then Gabriel smiled when he told Ramsey about the gift he and Isabelle were giving Andrew for his birthday. Gabriel wanted to be certain their plan wouldn't interfere with the small birthday celebration they planned for Andrew, but Ramsey couldn't make any promises.

Ben must have seen to his horse because it was no longer out front. He found Ben near the barn site and walked over to meet him.

"How is she?"

"She should be fine in a few days; she just took a fall," Ramsey said casually, as though it happened often. Ramsey wished that were true, but this injury following so soon after the shooting concerned him because he doubted they could keep her down for long. Ramsey prepared to mount up and head out to help

Gabriel. However, the sound of riders drew his attention. Ethan, Gabriel, and Connor approached and then dismounted a short distance away. Gabriel's coat was open, revealing a blood-stained shirt left behind from the wolf.

"Did the wolf—"

"Is she hurt?" Ethan interrupted Ramsey and then moved past his own question. "Because if she's not, she will be. What was she thinking riding into a pack of wolves like that?"

Ramsey and the other men exchanged glances and hid their smiles while Ethan's temper simmered. Ramsey said, "From what I understand, she did it to help Amanda get away. She's a little sore and bruised, but that's all. Elizabeth is doctoring her up now."

"That pack had to have been desperate not to have run after the first warning shot," Ethan said.

When Ethan had calmed down, Ramsey told them about Eliza's request to speak with all of them that evening.

"Did she say what it's about?" Ethan removed his hat and ran a gloved hand over the brim.

Ramsey shook his head. "All of the women were there at the time, but it sounds important."

"There's not much daylight left, and I'd like to check on her before dinner." Ethan began walking his stallion toward the stable and the others followed. "Gabe mentioned one of the prisoners talked about Tyre. Do you know if it was true?"

"Not yet, but it's not much to go on," Ramsey said. "Did he tell you what else we talked about?"

Ethan nodded. "I'd like to wait and tell Brenna and the others after we've had a chance to go over the details. No sense in scaring them yet."

21

Eliza waited with Ramsey in the library later that evening. After the days' events, having him beside her on the settee made her grateful for the comfort his closeness gave her. She wanted to tell Ramsey about Tyre Burton, and how close he'd been when Amanda overheard him at the saloon. She wanted to reach out and entwine her fingers with his because she knew how wonderful his strength would feel. Eliza didn't know for certain if Ramsey would leave once they found Hunter, but she did know with certainty what she wanted if he stayed.

Eliza counted on Ramsey, possibly even more than she did her brothers. She could remain the sister, the aunt, the sister-in-law, and be wonderfully content. But with Ramsey, she imagined a life with someone who could understand her devotion to the ranch and family—not a different life, but a more fulfilling one. Eliza had yet to figure out how to tell Ramsey that she wanted him in her life, but she hoped he knew and believed he felt the same.

As they waited in silence, it was Ramsey who reached out and joined his hand with hers. He held on, even when her brothers walked into the room. Gabriel walked to the liquor cabinet and pulled out a bottle of their father's favorite Scotch and asked if anyone else wanted a glass. Eliza remembered when her father had brought home a case of the whiskey from Scotland. He wasn't much of a drinker, but he enjoyed a small glass each night after supper. Her brothers didn't drink much either; four bottles of their father's whiskey still remained in the cabinet. Ramsey and Ethan both nodded to Gabriel's offer, and everyone waited until Gabriel had passed around the drinks and took his seat. Ramsey released Eliza, leaned forward, sampled, and then savored the Scotch.

"That's good stuff." Ramsey leaned back again, as though anxious.

Ramsey turned to her brothers. "Are you sure you don't want Brenna and Isabelle in here?"

Ethan and Gabriel both shook their heads. Ethan said, "They'll worry, and I don't know about Isabelle and Andrew, but when Brenna's upset, Jacob feels it. I'd rather we wait until we know what's going on."

Eliza tried to scoot forward on the settee, but her right hip still smarted from the fall off her horse. Instead she leaned all the way back and used Ramsey's body for support.

"Amanda told me something on the ride today—about Tyre Burton."

All three men sat forward in their chairs. Gabriel lowered his head as though in pain, Ethan looked surprised, and Ramsey's eyes focused intently on her. Uncertain about their reactions, Eliza continued on quickly. "I planned to disclose and warn Amanda about the possible danger she could be in living at the ranch, but she said she'd already heard some of what had happened from a couple of men."

Ethan looked at his sister. "Did Amanda say it was Tyre?"

"She didn't know his name, but he was tall, with long, dark hair like an Indian, and pale blue eyes." Eliza waited. When no one responded, she said, "This was three days before we brought Amanda to the ranch. If Tyre Burton is here, then we can bet that Hunter is here, too, or at least close by."

"Eliza . . ." Ramsey looked to Ethan and Gabriel first, and at their nods, continued. "One of the prisoners we caught from the store robbery mentioned Tyre. He said Tyre bragged about shooting a woman and leaving her for dead."

"And you believe he meant me." Eliza sensed the anger roiling below the surface, but her temper wouldn't solve anything. She breathed deeply. "Did this man know where to find Tyre?"

"I don't believe so, but I sent a wire to try and confirm what he did tell us." Ramsey reached into his pocket, pulled out a folded piece of paper, and handed it to her. "This telegram was waiting for me."

Eliza looked at her brothers. "Do you already know what this says?"

Gabriel said, "We both read it."

The telegram contained three short lines.

> *Nathan Hunter was here.*
> *Confirm departure last week.*
> *Be advised, he rides with gunslingers.*

The telegram had been sent from a Sheriff Plummer in Bozeman.

"You have been looking for him." Eliza knew she shouldn't be surprised, but they'd spoken so little of it. "Why didn't you tell me?"

"I didn't tell your brothers either, at least not everything," Ramsey said. "I've sent out a dozen telegrams, and none have produced anything until now. I wasn't going to send us off to chase unknowns."

Eliza allowed herself a minute to realize her anger wasn't directed at Ramsey but at the situation. "You believe he's back at the Double Bar." It wasn't a question, and she saw the confirmation in Ramsey's eyes. "Then we're exactly in the same place we've been in for years."

"No, we're not." Ramsey set his drink down on the table and shifted so he faced Eliza. He then looked at Ethan. Eliza's eyes followed the looks passing between Ramsey and her brothers.

"Enough! Tell me what you've planned."

Ethan said, "Hunter allows Ramsey to arrest him peacefully, or we end up in a fight that could cost the lives of our men."

Eliza threw her hands up. "That's not a plan."

"No it's not, but you won't like it," Ramsey said.

"I don't like any of this—tell me."

"I want to convince Hunter to sell me the Double Bar."

Utter disbelief was the only emotion Eliza could manage. "Why do you think he'll . . . you want to let him go?" Eliza stood and paced and then returned to her seat, shaking her head all the while. "You can't possibly be considering this!" Frantically, she glanced at her brothers.

Gabriel said, "I had the same reaction when Ramsey told me, but hear him out."

Eliza looked at Ethan. "You agree with this?"

Ethan nodded. "I don't want it, Eliza. I'd rather Hunter rot in a shallow grave, but we have to consider how many lives could be lost if we have to fight him. We've talked about this often enough, but I don't think we really thought about the potential loss. We've lost too many already, and when we almost lost you—I won't risk it."

Eliza sobered and forced back the tears beginning to form. Her friend—innocent lives who will never know justice. The pain was nearly unbearable, but Ethan was right; they couldn't risk losing anyone else. Eliza shifted to face Ramsey. "Assuming Hunter agrees, why do you believe he'll simply leave, and what about Tyre Burton?" Eliza body trembled.

Ramsey carefully reached up to wipe away a single tear she didn't know had fallen. He said, "I'm sorry for not saying this first—justice will be had. Perhaps not for the crimes here, but I'm going to make him an offer." Ramsey obviously didn't worry about what her brothers thought because he reached for her hand.

Ramsey said, "Hunter is wanted in Texas. The sentence for his crimes down there won't be enough to make up for what he's done here, but there's a good chance he won't live through it." Ramsey wiped another tear from her cheek. "As for Burton, I need you to trust me."

"He'll fight you, all of you," Eliza said. "The only way a man like Burton will go down is if you kill him."

Ramsey nodded. "That's a possibility."

"Then why let Hunter go? Tyre Burton is far more dangerous, and drawing him into a fight is a greater risk."

Ethan said, "It's not, and this is one time I need you not to ask and not to question."

Eliza considered her brother carefully. Eliza knew that Ethan, as the head of the family, carried a greater burden of responsibility than any of them—at least, he believed that—but he'd only pulled rank on her once before. They were a family and they worked together, even when they disagreed. For Ethan to ask this of her meant her brothers were removing her from the danger but not themselves. Fear coursed through her as her rampant imagination took over. "Who's going with you?"

"Eliza." Ethan's warning tone told her to leave it alone. Of course she wouldn't.

She stood again and looked carefully at each one of them. "When did this family stop trusting each other? When did you stop trusting me to know what in the hell I'm capable of handling?" Without waiting for an answer, Eliza left the room.

Ramsey stood to follow her, but Gabriel stepped in front of him. "It's time we have that talk."

Ramsey looked at the empty doorway, wanting to go after

Eliza, but Gabriel's expression told him that wasn't going to happen yet. A quick glance at Ethan told him that he'd better sit back down. He remained standing.

"If you want to hit me, do it, but I'm going to talk to her."

Ethan slowly stood and leaned casually against the side of the chair. "As soon as you tell us what's going on."

Gabriel glanced sideways at his brother and elaborated. "When there was something to tell, you agreed to let us know. We've all seen what's been happening between you and Eliza, but you have to be fair to her. We're doing our best to come up with a solution that doesn't get anyone killed, but I gather you're willing to risk catching a bullet in order to end all of this."

"You've known this from the beginning. I've always been honest to you and Eliza about what I'm willing to do."

Ethan said, "There's no disputing that, but I see my sister in love with someone who's willing to give his life in order to help her family, and I worry. I commend you for it, but I worry about what will happen if we have to bring you home, draped over your horse."

Ethan's words created a vivid image of Eliza waiting on the front porch of the house for him to return. That picture was followed with her standing over his grave, her black dress whipping in the cold winter wind, her hands bare, and the ring—everything he could ever hope to have would disappear before he even gave them a chance. Ramsey didn't fear death, but he feared not being with Eliza. A stampede, a fall from his horse, or any number of things could end the life of someone on this wild land. They would have no guarantees.

"You'll always be afraid for her," Ramsey said, "and I can't promise there won't be a day when I can't return to her, but you both know that same fear. Ethan, I don't believe there's a better man on this earth for my sister; I trust you with her life. Now I need you to trust me."

Eliza's eyes were darker than her brothers, but otherwise Ramsey saw no difference in the eyes staring back at him, as though considering his worthiness. Whatever Ethan and Gabriel decided, he needed them to hurry.

"It's different when it's your sister," Ethan said, "But I didn't have to prove myself to you—you weren't given that chance. I won't stand in your way."

Ramsey looked to Gabriel next. He didn't need their permission, but he wanted it from both of them. They would do anything for their sister, and they knew Ramsey understood that. Gabriel said, "Go. Talk to her."

Eliza disliked pouting, and always thought it was something weak women did to gain attention. She disliked those women even more than the pouting. She didn't pout, she got angry, and right now, she needed to work off the mad before going downstairs to apologize to Ramsey and her brothers. She couldn't fault them for trying to keep the family and the men at the ranch safe. The idea of allowing Hunter to go free sickened her, and she prayed they would find another way.

She thought to remain upstairs until Elizabeth and Amanda retired for the evening. When she had passed the kitchen and saw them staring into the hallway, she realized they had heard her outburst. Her anger and pride prevented her from immediately returning to the library to offer an apology she knew they all deserved.

The soft knock at her door brought her pacing to a stop. If it was one of her sisters-in-law, she didn't want them to think her surly. She wasn't certain what Ethan and Gabriel had told their wives to keep them from the discussion in the library tonight, but if it had been her in their position, she would have been livid. The knock came again, this time louder. Reluctantly, and feeling petulant, Eliza walked across the room and opened the door.

Ramsey's eyes roamed from the dark hair hanging over her shoulders, to the wrinkled skirt and stockinged feet.

"Is this a bad time?"

"So long as you're not kind to me because, right now, I don't deserve it." She opened the door enough for him to enter, and he didn't miss the fact that she kept it partially opened. He smiled at the action.

"Do you mind if I sit?" Ramsey indicated the chair he had once sat in while keeping vigil over her.

"Sorry, please sit." Eliza sat on the bed facing him, but it took her a minute to look him in the eye.

Ramsey moved the chair directly in front of her and patiently waited. What he planned to say might be ill-timed and unexpected, but he was going to say it, and he didn't want her angry when he did. "We deserved the lashing you gave us, me especially," Ramsey said. "I approached your brothers with the idea of handing Hunter off to the sheriff in Texas. It's not what I want either; I'd rather see him charged with the crimes he's committed here, but there are no witnesses who personally saw him do any of it. A judge is going to ask for any witness to step forward, and when they don't, Hunter will walk."

Eliza took a deep breath. "Even if a U.S. Marshal testifies? What if I testify about what happened to Mary?"

Ramsey shook his head. "I'm sorry, but Hunter wasn't there, and I can tell a judge everything I know Hunter has done, but when the court asks if I actually saw any of it, I have to tell the truth."

"So the only real justice would be if he was killed." Eliza spoke the words softly, but Ramsey heard an edge in her voice.

"Look at me," Ramsey whispered. He reached out with both hands and covered hers. "Do you want him dead? Is that how you want him to pay for his crimes?"

Eliza stared at him. "You would do that?" Eliza shook her

head. "No, God no, I don't. I mean I do, but—Ramsey, I keep hearing Mary's screams and seeing Gabriel carry Mabel's limp body from the fire. I don't want him breathing in a world when their lives were taken away." Eliza moved one of her hands away and lifted it to his face. "But not this way, not out of vengeance. Forgive me."

Ramsey turned his face into her hand and kissed the palm. He entwined her fingers with his and brought their joined hands to rest against his chest. "There's nothing to forgive."

Eliza closed her eyes and breathed deeply. "I expected you to be the one to kill him. I honestly don't know if that was even part of the reason I went to Kentucky. I didn't want it to be Ethan or Gabriel, and I knew I couldn't get close enough, and then I thought of you, but it can't be you."

Ramsey quickly moved to her side on the bed and pulled her into his arms. She relaxed against him and murmured against his chest. "I have a bad habit of crying around you. I'm not this weeping woman who needs rescuing, and I don't cry."

Ramsey's lips spread into a smile, but she couldn't see it. He kissed the top of her head and pulled her closer. "You're the strongest, toughest woman I've ever known, and it's okay to be soft sometimes."

Eliza pulled back but not enough for his arms to lose their hold around her. She wiped the tears away and took in a few deep breaths. "I don't want be soft and weak."

"Well, you can spend the next forty or fifty years convincing me you're not."

Ramsey hadn't expected it to come out like that, and by the shocked expression Eliza now wore, she hadn't expected the backdoor proposal either. However, he meant every word. She continued to silently stare at him.

"I've told you more than once that I don't know what will happen, and that I couldn't guarantee I'd be around, or that I'd even remain in the territory." Ramsey reached up to smooth a fallen lock of her hair. "I said those things to protect myself. I thought I was protecting you, but it was me. I knew how easily I could love you, and the idea of anyone counting on me that much was terrifying. I won't be an easy man to live with, but I'll never give you a reason to regret it, and I will always love you. All I ask is that you want me in your life and in your heart."

Eliza beamed. "I won't be easy to live with either." She then pulled him back to her, leaned in, and kissed him. Ramsey didn't question the action and instead deepened the kiss. Too little time had passed to suit Eliza, but Ramsey murmured something about footsteps in the hall and slowly pulled away from her. She opened her eyes, and his smile warmed her heart.

Thankfully, it was Brenna standing at the open door, because no matter what her brothers knew, she didn't want one of them walking in on her and Ramsey.

Brenna smiled at them both. "I didn't mean to disturb you."

"It's good that you did," Ramsey said, his own grin unrepentant. He stood when Brenna walked into the room.

"Is everything all right? I didn't hear Ethan and Gabriel come upstairs."

"Oh, everything is fine, but I wondered if I might have a word with you."

"Of course," Eliza said. Ramsey moved to leave the room, but Brenna hurried to ask, "Would you stay too?"

Uncertain about what Brenna could need with them both, but now concerned, Eliza motioned her to sit on the bed. Ramsey waited for Brenna to sit and then moved the chair a few feet away.

"What is it?"

"Never have I known a man to be more honest with me than Ethan, but at times, he tries to protect me, especially since Jacob has come."

Eliza said, "I think a wife would welcome those traits in a husband."

"Yes, but if there's a chance something might happen to him, he'll soften the truth for me." Brenna looked at Ramsey. "I'm counting on my brother not doing the same. I need to know how much danger my family is in. I was troubled when Ethan said that he and Gabriel needed to speak with the two of you alone, but I assumed at the time they wanted to discuss, well, you."

Eliza covered Brenna's hand with her own. "I'm the one who asked for the meeting, but it was to discuss news about Hunter. Well, actually about Tyre Burton, but we discussed Hunter."

Ramsey leaned forward. "Had I been Ethan or Gabriel, I would have done the same thing. They don't want you to worry before they know what's going to happen."

"Of course I'll worry, but I'd like to be prepared," Brenna said. "But this has become a conversation I need to have with Ethan now. Just tell me how much danger he'll really face."

"I promise you, he's faced worse, and I will make sure he comes home to you."

Brenna smiled at Ramsey. "We missed out on so much, but I'm glad you're here now. I rather enjoy having a brother."

"Wait a few years." Eliza smiled at Brenna. "It gets better."

Brenna rose, but then hesitated. "Amanda seems to have handled the incident with the wolves well. Perhaps too well."

"She and I didn't have the opportunity to speak alone afterward," Eliza said. "Did she say something to cause you concern?"

"With us both in the house most of the days, we've become friends, and I know Isabelle and Elizabeth feel the same way. While you were in the library, Isabelle and I returned to the kitchen after the children went to sleep. Elizabeth had already retired, and we found Amanda sitting alone. I don't know for certain, but it appeared as though she had been crying."

Concerned for a woman she now considered a friend, Eliza chastised herself for not thinking of Amanda after the ordeal. "I'll speak with her in the morning. I sometimes forget—I'll speak to her."

"I like her, and I hope she stays a while. It's comforting having more people in the house," Brenna said and then quietly exited the room.

"You sometimes forget not everyone is used to this life." Ramsey finished her earlier statement.

"I take for granted that I had a father who allowed me great liberties to learn the ranching business. Even my mother stopped balking when I began to wear pants on the range. Our compromise was that I don't wear them anywhere else." Eliza smiled at the memory of her parents. "My brothers teased at first, but then they began to teach me. I was lucky to have a mother to show me everything mothers do, and brothers who respected me enough to trust me on the range. You should know that most of the household learning didn't stick."

Ramsey laughed. "I've figured that one out, and it's easy enough to hire someone."

Eliza returned the laughter. "We'll have to or starve." Then she sobered. "You promised Brenna that Ethan would come home to her, and I'm going to ask you to promise you'll come back to me."

Ramsey returned to the bed, filling up the space next to Eliza. "I'll never break a promise, but you know I can't promise nothing will ever happen out there, just as I can't ask you to promise you'll stay inside the house where I know you'll be safe. It's not who we are."

"I know," she whispered. "But promise you'll always try."

Ramsey leaned forward and lightly kissed her cheek. "I will make you that promise because I know nothing will ever keep me from wanting to come back to you."

22

Ramsey stood on the front porch with Gabriel, sipping hot coffee, while Ethan spoke to the ranch hands. Ethan wanted to be the one to explain to the men that they wouldn't all be going with them to the Double Bar.

Ethan had sent Connor to Hunter's ranch at dawn to determine if anyone was living there again. Connor reported back that there were horses in the corrals and smoke from the chimneys, but he didn't see anyone. He also told them about a set of tracks he followed from the Double Bar to the edge of their land. The tracks stopped on Hunter's side of the fence and then veered north into the mountains toward Dwight Dicken's old cabin. Dwight had passed away two winters ago, so it would be empty. Hunter knew about it, but the cabin stood on Gallagher land.

Gabriel said, "I told Isabelle last night what we were planning, and then I spoke to Ethan. We want them and the children to stay at the cottage in town. I asked Elizabeth and Amanda to go with them."

"Eliza won't go," Ramsey said.

"Well, if Ethan's logic and demands don't work, I'll guilt her into it." Gabriel set his cup down on the top of the railing. "We'll all have a better chance of getting through this if we aren't worried about them."

"I agree, I just don't think she'll do it." Ramsey watched Ethan step outside of the bunkhouse with Ben and Connor. "You'll send a few of them with the women?"

Gabriel nodded. "Ethan wants Colton and Henry to bunk above Loren's store."

Ramsey said, "With Jake and Tom still in town, the women will be more than covered. People are going to start asking questions if they see so many of you in town at once."

"Then let them ask." Gabriel glanced at Ramsey. "You really think Eliza will fight us on going?"

"You've known her longer than I have."

Gabriel smiled and shook his head. "Doesn't mean we know her better—not anymore. I'm behind you, and so is Ethan."

"I appreciate that."

"Did you speak with her last night?"

Ramsey nodded. "I did, but I'm not going to tell you about it." Ramsey smiled at Gabriel.

Gabriel laughed and said, "I'm glad it's you. She's going to give you hell."

Ramsey shared in the laugher. "I'm looking forward to it." The camaraderie mellowed when they spotted a wagon coming toward the ranch. The ground had cleared enough for the wagon to move along at a steady pace, but they weren't expecting company. As the wagon neared, Ramsey saw it was Otis with a full wagon.

Otis pulled the team to a stop near the porch. "The rest of your supplies came in."

Gabriel stepped off the porch. "Kind of you to bring them all the way out, Otis, especially this early in the morning. We have men going into town with a wagon later."

Otis said, "It wasn't any trouble. My bones have been telling me we got weather coming, and you need that barn raised."

Gabriel looked back up at Ramsey, who stepped off the porch

to join them. Ramsey said, "Truth is Otis, we won't be raising that barn for a few more days. We'll just have to hope the worst of the winter accommodates us."

Otis scratched his chin. "I got plenty of men from town ready to help. We're all grateful what you've done for this town, for Loren, and for putting your men at the jail. Folks feel safer, and they want to help." Otis narrowed his eyes at them. "Is this about that trouble you've been having? One of the men from the Double Bar stopped by last night when his horse threw a shoe. I figured that—"

"A hand from the Double Bar? You're certain?"

"Well, sure. I don't know most of those boys, but I recognized him. Can't recall his name, though."

Gabriel shouted out to Ethan and waved him over. "Otis, we need to get this unloaded, and you better head back to town."

"Now if there's something I can do to help, I'll stay."

Ramsey said, "We're all grateful, but Gabriel's right."

Otis slowly nodded. "If I can get a couple of your men to help me unload this lumber, then I'll be on my way."

Ethan walked up, followed by Ben and Connor. "What's wrong?"

"Nothing," Gabriel said. "We're going to unload this wagon."

The look that passed between Gabriel and Ethan silenced any questions Ethan might ask. Instead Ethan nodded.

Ramsey ran his hand over the flank of one of the horses. "Otis, do you know how Loren is doing?"

"I stopped by last night. He doesn't keep his eyes open for long, but the doc says he's on the mend. He wanted me to tell you that you'll be able to talk with Loren in a few days about the robbery."

"I'll be there," Ramsey said.

Ben said, "If you want to follow us, Otis, we'll help you with that." Connor and Ben walked the distance to the barn, and after a moment of hesitation, Otis released the brake on the wagon and followed.

Ethan turned to Gabriel and Ramsey. "What's going on?"

Gabriel said, "Otis told us that someone from the Double Bar stopped by his place last night when his horse threw a shoe."

"Did he know who?"

Gabriel shook his head. "The women will be done packing soon. We can get them into town and ride over."

Ethan said, "I haven't talked with Eliza yet, have you?"

"No, but Ramsey here doesn't think she'll go."

"Ramsey's right." Eliza pushed open the front door all the way and stepped out onto the porch. "When Andrew rushed into the kitchen to say they were going to the cottage for a visit, I asked Isabelle what was going on. By the way, Gabriel, Andrew is excited. He thinks he gets to go back to school."

"In our defense, you weren't awake yet. We were coming in to talk with you. Well, Ethan was."

"It wouldn't matter who tried, I'm not leaving." Eliza walked down the steps to stand in front of them.

If the situation wasn't serious, Ramsey would have enjoyed it more.

Eliza said, "Unless you're planning to bring Hunter back here, I don't see why I should leave. Neither do the others, but they're married to you, and they're nicer."

Ramsey stepped toward her. "Is there anything we can do to convince you to go with them?"

"Are you sending any of the men into town?"

Ethan nodded. "Colton and Henry."

"Then they don't need me." Eliza shook her head when her brothers would have argued. "Ignore what I said about letting you tell me what to do. I'll stay at the house with whoever else you're leaving behind, but I have as much right to fight for this place as you do, and if I can't go with you, I can at least stay here.

Besides, you won't be gone long."

"Whether Hunter agrees to turn himself in or sell the land, we'll be there long enough to see that he leaves, or I'll be taking him back to the jail."

"And I'll be here when you all return." Eliza ended the discussion by turning back and walking up to the porch. "I'm going to help them finish packing. It's only for a few days, correct?"

Ethan nodded. "Yes."

When Eliza was back inside, Gabriel turned to Ramsey and smirked. "You know, she wasn't this difficult before you came along."

"Then we were living with different sisters," Ethan said. "Connor and Ben are coming with us."

"You didn't want to put any of your men in danger."

"I still don't, but they made a valid argument that only three idiots would go up against gunfighters alone. Besides, Connor is the best tracker around these parts, and Ben is a hell of a shot."

Gabriel said, "Then let's see what we can do about getting the women ready to go. I'd as soon get this over with. Jake and Tom will want to know what's going on."

Ramsey nodded. "I'll send a message into town with Colton."

They spent the next thirty minutes loading the wagon with everything the women deemed essential, which was surprisingly less than what Ramsey expected. Gabriel then informed him that the women didn't pack more because they fully expected to return home within two days. They were simply giving Andrew a chance to play with some of the children in town and to order a few items they wanted from the catalogs. No one reminded them that the reverend may not know how to place special orders or that it was too cold outside for most of the children to play. Eliza told Ramsey and her brothers to let things be. The women were doing their best to play down their worry and make the most of an awful situation.

Ethan and Gabriel kissed their wives and helped them into the first wagon. Ethan handed a bundled Jacob into his wife's arms once she was comfortably settled. Ramsey brought out extra blankets for the cold ride into town and then helped Elizabeth into the second wagon. Gabriel moved to assist Amanda, but Ben had returned and beat him to the task. Eliza stood on the porch and waved to Andrew, who looked excited about the prospect of getting outside. Eliza couldn't blame the young boy. Ever since someone shot at Ramsey and Andrew, Isabelle had worried too much to let him play outside often, and when she did, he wasn't allowed past the corrals.

Ramsey noticed Andrew's animated gestures and turned around. Bundled in her winter coat, her hat, and a heavy scarf, Eliza stood on the porch wearing heavy skirts and her riding boots. Her appearance was a contradiction, but she was beautiful. He knew the skirts were her way of telling them that she wouldn't leave, but she'd remain at the house. Ramsey climbed the steps to stand beside her, his arm brushing up against her shoulder.

"You're all worrying so much," Eliza said quietly so that only Ramsey could hear her. "How is this time any different than previous attempts by my brothers to bring Hunter to justice? You still have no proof, and you're riding over there, hoping he'll cooperate now. I comprehend the plan, but I don't understand the trust you're placing in Nathan Hunter to agree with you."

"I don't believe he will."

Eliza's surprise was apparent. "And that's why you're sending them into town," she said, indicating the wagons that were now rumbling away from the ranch. "You expect him to turn down your offer and fight back."

"To be completely honest, I'm not worried about Hunter," Ramsey said. "I'm worried about the men working for him, who hate someone here so much that they're willing to burn down a barn, shoot at women and children, and slaughter cattle."

"But Hunter—"

Ramsey shook his head. "I don't believe it was him. Everything up through Andrew's kidnapping, yes, but someone else is behind what's happening now."

"You've shared this idea with my brothers?"

"They're smart men. They have their own suspicions."

"But you have no doubts?"

Ethan and Gabriel had been in discussion with Connor and Ben, but they were dispersing now, which allowed Ramsey to avoid explaining his reasons to Eliza. He planned to tell her all of them, but only Tyre Burton could confirm his suspicions.

Ramsey said, "No doubts." He leaned into her and lightly kissed her forehead. "You won't even have time to miss us." Ramsey quickly walked down the steps and joined the others. Ben and Connor started for the stables. Ramsey and Gabriel were behind them, but they stopped when Ethan turned to face his sister. "Kevin, Pete, and Jackson are with the cattle, but they'll be checking in on you every so often."

"You're riding to the trouble, Ethan, not bringing it back here. I'll see you later today anyway." Ethan stood and stared at his sister another minute before turning around and walking with the others to the stables.

Eliza wished she could dampen the unsettling emotions of her mind, but her heart pounded, and only deep, steady breathing kept her calm until she saw the men riding east over their land to the Double Bar.

Her gaze followed the line of their land where it touched the trees, sloped up the mountains, and finally settled on the cattle moving to the feed line. One man drove the wagon while another, she couldn't tell from the distance, pitched hay onto the snow. Eliza envied them the task of watching over the cattle. Her greatest desire in that moment was to be out there with them or riding her horse. The aches had left her body, though she did have a few bruises to show for her fall off the horse.

Filled with frustration, Eliza turned away from the scene and walked back into the quiet house.

The men stopped at the crest where the land sloped down and opened up onto the Double Bar. The expanse of acres surrounding the ranch had been empty of cattle for nearly two years—ever since Brenna's return and Hunter's subsequent efforts to battle the Gallaghers. Ramsey had heard that Hunter sold off his entire stock at once to an outfit in Chicago. He knew that the only reason a rancher sells out is if he's planning to give up on the life. What Ramsey didn't know from Loren's letters, he learned from conversations with Eliza and her brothers. That knowledge, coupled with the more recent and drastic events, was what led him to believe Hunter wasn't giving all the orders.

Ethan said, "They haven't run off again. I don't know if that's a good sign or not."

"There are two more horses now," Connor said.

Gabriel shifted in his saddle. "They could have kept them in the barn."

"Possibly," Ethan replied, though he wasn't looking at the barn or the horses but at Connor. "What do you see?"

"Someone has made a fire in the trees, but I see no one." Connor handed his looking glass to Ethan. "Look about one hundred yards to the east of the fence line.

After a few seconds, Ethan lowered the glass. "When we ride up, keep an eye on those trees."

Connor nodded.

Ramsey said, "If Hunter is down there, he's less likely to shoot if he sees me first."

"Don't get dead, or we'll be the ones to answer to my sister,"

Gabriel said and smiled.

"I wouldn't dream of it," Ramsey replied, returning a grin of his own.

"You're both a little crazy, you know that?" Ethan said. "Ramsey, we're on your back."

They rode down the hill, picking up speed where the snow had melted, Ramsey in the center, and the others spread out beside him. A shot rang into the air from somewhere behind them, but they didn't stop or slow down. It was a warning signal to everyone at the ranch that riders were approaching.

Men emerged from the bunkhouse, and Ramsey searched every face for Tyre Burton. He wasn't there. They slowed their horses at the edge of the corrals and cautiously walked the animals until they stopped near the bunkhouse where the men had formed a line. Ramsey recognized only one man in the group—Paton Densely. When Ramsey worked at the Double Bar, Paton had been someone Hunter hired to protect the ranch. He believed Paton had moved on, hiring out his quick draw to the highest bidder. Ramsey searched again for Tyre.

"You got nerve coming here, Ramsey," Paton called out. Some of the men hadn't bothered with coats and hats, but they all wore guns. "Taking up with these Gallaghers was a fool's mistake."

"I'm here to see my grandfather, Paton. You'd be wise to tell him I'm here or move aside and I'll find him myself."

Paton and his men laughed. "Who are you to be giving me orders?" Paton sneered and seemed to want a fight. His hand loosely draped over the gun at his hip.

"I was a faster draw than you back then. I'm willing to see who's faster now." Ramsey kept his voice calm, but it contradicted the slow-building anger churning within.

Paton's expression sobered, and the men around him exchanged curious stares. None of them knew Ramsey, and from their blank expressions, he'd guess they didn't know Ethan or Gabriel either. From their stances to the way they wore their guns, Ramsey surmised they were all hired guns. They certainly didn't hire on as cowpunchers for a ranch without a herd.

Paton called out, "Hunter ain't here no more! Get the hell out of here and take those yeller Gallaghers with you!" Paton pulled his gun. "Or I kill you now."

Ben and Connor raised their guns in response.

Ramsey said, "There's no way out of this for you, Paton, unless you drop that gun."

"I don't see no gun in your hand." Before Paton could fully pull the trigger, Ramsey unsheathed his pistol and fired. Paton's gun went off, the bullet flying somewhere above them. Ethan and Gabriel now held guns on the remaining men.

Ethan said, "You boys only number five now, and those odds aren't worth you risking your lives for Hunter. We won't miss if we shoot, so unless you have a spot picked out for your grave, you'll drop those guns."

The standoff didn't last long. One by one the men dropped their guns, some of them not taking their eyes off of Paton's limp body.

Ramsey dismounted and walked toward the standing men. "I'll ask you again, where's Hunter?"

One man finally looked at Ramsey. "He ain't here."

Ramsey shook his head. "We'll have a look around just the same."

Ethan dismounted and handed his horse's reins to Gabriel. "Connor, Ben, tie these men up. Ramsey, I'll go in with you."

They walked the short distance to the main house, both men with guns drawn. Ethan motioned to the back of the house and disappeared around the side. Ramsey slowly pushed open the front door and was met with silence. The wood floor creaked beneath his boots, but it was the pervasive scent of filth that drew his notice. Each step raised dust from the floor. He passed the kitchen where dirty dishes littered the table and at the center sat a platter of half-carved meat. The door opposite the kitchen opened. Ethan walked through, met Ramsey's eyes, and shook his head.

"You finish down here, I'm going upstairs."

Ethan nodded and continued through the lower level of the house. Ramsey walked down the hall to the large staircase but stopped on the first step when he heard Ethan's shout. His heavy footfalls echoed through the house as he followed Ethan's voice to a room he remembered Hunter once used as his study. Ethan stared at the floor behind the cluttered desk, his gun resting against his thigh.

Ramsey walked around the desk, but he didn't have to go far to see Hunter's lifeless body, surrounded by a pool of thick, red blood. Ramsey holstered his gun and knelt at the edge of the blood pool. "Give me a hand."

Ethan holstered his own gun and leaned down to lift Hunter while Ramsey carefully pulled until the body faced upright. Ethan stepped back. "The barrel couldn't have been far from his face."

Ramsey stood. "He trusted whoever did this enough to let him in here." For the briefest moment sorrow clouded his mind, not for the death of a man he learned to hate, but for the grandfather he never was and could have been.

Ethan pulled a lap blanket from the back of a chair and covered Hunter's body. "It wasn't the fight we expected and that's what bothers me."

Ramsey nodded. "We need to get back to your ranch."

"Tyre Burton?"

Ramsey nodded. "We'll find a wagon and get the rest of the men into town. They're going to be the new marshal's problem."

23

Eliza bided her time in the library as it was the only room on the ground level to provide her with the view she wanted. When Ramsey and her brothers rode back, she'd see them. Hoping to distract herself, she opened the ranch account books, only to find that Ethan had them in order. She then turned to the bookshelves and pulled down one of the novels Isabelle had added to their collection, but after a few pages, Eliza lost interest. The small bell they kept hanging by the front door rang, and Eliza rushed out of the library, grateful for the distraction.

"Jackson? Is everything all right?"

"Nothing urgent, but we have some logs damming the creek up a piece. I need to take Kevin with me. Pete's out with the cattle, but your brothers wouldn't be happy with us leaving you alone."

"And the longer the creek is dammed, the greater chance it will freeze. Go, I'll saddle up and stay outside with Pete." Eliza rather liked having a valid reason for leaving the house.

"We won't be but an hour." Jackson's eyes nearly pleaded with her. "But I know I'd feel better if you stayed here."

"I'm sure you would." Eliza wouldn't back down. When she heard Jackson's heavy sigh, she knew he had come to that conclusion.

"I'll tell Pete you're coming out," Jackson said before leaving.

Eliza grabbed her coat, scarf, and hat and stepped back outside. Her skirts would suffice for what she had planned. Most of the snow had melted down to form a surface of hard earth covered in small patches of ice. Her boots left small indents in what was left of the snow, and it was with great pleasure when she opened the stable doors. Her mare seemed as anxious to get out of the stall as Eliza was to be out of the house. She enjoyed a few minutes with the horse and then fed the mare oats from her hand. The stable door opened, and the mare whinnied.

"Tell Pete I'll only be a moment, Jackson," Eliza said from the stall. Heavy boots walked across the boards of the stable floor, so Eliza glanced over the stall door. "Jackson?" When no one answered, she turned back to her horse. "Let's get you outside into what little sunshine we have today." Eliza led the mare from the stall and tied her to a hook to finish saddling the horse.

"Is that the man's name with the cattle? He's busy."

The menacing tone sounded unfamiliar, and Eliza's hands began to shake. Slowly she lowered the saddle to the ground and turned around.

"I can see you didn't expect me," Burton said. "But imagine my surprise when we discovered you're the only one here. Brenna was the prize I sought . . . but you'll do."

The heavy-laden wagon slowed their departure from the Double Bar. It barely made the climb over the hill through the snow, but once they reached the crest, the land flattened out all the way to Hawk's Peak. Connor rode ahead with Gabriel behind. Ben drove the wagon and Ethan rode along the right side in the event any of the men decided to cause trouble. They had all voiced complaints when Ethan and Ramsey slid Hunter's body into the wagon with them. Connor called out from ahead, and Ramsey and Ethan both rode forward.

Ethan waited until his horse was next to Connor's. "What do

you have?"

"Horses, three of them," Connor said. "They came down from the north but turned here."

Ramsey looked at Ethan. The only thing west of where they stood was Hawk's Peak.

Ethan shouted for Gabriel and then said to Connor, "You and Ben get these men into town and then head back out to the ranch."

Gabriel rode up and immediately sensed his brother's mood. "What's wrong?"

Ethan said, "We're going back to the ranch. Ben and Connor will take the men in."

Ramsey looked at Connor. "Tell Jake to wire the U.S. Marshal's office and the circuit judge. They need to know what's happened. Ask the doc to tend to any wounds at the jail."

"Do you know who it is?"

Ramsey nodded. "Make sure Jake wires the marshals." Ramsey, Ethan, and Gabriel turned their horses west and rode toward Hawk's Peak.

24

The rope burned Eliza's skin when she attempted to loosen the knot around her wrists. Tyre had found the knife she kept in her boot during a thorough search of her body and clothing. She closed her eyes as his hands roamed every fold of her skirt and then down her legs until he found what he wanted. The knife was the only weapon she had on her. Her rifle remained with her saddle in the stables, but it was of no use to her in the kitchen. Each of her hands was tied to an arm of a chair, but unless she could find a way to get free before Tyre returned, the knives in the kitchen drawer would do her no good.

They had to clear the creek once in spring and once before winter where it dammed up—the same place every time. That section of water was nearly a mile away, and they wouldn't hear her screams.

She heard footsteps in the hall, but when Tyre stepped into the kitchen, he wasn't alone. Eliza recognized the other man as the former deputy, Deputy Lewis, who had helped Hunter's men escape and killed the old sheriff. His leering smile sickened her, and she flashed back to another day when she felt helpless, struggling for her life and the life of her friend. His face floated through her memory, and she saw him laughing, pushing Mary into the ground as the other men dragged Eliza away. She pulled against the confines of the ropes and even tried to stand, but to no avail.

"I see you recognize me." Lewis's words taunted Eliza and she struggled even more, feeling as defenseless as the last time she had seen him.

"Do you plan to finish what you couldn't back then?" Eliza pulled against the ropes. "They'll gut you, if you touch me. They'll tear you apart and leave you for the wolves."

"If Ramsey doesn't kill him first, you mean," Tyre said. "Yes, I know about the two of you."

Eliza remained silent.

"Ah, I do prefer women when they shut their mouths, but my friend likes to hear their screams." Tyre's pale blue eyes mocked her. A sickness simmered in her stomach, but she wouldn't allow them to see her fear. "I need you to draw Ramsey here, but I don't see why Lewis can't have a little fun first."

Eliza watched Lewis's eyes roam her body. "Ramsey was right; Hunter hasn't been the one attacking us."

"Of course not," Tyre said. "That foolish old man lost his mind months ago."

"Why us? We didn't even know you."

"You ask the wrong question," Tyre said smoothly. "It is not you or your family I wish to ruin. I want Ramsey and his pretty twin sister."

Eliza couldn't control her surprise. He wasn't with Hunter when Brenna was kidnapped.

"What do you want with them?"

Tyre ignored her question. "Do you know what happens to a half-breed child? If the child is lucky, the tribe will accept him, but that is not always what happens. When the white man who defiled my mother turned her away because he had a family, we were left on our own. The tribe took my mother back, but not me. I survived, though."

"And you blame Ramsey and Brenna? Why . . ." One glaring possibility surfaced in Eliza's mind. "Hunter is your father."

"He was my father. The old man lost his mind months ago and did not recognize me, but I remembered him. All that remains is to get rid of his heirs."

Was his father? Brenna is safe in town, but Ramsey . . . Eliza shifted to look at Lewis, hoping to draw out the conversation and keep them in the kitchen. "How did the sheriff not know about you?"

Lewis shrugged. "It's simple to fool a fool, but you almost recognized me the last time I was here with Marshal Pickett. I figured you'd remember that day in the fields. That sweet young friend of yours, what was her name? Yes, Mary. But it didn't matter if you did recognize me after that hero brother of yours saw me helping Hunter's men escape from the jail."

Eliza took two deep breaths to calm her churning stomach. "You won't get away with this. Leave now and you might have a chance."

"I'm already a wanted man, thanks to your brother. Enjoying and killing you won't change that. Besides, I'll be far from here before anyone figures out what's happened."

Eliza didn't respond, her eyes shifting over surfaces and to the doors and windows. Soft rays of sun shone through the glass, but there would be no escaping through them. "Ramsey and Brenna don't want anything from Hunter. Leave them alone and they'll let you go." The lie came easily but wasn't any more believable to her ears than it was to Tyre's.

"What I do with them is none of your concern," Tyre said. "Worry now about pleasing Lewis while we wait for your man and brothers. They should be on their way to town with the fools left at the Double Bar, so we have some time."

Lewis's eyes and smile told Eliza exactly what he planned to do with her. He pulled a knife from his belt and held it against her neck. His foul breath reached her nostrils when he leaned forward to speak. "You do what I say, and I won't touch that pretty face of yours." He slid the knife down her arm and sliced through the rope and then did the same with the other. Tyre's eyes remained fixed on Eliza, and his hand rested on his gun. Lewis held the knife against her neck and forced her to stand.

"Enjoy yourselves."

Eliza closed her eyes at Tyre's words and walked stiffly in front of Lewis.

Ramsey pulled his horse to a stop near the edge of the lower pasture. The herd was intact, but he couldn't see any of the men Ethan had left behind. His eyes scanned the ground, and the tracks confirmed the riders had come through here.

"If any of the men had seen Tyre coming, they would have stopped him," Gabriel said. "Eliza's in there, damn it."

Ethan said, "And if we rush in there, they'll kill her."

Ramsey couldn't squelch the image of what Tyre was capable of doing to Eliza. "Not if I go in alone."

"Not a chance," Ethan said. "He hurts her and we kill him."

"He doesn't want Eliza! He doesn't want any of you."

Ethan's horse danced beneath him. "You know something you didn't tell us?"

"Nothing I could confirm, only a suspicion. Be angry at me, but I'm the one he wants. Let me get her out of there alive."

Ethan stared at Ramsey. "Is this about you?"

"It's about Hunter's grandchildren."

"You're telling me Brenna is involved? How?"

"The worst of everything began when Brenna arrived. I don't believe that's a coincidence. Hunter is guilty, no question, but he had motivation from someone else. Tyre simply took over."

"That doesn't answer—" The sound of horses interrupted Ethan. Seconds later, Jackson and Kevin rode up.

"We didn't expect you back so soon," Jackson said. "The creek was dammed up."

Gabriel swore. "Was Pete at the house when you left?"

"He was with the herd. Eliza was on her way to the stables when we left. Planned to stay with Pete until we got back." Jackson sat up in the saddle and looked around. "Where's Pete, and why you three standing here?"

"Three riders came this way, and we're pretty sure they're inside with Eliza," Gabriel said.

Ethan looked once again at Ramsey and then gave orders. "We'll split up. Jackson, see if you can find Pete. If he's still alive, get him into town. Kevin, loop up toward the trees and then around the house, and come in at the back. Gabe, come in from the South. I'll go through the kitchen." Ethan faced Ramsey and pulled his gun out. "I'm trusting you."

Ramsey held Ethan's stare for a breath and then nodded. The men dispersed.

Eliza tried to block Mary's screams from her mind, but with the knife at her throat, she couldn't risk fighting back, and the screams were all she heard. The tears flowed from her eyes but without sound—she wouldn't give him that pleasure. He finished tying her hands to the bed posts. It took longer because he held the knife, taunting her with it, telling her every vile thing he would do. Eliza squeezed her eyes closed and then heard it. Three long calls of a hawk, but not the kind she watched soar through the air. As children, she and her brothers competed to see who could mimic the sound of a hawk first. Hers always sounded like a crow squawking, but Gabriel's was perfect.

A rush of hope coursed through her, and she tugged slightly to check the tightness of the rope. It wouldn't budge. Lewis finally finished tying her to the bed. He ran the knife along the edge of the buttons on her shirt, slicing through the thread until every button lay scattered around her on the bed. He sheathed the knife and began undressing, starting with his boots.

Ramsey dismounted at the corral, leaving the reins of his horse over the railing. He deliberately walked where anyone watching could see him. A few yards from the house he stopped when someone shouted from the window. "We didn't expect you so soon!"

"Happy to disappoint you. Send her out, Burton!"

"She's the only one who's going to survive this. Leave the guns and walk slowly inside."

Ramsey dropped his gun belt, confident that Tyre couldn't see the one secured in his belt against his back. He moved closer to the side of the house now and walked cautiously up the steps. He pulled the gun from his belt and slowly opened the front door, but the hallway was empty. He checked each room as he went, but they, too, were empty. When he faced the kitchen, he saw Ethan stepping inside. Ramsey shook his head and proceeded down the hall. The only place left to go was up. Ethan followed him up the stairs. A rifle shot sounded from the back of the house where Kevin was supposed to be.

Ramsey turned to look at Ethan, but he indicated with his gun for Ramsey to continue on. At the top of the stairs, Ethan turned right and Ramsey turned left. Ethan checked the rooms but found nothing. Ramsey passed Eliza's room and found it empty. He began to make more noise, and a gun shot hit the banister outside of Elizabeth's room.

Ramsey pushed his back up against the wall. "Tyre, you bastard! Let her go!"

Ethan moved up behind Ramsey and then jumped across the hall to stand on the other side of the bedroom door. Ethan's movements brought forth a spray of bullets, but Tyre yelled at someone to hold his fire.

"You brought friends, Ramsey. Is that one of Eliza's brothers? She's comfortable in here, so I don't believe we'll let her go yet.

You come in and we'll talk."

"No, Ramsey!"

"Shut your mouth!" A hard slap was accompanied by Eliza's cry of pain.

Ethan peeked around the door, but another shot rushed past him. Ethan held up two fingers.

Ramsey said, "Tyre, this has nothing to do with them. You let her go and do whatever the hell you want with me."

"You know why I'm here?"

"You're Hunter's son."

Ethan whipped his head around to look at him, but Ramsey ignored the look. "My guess is that you found out about your white father, but Hunter didn't welcome you the way you thought. You're caught between worlds, Tyre, and neither wants you."

"I deserve that ranch! That foolish old man didn't even know me. It took him a year to realize who I was, but he swore a half-breed would never inherit. I heard about you and your Scottish whore of a sister."

Ramsey shook his head quickly at Ethan when he would have entered the room. Instead, Ramsey let Tyre continue his tirade. "Is that why you killed him? He didn't know you?"

"I only have to get rid of you and your sister, so if you want your pretty woman to stay pretty, you're going to walk in here and take the bullet."

"I don't have a problem with that, Tyre," Ramsey said, "but then her brothers are going to kill you and whoever's in there with you."

"Why don't we find out?"

Ramsey held his gun hand out in front of the open door and then stepped around the corner and entered the room. His eyes went immediately to the bed and took in Eliza's position. Her hair lay in disarray, her shirt torn open, revealing her white camisole beneath. The side of her face was still red from where Tyre had slapped her. Ramsey clamped his jaw shut, trying to control his body from leaping for Tyre. His eyes studied the man who held a knife to Eliza's neck, recognizing him from another time and place. Ramsey finally faced Tyre and the gun barrel pointed at him.

"I'm here, Tyre, but you're crazy if you think you'll get anything out of this except a bullet and a pine box."

"I'm his son! If I don't get that ranch, no one will."

"We never wanted it!" Ramsey continued to watch Tyre and the gun. "I left a long time ago. Brenna never wanted it. Hunter would have burned it down before giving it to anyone, but you saw to it that wouldn't happen."

Tyre faltered, but his hold on the gun didn't waver.

Ramsey looked back at Eliza. When he left this earth, he wanted her face to be the last thing he ever saw. Tyre pointed, but the shot Ramsey heard didn't come from Tyre's gun—it came from the balcony.

Ethan shouted to Ramsey and tossed him his gun. Ramsey pointed at Eliza's captor and pulled the trigger. Everything happened too quickly after that, but Ramsey saw only Eliza and rushed to her side. He pulled the knife from his boot and carefully cut through the ropes. Gabriel came through the door from the balcony, and Ethan walked to the bed. Ramsey ignored them and pulled Eliza into his arms. She crushed her body against him and allowed the tears to flow freely.

Eliza needed only a few minutes to calm down, and Ramsey knew Gabriel and Ethan waited. He pulled back and gently wiped tears from her cheek. She finished the job and looked up at her brothers. "Would it be completely horrible if I said thank you but I would have preferred to put a bullet in Lewis myself?"

Eliza moved off the bed, and Ethan immediately pulled her into his arms. "I'm locking you in your room from now on."

"I figured." Eliza laughed, surprising them all. She walked into Gabriel's outstretched arms and with her arm still around his waist, turned away. "Is it over?"

Ramsey nodded. "It's over."

They all looked down at the bodies on the floor of Elizabeth's room. A shout reached them from the ground outside of Elizabeth's window. Ethan walked over and called down to Kevin. "It's over!"

"I'm coming around!"

Ethan said, "Ramsey, would you take our sister to her room? We'll take care of the bodies."

Ramsey was surprised at Ethan's suggestion. Ramsey nodded and guided Eliza from the room.

He waited with her until the bodies had been removed. Her wrists needed wrapping and the side of her face would require something cool to prevent swelling, but Ramsey predicted a bruise would form, much to Eliza's chagrin. They remained silent most of the time, listening to the sound of her brothers removing Tyre and Lewis.

Eliza knew Kevin was all right, but she forgot to ask about Jackson and Pete.

"Jackson is safe. He and Kevin rode back from the stream after we'd arrived. I don't know yet about Pete." Ramsey reached up and brushed a loose bit of hair away from her face, something that had become one of her favorite gestures.

Ramsey hesitated to ask the one question he and her brothers had avoided asking, but there had been time for worse. "Eliza, did they . . . hurt you?"

Eliza turned Ramsey's face toward her and shook her head. "No, but if they had, I would still be all right."

Ramsey leaned in and gently pressed his lips to hers. "I love you."

"I love you," Eliza whispered and returned the kiss. "And I

can think of nothing I want more than to be here with you, except a bath." Eliza's laugh was one of relief, and then she sobered. "I need to wash everything about them off of me."

Ramsey kissed her again, this time pulling back slowly. "It should be safe enough to go out. I'll go and heat the water."

"That's not necess—"

Ramsey silenced her with another kiss. "Yes, it is."

Ramsey met Gabriel at the foot of the stairs and paused when he saw the blood on Gabriel's shirt. Gabriel looked up at him and said, "How is she?"

"She's Eliza. I imagine she'd survive anything," Ramsey said. "Where'd you put them?"

"In the woodshed. I'll ride into town with Ethan, and he'll send Henry back with a wagon. We'd like to get the bodies off the ranch before we bring the others back."

Ramsey stepped down to the main level next to Gabriel. "Your family's safe now, at least from this threat."

"You kept what you suspected about Tyre to yourself. How long have you known?"

"A few days." Ramsey rubbed a hand over his tired eyes. "I put together pieces of what I'd learned about Tyre when he arrived, but mostly, I couldn't figure out why he was so invested in Hunter's cause. When I went to send the telegram to confirm Hugh's story, one was waiting there for me. Apparently I'm not the first to suspect Tyre's parentage, except Tyre turned out to be crazier than the old man."

Ethan leaned against the wall. "Do you know how he came to find out or when your grandfather—"

"The only two people who have answers to those questions are Tyre and Hunter," Ramsey said.

"At least all of us were spared becoming Hunter's executioner," Gabriel said, "and Buxley Whit gets justice for his brother. You'll let him know?"

Ramsey nodded. "I'll meet the authorities at the sheriff's office when they arrive from Texas." Ramsey looked up and stared at Gabriel. "I would have killed him, Gabe. My own grandfather. I just can't help think that my family brought this on yours. It won't be easy to get past that."

"We can't know what any of us would have done if Tyre hadn't killed him first. Next time you know something important, tell us. Right or wrong, we'll stand by you. If you had been here when Brenna was kidnapped, you might have given Ethan a good beating. We don't always get it right, either."

Ramsey pointed to Gabriel's shirt. "It really is over."

Gabriel looked down at the drying blood on his shirt and nodded. "I thought it would feel different."

"Ending it or killing them?"

Gabriel pondered that. "I never set out to do harm to anyone, but when it comes to my family, I've discovered the limits to which I'll go. I feel no guilt for that. I'd also like to tell you that tomorrow we rest, but we have a barn to build, and I hear you want to breed horses."

"You talked to Ethan?"

"He likes the idea," Gabriel said. "It will expand what we do here, and it will keep you close. There are two women he wants to make sure stay happy."

"I'd hate to disappoint them." Ramsey began to feel free from a burden he'd carried since the day he left the Double Bar. He sustained no apprehension about giving up his drifter ways. His family and his future were here.

Gabriel moved toward the steps. "I'll clean up and then Ethan and I will drive into town. You'll stay with Eliza?"

Ramsey swept his eyes upward, first touching on Eliza's closed door and then settling briefly on Gabriel. "Try and keep me away."

25

Hawk's Peak
November 8, 1883

The wagons rolled in the following morning under a dusting of light snowfall. Eliza watched Andrew bounce up from his seat in the back of the wagon before Isabelle settled him down. Eliza returned his enthusiastic wave with one of her own. She attempted a smile but cringed instead. Her fingers reached up and gently pressed on the tender skin under her eye.

"You should still be resting." Ramsey stood with her and watched the family proceed toward the house. Concern evident in his voice, he said, "Your brothers will have told them some of what happened, but explaining your condition to Andrew may prove more difficult."

"I'll figure something out," Eliza said. "But would it be so wrong to tell him the truth or a semblance of it? He's a bright boy, and lying doesn't sit well."

"He's only five."

"Almost six. Besides, I don't condone lying to children."

Amused, Ramsey glanced down at her. "Have you ever been less than truthful?"

Eliza's face warmed, but she shrugged. "I'm certain I have, but

I'm also certain it was warranted."

Ramsey's deep laughter was a reassuring reminder that life continued on after tragedy and hardship. Serious and determined to exact revenge one day and laughing the next—the man was a curious contradiction of emotions, and his smile proved infectious. Despite the soreness in her face, Eliza managed to wear a smile when the wagons came to a stop. Ramsey descended from the porch and held the reins of the first team while Ethan and Gabriel helped the women down. Ethan motioned Ramsey over and handed Jacob into his arms, much to Ramsey's surprise, and then raised his arms to lift Brenna and Elizabeth out of the wagon.

Eliza's smile grew as she watched Ramsey hold the baby and then almost reluctantly pass Jacob back over to his mother.

Ben and Connor helped unload the bags and supplies from the wagon and then led the horses to the stable to give Henry and Colton a chance to stretch their legs from the drive.

Eliza called down to Andrew. "Did you enjoy your stay in town?"

"I got to play with school friends, Aunt Eliza!"

Brenna and Isabelle glanced up, and Eliza saw a noticeable cringe pass over their faces. Ramsey had informed her that the discoloring would last a while. Watching her sisters-in-law, she was oddly grateful she had been at the ranch and not them.

Brenna said something to Isabelle, carried Jacob to the porch, and stepped up until she stood next to Eliza. "Don't worry; I imagine it feels worse than it looks."

Eliza instinctively brushed her fingers over the bruise. "It doesn't look that bad?"

"Oh dear, it does." Brenna blushed and then whispered, "I thought only to make you feel better."

Eliza laughed, ignoring the pain it brought to her body. "Only two days, but I missed you."

Brenna leaned in and kissed Eliza's cheek. "We missed you, too." Brenna sobered. "You are all right, aren't you? Ethan didn't go into much detail."

Eliza slowly nodded and found herself searching for Ramsey, who was presently tossing Andrew into the air. "I'm more than all right."

Andrew's squeals of joy had the adults around him chuckling. Ramsey tossed him up once more and then set him down. Leaning over, he said, "I think it's time you named my horse."

Andrew's big gray eyes looked at Ramsey as though he didn't believe him. "Yes!"

Ramsey was absolutely delighted with the child. "He's in the stables."

Andrew jumped up and down in front of Gabriel. "I get to name Ramsey's horse now!"

Colton walked up behind them and offered to take Andrew to the horses. He and Gabriel exchanged knowing glances before Colton followed Andrew. Ramsey watched Eliza's awkward movements as she stepped down from the porch to walk with the women into the house. He wanted to pick her and carry her inside, and while he believed the gesture romantic, he didn't think she'd appreciate it in this instance. The evening before, she had expressed her wish that the family not look at her as weak or damaged. He wondered if she would feel the same way when heavy with their child. He grinned at the idea.

Ethan interrupted his daydream and pulled an unopened envelope from his jacket pocket and handed them to Ramsey. "It's from the judge. Jake also said that the sheriff down in Wyoming will arrive today to pick up Hugh."

Ramsey nodded absently. He opened the telegram and relayed the message aloud. "The judge says that one of the other circuit judges will be passing through here in two weeks and has offered to sit in his place." He then turned the other envelope over—it was from Governor Robinson. When he didn't say anything for a few minutes, Gabriel finally broke through his concentration.

"Good news?"

"I'm not sure." Ramsey folded the paper back into the envelope. "Apparently Washington is willing to appoint me permanently to the office."

"Remain a U.S. Marshal?" Gabriel's surprise was evident. "Is that what you want?"

Everything Ramsey ever dreamed of having was already his— a woman to love and a family worth risking everything to have. "I honestly don't know." Ramsey slipped the telegrams into his own pocket and asked Ethan about Loren.

"He's awake now and complaining that the doc won't let him leave the clinic. Brody expects him to be back at the store next week, though it will be a while before he can do everything on his own."

"I'll ride into town tomorrow to speak with Loren and wire the judge back," Ramsey said.

"Do you think the Peelers have a chance?"

"No honest and law-abiding judge will let them go," Ramsey said. "I expect they'll be sent to Deer Lodge, but it won't be for murder."

Andrew came running back from the stables, followed closely by Colton, who tried to keep the boy from falling on the ice stuck between wheel lines and hoof prints. He nearly fell forward once, but Colton managed to catch him. Back on his feet, he moved a little slower, but only for a few steps. "Uncle Ramsey!" Andrew eagerly called out. By the time Andrew reached them, he sounded out of breath, and his face was red from the cold.

Ramsey reached down and lifted Andrew into his arms. "Well, does he have a name?"

Andrew grinned, showing a line of small white teeth. "I

named him Prince!" He squirmed away from Ramsey. "I want to tell Ibby!"

Isabelle stepped outside, her heavy shawl wrapped around her shoulders. "Amanda has put together a lunch of cold meats and bread if you're at all hungry."

"Famished." Gabriel walked up the porch steps. "Did Andrew tell you his latest news?"

"That he finally named Ramsey's horse? Yes, and Prince is a fine name."

"He certainly lives up to it." Ramsey stepped closer to the front porch and leaned against the handrail. "How's Eliza doing in there with everyone?"

Ethan moved closer when he heard Ramsey's question. The concerned expression Isabelle wore did little to ease Ramsey's worry.

"She's strong, but I think she's in some pain and won't admit to it."

Gabriel settled his hand gently against his wife's back. "Let her be strong. She'll feel better for it."

"We'll slip something into her drink tonight."

Ramsey didn't doubt that Ethan meant it.

Confused, Isabelle said, "But Eliza rarely drinks spirits."

"She will tonight," Ramsey said.

Three days later, snow dusted the land but that didn't stop the family from moving forward with the barn raising. The frame of the new barn was already constructed, when nearly two dozen men arrived in a wagon and on horseback. Otis climbed out of the wagon and walked toward Ethan, who handed a cup of coffee back to his wife.

"You don't get to have all the fun without us, Ethan."

Ethan chuckled and shook Otis's hand. "Glad to see you, Otis. We could use the help before the storm hits."

Otis said, "Oh, and I brought the package Gabriel asked about."

Ethan looked past Otis to the group of men and shouted for Connor to come over. Connor moved easily on the snow, but his red face attested to the time he'd spent outside already that morning. Most of the men had grown their beards out for the winter months, and Connor was no exception. "Do you need help unloading anything else?"

Ethan said, "Otis has a special delivery that we need to keep in the bunkhouse for a few days."

Connor nodded in understanding, having been with them in town when Gabriel and Isabelle picked out Andrew's gift. "Consider it handled. Andrew will notice if any of you are gone for long, so me and the boys will take shifts."

"Appreciate it, Connor."

Connor shrugged. "Anything for that kid." He said a quick hello to Brenna and then followed Otis to the wagon.

Now alone, Ethan pulled his wife against him. "I better get back." Ethan pressed his lips to hers. "Your skin is cold—better get back inside."

Brenna laughed. "You forget that Highland blood runs through my veins."

"It won't happen again." Ethan leaned in and kissed her again.

The front door pushed open and Ramsey stepped out.

Ramsey coughed loudly, but he'd already caught Ethan's glare. He smirked at his brother-in-law and sister. "I believe we have a barn to finish."

Ethan grinned, showing no shame.

For the noon meal, all of the women gathered in the kitchen to help prepare a satisfying feast for the men. Eliza was amazed the women managed to keep their composure when they told her it was unanimously decided that Eliza should rest. At Isabelle's urging, she sat down, but after a few minutes, she'd had enough.

"If I can't work outside, then you're going to have to allow me to do something in here." Eliza looked around and her eyes settled on the loaves of bread that needed to be sliced. She reached across the table, but Elizabeth stepped over and slapped her hand away.

"Mind your manners, Eliza Gallagher. Your feet work; walk around the table." Eliza grinned at Elizabeth, silently thanking the woman for not treating her as weak or wounded. "But don't touch anything else. These men deserve a good meal."

Eliza laughed and moved to stand at the other side of the table. "You have nothing to worry about. In a few days, I'll be out of the house and back with the horses."

Brenna and Isabelle exchanged conspiratorial glances not lost on Eliza.

"It wouldn't hurt to learn a thing or two in the kitchen, Eliza," Brenna said, "before you set up a house of your own."

Eliza paused, the knife in her grip hovering above the second loaf of bread.

Isabelle said, "I was never one to spend time in the kitchen, either, but I imagine most men enjoy a nice hot meal at the end of the day."

Eliza set the knife down next to the bread. "Who have you been talking with?"

Brenna laughed, as did Elizabeth and Isabelle. Even Amanda smiled. Brenna settled her mirth and managed to say, "Had Ethan not told me what he'd seen between you and Ramsey, we would have known anyway."

Eliza looked from one face to the next. "It's that obvious?"

"Afraid so, child." Elizabeth brushed a few strands of hair away from her face. "Now finish that bread, and then go tell your brothers and my grandson that the stew is ready. They can eat here in shifts."

Eliza finished slicing the bread, but on her way out of the kitchen, Elizabeth stopped her. "I am glad you're the one for him. It's what I always had hoped for."

Surprised, Eliza stepped closer. "I don't understand."

"From the first day he met you, all those years ago, Ramsey was smitten, only he was too young and foolish to know it at the time."

Elizabeth sounded so certain that Eliza couldn't help but wonder if she was right.

"Go now. They'll be hungry."

The cold winds and fresh snow prevented Andrew from spending more than a few minutes at a time outdoors. By the time his birthday approached, he managed to expend every bit of his stored energy, and Isabelle threatened to send him to boarding school. Although she didn't mean the threat, Isabelle was saved from making that drastic choice when Ethan announced that the storm had cleared and he fully expected the sun to come out for a few hours.

Elizabeth and Amanda had been busy in the kitchen, preparing a meal suited more to Andrew's tastes.

"There will be enough fried chicken to feed everyone at the ranch twice over," Amanda said.

Elizabeth chuckled. "If we left the choosing entirely up to Andrew, we'd be eating nothing but cherry pie and chocolate cake."

"It looks like he'll still be getting his wish, unless I'm mistaken about that being cake batter in that bowl."

Elizabeth smiled. "You try saying 'no' to him."

Amanda wiped grease off her hands onto the edge of her apron and glanced at Elizabeth. "I've already tried. He came into the kitchen yesterday asking for a third cookie. Against my better judgment, I gave him one."

"Don't fret—Isabelle gave him another one, too, though at the time I don't think she knew he'd already had three!"

Brenna walked into the kitchen, carrying Jacob. "Something in here smells wonderful!"

"That would be the cherry pies Elizabeth has cooling," Amanda said.

Brenna winked at Amanda. "They smell good enough to sample."

"Your husband already tried that." Elizabeth brushed the flour off the top of her apron and held out her hands. "Hand that child over for a minute."

Brenna smiled and carefully transferred Jacob into his great-grandmother's waiting arms. "Did I hear something about cookies?"

Amanda set the chopping knife aside. "Would you like me to fix you something to eat?"

Brenna shook her head and lifted a cloth from a fresh loaf. "Don't fuss over me; I can manage with a slice of this bread. I seem to be hungry all of the time."

Amanda motioned toward a covered plate on the sideboard. "There are a few cookies left."

"Even better!" Brenna walked over and helped herself to two and recovered the plate. "Is there anything I can do to help?"

"Little Jacob could use a change." Elizabeth cooed and rocked the baby. "I firmly believe that is the job of the parents. Great-Grandmas just get to do the fun stuff."

Brenna laughed and held her hands over the sink to wipe off any crumbs. She lifted Jacob from Elizabeth's arms. "Oh, he does, and perhaps a bath before supper!" Brenna looked at the women. "I'd best get him out of here. Thank you for the cookies."

Ethan passed Brenna outside the kitchen door. "Do you want

to handle that?"

"I'll manage." Brenna welcomed Ethan's quick kiss and continued down the hall toward the stairs.

Ethan peered over Elizabeth's shoulder. "Have you changed your mind about the pie?"

"You keep your hands off the food," Elizabeth said, not bothering to turn away from pouring batter into pans. "You may finish off that plate of cookies if it won't spoil your supper."

Amused, Ethan walked over to the plate from which he'd pilfered a cookie earlier.

Elizabeth slid the pans into the oven and turned to look at Ethan. "Did Gabriel get him?"

Ethan nodded. "Best of the litter. Thinking of getting one myself."

"Brenna mentioned you used to have a dog, but she only saw him once."

"He wasn't really ours—mostly wolf and mostly wild. He comes back around once or twice a year, but if he's found a pack who will take him, or a mate, then he may not come back." When Ethan reached for another cookie, Elizabeth looked pointedly at his hands. "I promise I'll be hungry for your fried chicken." Ethan finished the cookie and filled a glass with water from the pump. "This is a bit stiff. Has it been giving you problems?"

"It's a little fussy, but not too bad," Amanda said.

"I'll have a look outside. I'm headed out anyway," Ethan said.

"Mind you tell those boys out in the bunkhouse that supper is at six o'clock."

Ethan leaned over and kissed Elizabeth's cheek. "Yes, ma'am."

26

Eliza smoothed down the skirts and frilly blouse she slipped into for the occasion. She had even allowed Brenna to fuss with her hair, lifting it off her back and into fancy clips. Her elegance would never match that of Isabelle, who had been raised under strict social standards, or even Brenna, whose mother had managed to raise her a lady despite her love for the outdoors.

Eliza didn't often consider herself beautiful, but she did on that day with her hair washed, brushed, and twisted up together until only a few strands draped her face. She felt even more beautiful when she walked down the stairs for supper. Ramsey waited for her at the base of the staircase, unmoving, his eyes following every step. He wouldn't let her pass when she reached him. Instead, he slipped his fingers through hers, cupped her face, and brought her down to meet his lips.

When they entered the kitchen, Eliza soaked in the love and laughter while everyone helped prepare the meal. The most important people in her life surrounded her and filled the house with an abundance of joy. She watched Gabriel share a moment of laughter with Isabelle. Ethan and Brenna doted over their son, whose animated hands and face were responsible for their glowing expressions. Amanda, a woman lost and still somewhat of a mystery, had found a home at Hawk's Peak. Elizabeth, grandmother to them all, slapped Ramsey's hand away from the plate of chicken before he reached down and kissed her cheek.

Eliza's gaze settled on Ramsey, her heart overcome with a happiness she didn't yet understand, but one she was determined to never lose. Ramsey had turned down the permanent appointment as a U.S. Marshal to the governor's disappointment. He explained to Eliza that he wasn't willing to leave her behind, and the position would require him to travel often.

"I've purchased Nathaniel's remaining stock of mares," Ramsey said when he found a private moment with her. "Care to join me for a ride south?"

Eliza was in no hurry to venture that far from home again, but the idea of time alone with Ramsey was too appealing. "Absolutely!"

Ramsey smiled. "First thaw we'll leave for Kentucky. Nathaniel spoke with the farm's new owner, and he agreed to board the horses until spring."

"That will mean expanding the stables before we leave."

"Actually, I wanted to ask for your thoughts on an idea," Ramsey said. "I would understand if you're not comfortable with it."

Eliza tilted her head in question. "I won't know unless you tell me."

"With Hunter dead, it was simple enough to get his land turned over to Elizabeth—she's still his wife—but she doesn't want it. I'd like to buy the Double Bar from her."

Ramsey waited for nearly a minute. Andrew's giggles, caused by Gabriel's tossing him over his shoulder, and conversation among the other adults filled the quiet space between them. Finally, he said, "It's not something I have to do. I thought . . ."

Eliza slowly lifted her eyes to meet his. "You're the last person I expected to live on that land again, but I think you should."

Ramsey didn't even try to hide his surprise. "Are you certain?"

Eliza slowly nodded. "Yes. Truth is, worse has happened to all of us here than it ever did on the Double Bar." Eliza slid her hands into Ramsey's. "It's only land and buildings, Ramsey, but we can make it a home. I don't want to leave Hawk's Peak, either. This is my home and what we've all fought for. How would you feel about tearing down Hunter's house and building our own on the strip of land bordering the two ranches?"

"Tearing down the fence in the process?"

Eliza smiled. "That's the idea." Eliza's fingers played gently with the thick hair curling at Ramsey's ear. "Hawk's Peak is your home now, too, and I guarantee my brothers won't object."

Eliza welcomed Ramsey's soft kiss, and then her gaze passed over her family once more. She believed a more beautiful sight had never existed, even if Elizabeth was now slapping Ethan's hands away from the biscuits.

"Too many of you walking around in this kitchen," Elizabeth said. "Take a seat at the table or wait someplace else."

Andrew's delight was contagious, and he soon calmed down once he realized that everyone was there to celebrate him. Eliza teased him with a loud kiss to his cheek. He pretended to not like it, but his soft skin turned red as he blushed and hugged Eliza before moving onto the next adult. He wanted to show Gabriel the new book his grandmother bought him, but Gabriel had slipped away. Andrew's excitement escalated when the ranch hands knocked at the back door and slowly filed into the kitchen. It was the only room large enough to set up the barrels and planks to create a second table.

The men tossed Andrew from person to person until he had expended so much energy in giggling that Isabelle announced it was time to proceed with the gift giving and meal. Eliza caught Isabelle's nod, whispered to Ramsey, and slipped out to the hallway. Unfortunately, Andrew's gift managed to slip from Gabriel and scampered past Eliza to the open kitchen.

"A puppy!" Andrew jumped down from his sister's lap.

Eliza shook her head at Gabriel. "Wild horses, bulls, and outlaws, and you can't hold onto a puppy."

Gabriel shrugged. "You try it sometime. I swear that dog is some kind of bloodhound. The second we walked into the house, he could smell the food."

Eliza looped her arm through those of her brothers. "Spring might be a good time to build a new house."

"Funny, Ethan said the same thing." Gabriel joined in her teasing. "Speaking of houses, where would you like yours?"

Eliza smoothly skipped past the question and grinned at her brother. Andrew's cries and shouts of joy propelled them to enter the kitchen. "Into the fray, Gabe."

When they entered the kitchen, Andrew was attempting to lift the energetic puppy into his arms.

Eliza leaned over and whispered to her brother. "That thing looks more wolf than dog. Where did you get him?"

"Phineas Simms is giving them away." Gabriel smirked. "Do you want one?"

Eliza actually took a minute to consider it.

"You're serious?" Gabriel kept his eyes on Andrew and the puppy.

"I better wait until I have that house you mentioned." She grinned at him and then left his side to join Ramsey.

Gabriel knelt down on the floor next to Andrew and the puppy, now winding down. "You have to take good care of him."

"I get to keep him?" Andrew looked at Gabriel with wide eyes.

"He's all yours," Gabriel confirmed. "But he needs a name first."

Andrew pursed his lips and glanced around him as though searching for an idea. Eliza thought it possible that the boy had run out of names. In the past week, Andrew had named every remaining unchristened horse at the ranch.

"Did you ever have a puppy, Gabriel?"

"Well now, we did have a scrappy cattle dog named Cody when we were kids."

"Do you think Cody would mind if I called my puppy Cody, too?"

Gabriel lifted Andrew and the puppy onto his lap. "I don't think he'd mind at all."

Eliza stood over the graves, buried now beneath a foot of snow. Her eyes shifted over the land, settling on the completed barn. They had rebuilt on a foundation of strength and love where ashes once covered the ground. The barn was merely boards and nails to others, but to her family, it was a symbol of hope. The legacy their parents had begun would endure.

Eliza brushed away the snow from the tops of the three headstones, ignored the cold that seeped through her skirts, and knelt between her parents. "Andrew turned six years old today. Father, you'd be proud to know he wants to work the ranch someday. Don't worry, his sister is a schoolteacher, and she'll make sure he goes off to college. Ethan didn't like leaving, either, but Brenna will insist Jacob gets an education, too."

Eliza smoothed the snow over her mother's grave. "Mother, I'm still useless in the kitchen, but it turns out that's not as important as I thought it would be. Ramsey insists on marrying me, even though I can't sew, either. You remember Ramsey, don't you? You'd like the man he's become. I wish you could be here for the wedding, but we aren't doing anything fancy. We'll spend our first nights together in your cottage, just as you did. I promise he'll be as good to me as Father was to you."

Eliza stood then and moved to kneel beside Mabel. "Your house is in good hands now. I think you would have approved of Amanda. You weren't given a choice about leaving this earth, Mabel, and I'm the most sorry for that. We're all the better for the time we had you with us."

Eliza sensed him before she heard him. Standing and brushing off her skirts, she waited.

Ramsey slid strong arms around her waist and pulled her back against his chest. "You're not crying."

Eliza covered his arms with hers, drawing on his strength and warmth. "I wish they were all here, but it doesn't hurt the way it once did. A part of me will always ache from their loss, but my best memories of them are stronger than the sadness."

"We'll create more memories, and we'll stand here together and tell your parents all about them."

Eliza turned in his arms and she faced him.

"And there will be no regrets."

Ramsey shook his head. "Never, although I did warn you I wouldn't be easy to live with, so there's no changing your mind later."

Eliza returned his easy smile. "Bringing you home was the best thing I've ever done."

Ramsey gently brushed his lips against hers. "You saved my life that day. I could have spent my days wandering, never knowing a life with you."

"You'll never have to find out. Besides, one of my many flaws is stubbornness, and when I want something enough, I eventually get it."

Ramsey's laughter filled the early evening air. "How many flaws exactly?"

Eliza pretended to consider the matter seriously, but Ramsey squeezed her until she laughed. "I'm usually right."

"So I've noticed," Ramsey murmured. "You were right about almost everything. Family and love is worth every risk."

Her lips curved into a smile. "Wait, *almost* everything?"

"It's only fair that you be wrong about something."

"And will you endeavor to discover what that is?"

Ramsey's lips slowly curved into a smile. "I'll have a lifetime to find out."

The End

GALLAGHER'S CHOICE
BOOK CLUB DISCUSSION QUESTIONS

1. How do you feel Eliza measured up alongside her brothers as a prominent member of the Gallagher family? Do you feel her independent nature was a weakness or strength?

2. What draws Eliza and Ramsey together? How do their own strengths and weaknesses complement each other?

3. How important do you feel the family unit is to the success of the individual characters? Do you feel they rely too little or too much on one another?

4. Describe Eliza's relationship with Ethan and Gabriel. How does each rely on the other?

5. Which character in the story do you identify with the most? Tell why.

6. How would you describe Elizabeth's relationship with the Gallaghers? Do you feel she filled the void left behind by Mabel?

7. In your experience, and in this story, when people have endured great tragedy or loss, are they destined to live unhappily for long periods of time? In other words, does tragedy demand its due? Is "happily ever after" possible?

8. Discuss the ending. How did it make you feel about the series? Would you have changed the ending? If so, how?

Interested in reading more by MK McClintock? Try her British Agent novels—stories of romance, adventure, and mystery set in Victorian England. Available in print and eBook.

The Historical Romantic Mystery British Agent novels:
Book One – *Alaina Claiborne*
Book Two – *Blackwood Crossing*
Book Three – *Clayton's Honor*

Also try *A Home for Christmas: Short Story Collection.* A collection of three historical western short stories to inspire love and warm the heart, no matter the season. Set in Montana, Colorado, and Wyoming.

If you'd like to share your thoughts or comments with MK, feel free to email her at mk@mcclintockmt.com.

If you'd like to share your thoughts with others, consider leaving an online review.

Don't miss out on future books and special offers.
Sign up for MK's periodic newsletter at
www.mkmcclintock.com/newsletter.

MEET THE AUTHOR

MK McClintock is a multiple award-nominated author, entrepreneur, and avid photographer. She spins tales of romance and adventure inspired by the heather-covered hills of Scotland and the majestic mountains of home. She dreams of a time when life was simpler, the land rougher, and the journey more rewarding. With her heart deeply rooted in the past and her mind always on adventure, she lives and writes in the Rocky Mountains.

www.mkmcclintock.com
mk@mcclintockmt.com
facebook.com/mkmcclintockbooks
twitter.com/mkmcclintock

Made in the USA
San Bernardino, CA
06 March 2020